SPLIT by a KISS

D0784240

www.**rbooks**.co.uk

SPLIT by a KISS

Luisa Plaja

CORGI BOOKS

SPLIT BY A KISS
A CORGI BOOK 978 0 552 55680 4

Published in Great Britain by Corgi Books,
an imprint of Random House Children's Books
A Random House Group Company

This edition published 2008

1 3 5 7 9 10 8 6 4 2

The Random House Group Limited supports The Forest Stewardship Council
(FSC), the leading international forest certification organisation. All our titles that
are printed on Greenpeace approved FSC certified paper carry the FSC logo. Our
paper procurement policy can be found at: www.rbooks.co.uk/enviroinment

Mixed Sources
Product group from well-managed
forests and other controlled sources
www.fsc.org Cert no. TT-COC-2139
© 1996 Forest Stewardship Council

Set in Palatino and Kievit

Corgi Books are published by Random House Children's Books,
61–63 Uxbridge Road, London W5 5SA

www.**kids**at**randomhouse**.co.uk
www.**rbooks**.co.uk

Addresses for companies within The Random House Group Limited
can be found at: www.randomhouse.co.uk/offices.htm

THE RANDOM HOUSE GROUP Limited Reg. No. 954009

A CIP catalogue record for this book is available from the British Library.

Printed in the UK by CPI Bookmarque, Croydon, CR0 4TD

To the people who got me out of the ice rink

FIRST BASE

Lucky Break

I am in a cupboard, and I'm snogging the coolest and most gorgeous boy in the whole school. And it's a big school. And really, we're kissing, not snogging. In a closet, not a cupboard. They don't really have snogging or cupboards here – they would laugh and tell me those are dodgy British phrases. Except they wouldn't say 'dodgy'. That's just as dodgily British. And – quick tip – don't ever let them catch you saying 'tomato and basil' – that will have them laughing for like a year. I learned that the hard way.

But none of that is the point at all. The point is – I am kissing Jake Matthews, the coolest boy in the school! If not the entire world.

And the really amazing thing? I am seriously UNcool. Or rather, I was.

Let me tell you how it happened. Remember – if it can happen to me, it can happen to you. Not with Jake Matthews, of course – hands off! He's mine. But you'll find someone like him. There's one in every school.

These facts about me are probably not important for the success of your kiss-the-fittest-boy-in-school plan, but here they are anyway. My name is Josephine Reilly, I live with my mum, my dad is married to an empty-headed bimbo called Kelly, I have a sweetie-pie half-sister called Lolly-Lauren, who's three, and a best friend called Hailey.

The following facts ARE important.

Your mum has to qualify for the 'brain drain'. Or your dad has to, I suppose, but that doesn't apply in my case – my dad left my brilliant mum for Kelly, so he is certifiably brainless. Anyway, my mum went for the 'brain drain', which is a cool way of saying she got a job in the USA because of her super-clever egghead status. It has nothing to do with zombies. Although, you know, zombies would be cool too, but in a different way.

Then you need to have an accent that makes everyone stop and stare at you. Most of these people should say, 'I just LOVE your accent.' Any old accent will do, don't worry. My accent is from Boringtown, Boring County, England, and it's worked well for me. I suppose you could pretend to have an exotic accent, one that isn't your real accent, but inventing things isn't always the best way to go. You'll see what I mean about that later.

And then – and this is what makes the accent thing

work – you need to move to the United States of America.

That's it. That's what it took to transform me from Lady Saddo of Boringtown High to Cool Girl on the Block, complete with snogging Jake Matthews and everything. Brainy parent, accent, USA. You're thinking it can't be that simple. Anyway, dorky ducklings don't turn into hip-'n'-happening swans, except in fairy tales. In fact, seeing me now with Jake Matthews, you're seriously doubting I was ever remotely uncool.

I can see why you'd think that. So here are a few more details about the old me. Judge for yourself.

At the drop of a hat – and sometimes entirely unprovoked by any falling headgear whatsoever – I, Jo the Nerd, would quote, word-for-word, vintage episodes of *Buffy the Vampire Slayer*. I owned every available *Buffy* DVD box set. I was a regular in *Buffy* forums and chatrooms.

And it didn't stop there. I had a superior knowledge of straight-to-TV movies. You know the kind I mean – the ones where everyone sobs a lot and overcomes tragic problems, based on a true story. OK, I still have that knowledge and I still own those *Buffy* box sets. But now? I usually keep it to myself.

Here's more. My wardrobe used to come entirely from charity shops. That was out of no-money type necessity, not out of misdirected reverse-coolness (you know, when you are so uncool it's almost cool?). So I often looked a mess. I really did. I'm the first to admit it.

Also, I didn't wear makeup. This wasn't because of the money thing. I could have asked for Kelly's off-casts. I could have popped into Superdrug and used theirs. But I didn't think girls should wear makeup. I thought it was 'demeaning', trying to change my face to 'mirror a state of perpetual arousal'. I read that in Mum's feminist magazine. I used to recite it to the makeupy girls at Boringtown High, the ones Hailey and I call the Delicates. It wasn't just a convenient excuse for the fact that every time I tried to wear makeup, it fell off my face into my lunch and didn't taste very nice.

Do you believe me now? Thought so. That's how uncool I was. Utterly, unashamedly uncool.

Don't worry, I haven't changed completely. Jo the Nerd's still in there somewhere. But my Josie the Cool side has popped up for a party – a party for two in a cluttered closet. And I'm partying with – sorry, KISSING – Jake Matthews.

My partywear includes makeup now. And I think my party partner is wearing a lot of my lipstick too.

The old me might have said Jake Matthews was as 'demeaning' to girls as makeup. He's one of those boys who's so drop-dead gorgeous that he's never had to try – you know, he clicks his fingers and girls literally come running to him. Of course, the old me would not have experienced any finger-clicking action from any Jake Matthews types in the first place.

Here's more about how exactly it happened.

So Mum tells me she's been offered a job in the USA. She sits awkwardly on the edge of my bed and fiddles with the wooden beads on her necklace, and first of all she says, 'Boston,' so I say, 'In Lincolnshire?' and I can't believe it when she says, 'No, in Massachusetts.' And I wonder how I'll ever be able to spell that. Is there a rhyme for spelling it? Or am I thinking of Mississippi?

Mum tells me it's a great opportunity for her. She does technical stuff with computers and not a lot of people know the stuff she knows. So she was head-hunted. (There go those zombies again!) And she's been offered a job. In the USA. I already said that, didn't I? But it's such a big deal.

It would probably be temporary, about a year, and I don't have to go with her. Although she is allowed to get a visa for me. And I've just done my Big Bad GCSE exams, so it's OK to go now. It could be like a year out before A levels. The A levels I've chosen are pretty dull anyway – history, English, geography – compared with the things I've heard I can study in the USA, where it's all Psych 101 here and Advanced Trig there, and even plain old maths sounds more exciting without the 's'.

Or I can stay here and live with Dad and Kelly. Mum has discussed it with Dad, although she'd miss me so much. I can even have my own room at Dad's instead of having to share with Lolly, like I do when I visit now. I can go to Boringtown Sixth Form College with Hailey.

Mum goes on about how sorry she is to do this to me. In fact, the visa application isn't in yet, it might get denied, maybe she should turn the job down anyway? She would hate to ruin my life. She remembers what it was like to be fifteen and have your life turned upside down. She never quite forgave Grandpa for leaving Grandma in an exam year.

I have to contain myself. I can't seem too keen. It might make Mum suspicious about why exactly I want to go. It might put her off taking me with her.

But really?! Swapping my life in Britain, where I couldn't be much lower in the social pecking order, where I have no boyfriend and I hate school and there's nothing to do in Boringtown where I live? Where I've been thought of as weird and geeky since I was five years old and told everyone on my first day at school that I was related to Batman? (They still sometimes call me 'Batgirl' now. And, no, they're not laughing WITH me, either.)

I worry that they're going to tease me in America though, for being British. It could even be worse than the bat thing.

'Am I going to get called a Limey?' I ask Mum, because I remember studying that in history last year – about British sailors in the nineteenth century sucking limes to stop scurvy, or something, and the Americans using 'Limey' as an insult to Brits.

But Mum just laughs and tells me, 'Nobody uses that term any more, Jo-Jo, don't worry. Just be yourself. They're going to love you.'

But what about the people who love me now? I wonder. Will I miss Dad and his sleep-inducing words of ultra-sensible wisdom? Will I miss Lolly's gooey kisses? I know I won't miss anything about Kelly, so that's no problem. But will my best mate Hailey forget me in a year? Will she get a boyfriend before me, one I haven't vetted and approved?

Mum reminds me that there's always email and phones. And visits. It's not as if I'm going to the other end of the world. I can e-vet Hailey's potential boyfriends. Lolly can blow sticky kisses into the phone, with the hidden benefit that it would upset Kelly and cause a phone-disinfecting crisis in the house of the second Mrs Reilly.

Anyway, I know Hailey wouldn't hesitate if she was offered a chance like this, so I shouldn't feel guilty. I know it because she puts on an American accent all the time, and pretends to be an 'aaah-some' extra from an American TV movie. She totally fancies American actors in general, and Boston is at least in the same continent as the one most of them hang out in.

So would I swap being Batgirl for the life I've seen on so many telly programmes and films? A life filled with proms and sleepover parties and banana splits in ice-cream parlours?

'Mum,' I say, 'I think it would be OK. I mean, I think I would miss my schoolwork terribly' – here I pause and try not to snort – 'but I think I would survive. Besides, I'd like to be with you. To support you.'

Uh-oh. Maybe the 'schoolwork' and the 'support you' were a bit much. Mum gives me a strange look.

I add, 'And I've always wanted to see what a real American high school is like. Do you suppose they'll have jocks? Will they take mean-girl cheerleaders to dances?' I have a quick fantasy about being a straight-haired popular-girl type and going to a prom with a fit American football player.

Then Mum smiles and gives me a hug, because she knows me inside out really, and she understands I'm going to love this as much as she is.

'You're a good kid,' Mum tells me, mimicking a line from eight out of ten of the TV movies we watch together when one of us is ill or just miserable.

I smile and reply, right on cue, 'I luuuurve you, Mo-m.'

We pretend-sob at each other for about a minute.

The next few weeks are difficult. We have a long wait for visas, lots of worry and panic and packing.

I'm sadder than I expected about leaving Hailey. She comes round the morning before we leave, and brings my birthday present. I unwrap it right there on the doorstep. It's a framed photo of me and her – one she took last summer, with her new camera phone held at arm's length. We look like we're reflected in a giant spoon. We've got huge smiles on our distorted faces, my nose looks even bigger than usual, and you can barely see Hailey's lovely auburn hair around the edges. You can see my trademark curly brown mop, though – Hailey even has a strand obscuring one of her eyes.

I look at the picture and have a sudden worry that nothing will ever be the same between us again.

'I'll email you every five minutes,' I promise, my voice wavering.

'You will not. You'll be too busy having aaah-some fun.' She pouts and blinks a lot. Hailey never cries. She prides herself on being tough. Old people at bus stops used to call her 'laddie', until she got all curvy last year. Now they just purse their lips at her sporty hoodie and trainers and total lack of girliness. 'Don't worry about me, I'll be fine. I've got running club. And maybe I'll hang around with the Delicates next term. There's a two-for-one on false lashes at Claire's Accessories.'

'Oh, Hailey! Don't you dare change!'

'You're the one who's going to change, Batgirl. You'll probably have forgotten how to walk outdoors by the end of next week. They drive everywhere in the US, you know. They drive to malls and then power-walk around them for exercise.'

'I won't do that.'

'No, you'll stay at home by your luxury swimming pool, eyeing up bare-chested pool boys.' She smirks.

I've been kind of imagining the same thing myself. 'Oh, Hailey. Can't you get in my suitcase?' I sniff.

'Just go. You'll love it. Send me a lifeguard.' She gives a little wave, turns away and runs down the street, her new cross-trainers adding extra spring to her speed. I can't believe I won't see her again for months. I clutch the photo and sniffle for ages.

When Dad and little Lolly-Lauren come round to say goodbye later that day, I cry properly. I start the moment they walk in, and by the final goodbye I'm in floods.

'Bye bye, Lolly-Lol,' I manage through my tears. I squeeze her tight, making salt-water stains on her perfect miniature designer T-shirt. Kelly looks at me like I'm doing it on purpose.

'Bye bye, Jo-Jo-Jelly.' Lolly squirms out of my grip, climbs onto the sofa and launches off it. 'See my jump!'

'That's a great jump.' I sob.

I soak Dad's shoulder too as he puts his arms around me stiffly and says, 'Remember to check the exchange rates regularly – the dollar's not as weak as you might think. And brush your teeth at least twice a day.'

I sobbingly promise to do both those things. Then I give Kelly a peck on the cheek. That dries my tears up at last.

Dad tells me he'll come and visit before Christmas, which is only a couple of months away. But it might as well be years. Lolly will have done a term of pre-school by then. She'll be noticeably bigger and older. She might even be able to pronounce her real name.

Kelly says she's looking forward to shopping in New York. I don't tell her that I don't think she can pop on a bus from Boston to Madison Avenue for the day. It's not a good time to have another row with Dad about respecting Kelly.

Mum appears at the end of the big goodbyes. She nods slightly at Dad and says, 'We'll see you before Christmas as arranged. Excuse me, I've got lots of packing to do.'

I think how great it will be for Mum to get away. I touch Hailey's photo in my pocket, surrounded by the half-melted sweets Lolly just gave me to eat on the 'hairy-plane'.

I'll miss them, but I can't wait to go.

Stepping up to the Plate

In a minute we'll get to the juice – the Jake Matthews stuff. Hold on though. There are a couple more details you need to know first.

I'm in a suburb of Boston called Milltown, Mass. – and I can spell 'Mass.', no problem – USA.

It's nothing like the America I expected and I might have to sue some film producers. I've heard that's the thing to do, here in the States. Practically no one lives in high-rise apartments, and I'm not living on the 51st floor like Hailey said I would. Just as well I didn't pack my telescope. (It's a joke! I'm not that geeky! My telescope is broken. Joke again! I don't have a telescope.) (Any more.)

We're living in a large wooden-slatty building where each floor is a flat (OK, an apartment). It's called a three-family, and we're the family in the middle. Our place has the best shower I've ever seen in my life, but everything else is broken and even the doors don't close properly. It's more of a power shower than an apartment, really. It took Mum and me two panicky days of high-life hotel-living to find it. Mum did the panicking, I did the high-life bit. Ooh, they had the nicest doughnuts at that hotel!

Mum spent so much on deposits and fees and doughnuts that we had to sleep on the floor for three nights before she could transfer money from England to rent a bed. And we had to buy lots of house stuff from the Walnut Street Thrift Store, which is huge, and so much funkier than it sounds. And I mean 'funky' in a good way, not in the American smelly-cheese sense. I even bought myself some new clothes for school there.

Speaking of which, let me tell you about my first day at high school.

So. It's only a few days since our plane landed (on my birthday – I got an extra five hours of it this year!) and I'm still wide awake at four a.m., sore from sleeping on the hard floor, and sixteen years old! Getting to school on time is no problem even if the school day does start stupidly early, not to mention the fact that it's still August. This is much more like what I imagined when Mum first told me I'd been enrolled as an American high school junior.

The school's a big, factory-style building that everybody round here calls The Mill, although I've no idea why because it looks nothing like a mill, unless, uh, the mill happened to look exactly like a large school. But anyway. The Mill is the focus of Milltown. It's also just round the corner (or block) from our apartment in downtown Milltown, so I don't get to catch any yellow buses there in the morning. In fact, even though Hailey went on about the US and its car culture, so far I've walked everywhere here.

Mum's sad because I don't get a chance to shout, 'Bye, Mom, the SCHOOL bus is here!' which we'd been rehearsing back in England. I wouldn't have been able to do it anyway, because Mum has to leave really early for her swanky new workplace, Brain Drain, Inc. They also don't really believe in holidays for staff there, and after the Great Apartment Hunt she can't get any more time off work. So I have to walk to The Mill by myself.

But that's OK. That part is easy.

Then I stand in the shadow of the huge red-brick building and think, Now what?

There are groups of kids chatting and laughing, and they look pretty normal, really. I mean, take away a bright J. Crew sweater or two and add a scruffy Boringtown High navy-blue school jumper or two, make the scary-thug types slightly less mean-looking and more bored-looking, and these are pretty much the same kids. I think.

I see a girl with amazing sleek black hair that covers half her face. Most of her clothes are black too, and her red lipstick practically glows on her face in contrast. She's leaning against a pillar, lost in a book. I edge close and see it is called *A Teen Girl's Guide to Witchcraft*. Something about the way she pulls at her hair while she reads sort of reminds me of Hailey. What do I have to lose?

I open my mouth and speak before I can change my mind.

'Excuse me, could you please direct me to Principal Harwood's office?'

Oh, great start, Jo. Could I sound any more British? I have no idea why that came out in my poshest telephone voice. I've made the Queen sound like a total chav in comparison.

The witchy girl glances behind her at a boy with wild, just-out-of-bed hair. Next to him is a tall black girl who looks and stands like a catwalk model. I didn't realize the witchy girl wasn't on her own.

'First floor, turn left,' the supermodel says. 'Are you a transfer?'

The others stare at me. I think my accent has left them speechless. I nod my reply so as not to expose them to it again. I know from watching *Buffy* that I'm being asked if I'm from another school, not whether I'm an iron-on picture for a T-shirt.

As I walk away, I hear one of them say something that sounds like, 'Too cute,' and then lots of laughter, but I'm not sure who said it or whether it's about me. Or whether it's good or bad.

Ten minutes and lots of stairs later, because the first floor actually turns out to mean the ground floor around here, I find the office.

Principal Harwood's assistant gives me my timetable, only he calls it a schedule, and makes me choose some options, only he calls them electives. I choose lots of maths-related subjects because I want to say 'math' as much as possible. Then he tells me that based on my British school report I am an honour student (Hailey would call it 'girly swot') and pairs me up with another honour student, a girl who is all scrubbed and sensible. The clean girl shepherds me around all morning, babbling about 'school spirit'. I start to think we might be friends, if I can work out what she's talking about, but then she shows me to a huge room at lunch time and disappears with a quick 'See ya.'

I'm on my own! I know absolutely no one and I AM absolutely no one. I'm terrified.

That's when I see sleek-black-hair girl again. She's definitely on her own this time, but still wrapped up in the witchcraft book. Must be a good book. Maybe she'll let me borrow it some time. She's the first person in The Mill I spoke to. She's practically my best friend here.

'Excuse me,' I say. 'Do you mind if I sit with you?'

This time, the girl doesn't even look up. She speaks in a flat, casual voice. 'Get lost,' she says, and she follows it with a string of similar-sounding things, including lots of swearing, some that I don't understand. I think it might be Spanish. Definitely rude though. And then she adds, 'Limey.'

Huh! I thought no one was supposed to use that term any more. Trust me to pick the one person in the whole of the US of A who still says it.

Anyway! It isn't my fault I'm new, is it? And pardon me for speaking! I don't say either of those things, because as comebacks go, they're pretty rubbish. And while I stand there trying to think of something witty and cutting to say, I see this gang of perfect girls. They're slick, they're stylish, and they're heading for ME!

I've seen this crowd before in countless films. The popular crowd, who stride down the high-school corridors in slow motion so their glossy hair flies around making pretty patterns as they walk. I almost smile at them because they look so familiar. But then I remember that they never hair-swish in the direction of new-girl nerds unless it's bad news.

Uh-oh. Why have they stopped in front of me?

'Hi, I'm Chelsea,' says the lead girl, blonde and beautiful, smiling sweetly, 'and this is Kristy, and Chris, and the others.' Kristy and Chris stand one on either side of her. I don't know which is which. They remind me of Cinderella's Ugly Stepsisters, caked in makeup and attitude. Their clothes match Chelsea's, as if they decided together what they'd wear today. 'The others' consists of a goofy-looking girl, hanging back slightly, and another ordinary-looking girl.

I try to get some insults ready, just in case. I can't be a pushover on my first day. I'm not quite sure how to be anything else though. This is exhausting.

Chelsea rests her hand sincerely on my arm and whispers loudly, 'I know you're new and all, but I can't believe you talked to Rachel Glassman!' She tosses her perfect blonde hair in the direction of sleek-black-hair girl.

'Bite me,' says Rachel calmly. She still hasn't looked up from her book.

Chelsea narrows her eyes, but it's lost on Rachel.

Still holding onto my arm, Chelsea marches me away from Rachel, which I'm almost sad about. She was rude, but I think witches are far less scary than style princesses. Chelsea's making me nervous just by standing next to me.

But, hey, new beginnings! I want to reinvent myself, don't I? It's time for a whole new me. How hard can it be?

Then the questions start. I don't have much time to think. It's worse than any GCSE exam ever!

UGLY SISTER 1: Are you a junior? We're juniors.

ME: Yeah, I—

UGLY SISTER 2: What's your name?

ME: Uh, Josephine Reilly – my friends call me Jo, but, er—

CHELSEA: So, Josie, where are you from? You have the coolest accent.

ME: Er, England, it's—

GOOFY GIRL: England! Cool! Hey, my cousin Brad lives in London – do you know him?

UG SIS 1: Duh, Tori, you do NOT have a brain. So, Josie, why'd you come here?

ME: Um, er, it was my mum's job – she works near Route 128—

GOOFY GIRL, MUST BE TORI: Hey, do you know Prince Charles? Dad would be psyched! Or Prince Harry? He's so almost hot.

ME: Er, no.

ORDINARY GIRL: Tori! Duh! Josie, do you have a boyfriend?

UG SIS 1: We've all got boyfriends except Ana. I'm with Carl and Chris is with Anthony, Chelsea's with Bryce and Tori's with Greg. But Ana is SO getting asked out by Jonny Wells soon, it's totally obvious.

ME: Er.

ORDINARY GIRL, MUST BE ANA: Shut up, Kristy. Oh, I wish.

UG SIS 1, MUST BE KRISTY: You shut up, you totally ARE. She totally is, isn't she, Chris?

UG SIS 2, MUST BE CHRIS: So what's his name?

ANA: Yeah, what's his name, your British boyfriend?

ME: Um, um, Prince. No, um, William.

KRISTY: Huh?

TORI: She said William. Oh, he sounds hot. Is he missing you? I bet he is. Is he visiting soon?

CHELSEA: Come on, girls, it's time to eat. Come with us, Josie, we'll show you the only cool place to sit. Chris, get me an apple, would you?

UG SIS 2, OR RATHER, CHRIS: Sure, Chelsea. What kind of apple would you like? Should I wax and polish it for you?

OK, Chris doesn't say that last sentence. But she wants to, I swear.

So that's my first conversation with the coolest group of junior girls at The Mill. Not too bad, if you ignore the fact that I just invented myself an English boyfriend called William. See, I can do this! I can be one of them.

I sit with the it-girls at lunch, fitting right in. At least, I think I am.

19

And at the end of lunch Chelsea says, 'So, Josie, you going to Tori's party on Sunday night? Chris, tell her.'

There's a stunned silence. This is obviously a very big deal. Chris looks impressed. Kristy looks disgusted. Ana looks surprised. Tori looks not remotely annoyed that Chelsea is inviting people to her party.

'Tori's parents do this thing when they have parties,' Chris starts dutifully. 'We get to use the whole basement and they keep out of the way.'

Tori nods. It's like, even though it's at her house, the party doesn't have that much to do with her. Maybe she's just a useful source of party venue.

'And all the hot guys are going to be there,' Chris adds.

'Even Jake Matthews, and he's not dating anyone right now,' Kristy says.

'Yeah, but you are,' says Chelsea. 'And anyway, Josie doesn't even know who that is.'

Kristy glares at me. I pull my shoulders in, making myself smaller. If only I could make my hair blonder and my clothes mall-ier. I wish I was more like them.

'Josie, Jake Matthews is the coolest, hottest boy at The Mill.' Kristy's face softens and she sighs, the acid look leaving her face at the mere mention of this guy's hotness.

He must be something special. I can't wait to see him.

Chelsea yawns, though I thought she looked kind of

dreamy at the mention of Jake Matthews too. 'So anyway, be there, Josie. Come on, I'm getting out of here.'

She stands up, swishes that hair again and strides
away smartly, with Kristy and Chris falling into step,
one on either side of her. Ana and Tori scurry behind
and I'm not quite sure what to do with myself, until
Tori hurries back and says, 'Come on, Josie.'

My brain races with thoughts like: Help! Nothing to
wear! They'll realize I'm not cool! Save me!

And Tori does. She says, 'Want to come over later? I
could do you a makeover like you wouldn't believe! I
can lend you clothes too.'

I like Tori.

That afternoon I go home with Tori. Her house is
very different from my 'three-family'. There's room for
about five families in her house, but only hers live
there.

'Quick, let's go to my room,' she says as we walk
into a hallway the size of my whole apartment. The
walls and high surfaces are covered with framed
photos. I expect to see baby photos of Tori, but instead
there's mostly one familiar, older face. It's the Queen –
in at least ten different single-coloured outfits, posing
with a serious half-smile. There's a portrait hanging
further up the wall. It takes me a second before I recognize it's a painting of Prince Charles and Camilla,
wearing green wellies and standing by a horse.

Tori twitches. 'It's upstairs,' she says, leaping

towards a grand staircase that wouldn't look out of place in Buckingham Palace.

'Honey, did the ceramic corgis from eBay arrive yet?' a male voice booms from somewhere to the left of us.

'Upstairs!' Tori ushers me desperately, but it's too late. A door opens and a man in a tweed jacket smiles broadly at us.

'Ah, Victoria. I thought you were your mother. How was school? Who's your friend? She looks a bit different than the usual starved fashion victims you bring home.'

'Da-aaad,' Tori whines.

'I'm Jo – Josie,' I say. I'm not quite sure what my name is any more. Then, maybe because Tori's dad is staring at me as if I've just said something amazing, I feel compelled to add, 'I'm from England.'

Tori looks horrified. 'No,' she murmurs.

'Oh my! You're British! Oh my! Splendid! Do you say "splendid"? You really must. It's a marvellous word. You do say "marvellous"? Oh, my, Tori, why didn't you tell me you have a British friend? This is marvellous, splendid, ahhh, spiffing? Spiffing news.'

Poor Tori – I've never met a more embarrassing dad in my life. My dad, who has been known to bore Hailey about taxation law, looks positively normal in comparison to Tori's cringe-machine of a parental unit.

'Da-aaaaad. Please quit it.' Tori looks miserable.

'Would Josie like to take some tea? My nephew in London says it's true that the British drink tea all the time. He couldn't answer my other questions though. Josie, maybe you could help?'

I nod, even though Tori shakes her head and looks longingly at the stairs.

'Where do the princes mostly buy their clothes?'

'Sorry?' I don't know what I was expecting, but it wasn't this.

'Harry and Wills. Is their tailor contactable online? I'd really like to know. I want to buy my son a special suit for his eighteenth.'

'Dad. Josie and I have to study.'

'I'm really sorry. I don't know,' I mumble.

'Oh, my. I just love your accent.' Tori's dad gazes at me in admiration. 'Victoria, I must tell your mother how marvellous it is that you have a new friend. Josie, I have so many more questions. About Windsor Castle – oh, and as you know, our family name is Windsor – yes, that's right—'

'Mum's probably still in the pool. You should go talk to her there right now.'

'Splendid idea, Victoria. Farewell, Josie.'

Tori looks mortified as Mr Windsor strides away. But when I laugh, she joins in, and we giggle up to her room.

She sorts through a rail of designer clothes in her huge closet. 'I'll turn your cool British look into a cool American one in no time, Josie,' she says.

I'm pleased she thinks I have a cool British look, so I don't correct her, but she makes me feel comfortable enough to tell her I think I need all the help I can get, and not just today, either. So Tori says she can lend me lots of clothes and shoes. We have a slight problem with sizing – at first I think Tori must wear children's clothes, her size is so small, but her clothes seem to fit me snugly. Neither of us understand the shoe sizes, but through trial and error we work out I can wear most of Tori's shoes too.

For the next hour or so I have an amazing makeover session. I admit to Tori that I eat my makeup and I've never worn heels. She says I can borrow her 'flats', and she teaches me techniques to stop me snacking on my lipstick.

I let Tori fuss over me. She straightens my hair so that it doesn't have a mind of its own any more.

Then she calls in her older brother, who is a senior at our school, to evaluate my transformation from a male point of view. Tori instructs me to change in the closet and emerge at regular intervals in different outfits for Albie to rate.

'Albie's a singer and guitarist and a total musical nerd,' she says right in front of him, with a grimace. 'But he plays hockey with Jake Matthews and he's popular with the cool juniors and seniors, so his opinion sort of counts.'

He grins.

He doesn't look like a nerd to me. He has spiky dark hair and these deep Jake Gyllenhaal eyes you can lose yourself in if you're not careful. He's pretty fit, in fact, but I won't mention that to Tori, because he's her brother and because she probably doesn't know the term 'fit' anyway.

At first I cringe about standing in front of Albie in my different 'new looks', but he talks a lot and I relax. I could listen to his warm voice saying American-boy things like, 'All RIGHT!' and 'Way to go' and 'That looks cute' all night.

Sadly for me, after a few thousand outfits, Albie looks at his watch and says, 'Sis, I have to go now.' He edges towards the door.

'You're not going to Mrs Cook's again, are you?' Tori asks. 'Can't you stay a bit longer? It's important.'

Albie jiggles the door handle. 'No, I really gotta go,' he says. 'But listen, Josie, you look great whatever you wear and whatever Tori does to your face.'

And that's the end of the assessment.

After Albie leaves, Tori tells me that he doesn't usually notice girls, even when they fall all over him begging for a date, so she passes me with an A grade just on the basis of his last comment.

So thanks to Tori, by my second day of school I'm transformed into a cool girl. With my new looks and my old accent, I've arrived.

Playing in the Big League

Remember what I said about the accent? I'm finding I can get away with saying any old rubbish because no one listens to a word I say, just the way I say it. And they love me for that.

The exception to this is Kristy. She listens to me, which is annoying.

'So tell me more about William,' she says on Wednesday in the lunchroom, looking at me intently. Something about her expression makes me wonder if she suspects I made him up, but she can't possibly. I answer all her questions as quickly as I can. Thankfully, someone in a less-than-designer outfit comes in and distracts Kristy into a flurry of 'Omigod!' and 'LOOK at HER!'

By Thursday morning, when Kristy starts the questions again, I'm thinking I'd better dump William as soon as possible. He's trouble. And anyway, I decide, we've been growing more distant. It's very sad, but long-distance relationships can easily become strained.

I spend the morning moping around a lot, and the girls take me to the toilets, only they call it the restroom, for a lovely girly heart-to-heart. I've never been on the inside of one of these before. It's brill. The girly heart-to-heart, I mean, not the restroom. The restroom's on the disgusting side of the usual school uncleanliness scale.

Chelsea must think so too, because when we get there, she wrinkles her barely-there nose and signals to Chris. Chris reaches into her designer bag and takes out a can of cleaning fluid and a cloth and wipes some graffiti off the wall. Then Chelsea looks happier and she says to me, 'Tell us all about it, Josie.'

'It's William. I . . . I miss him so much.' I give a small, feminine sob.

The girls crowd round, hugging me and making soothing noises, while I cry a little more and streak Tori's mascara. (On MY face!) It's easy to squeeze out some tears. I think about Lolly, and my house on Normal Street, Boringtown. Part of me – my Jo the Nerd side – really is homesick. The rest of me – my cool Josie side – is loving the spotlight. The Limey-light.

'We might be breaking up.' I sniff.

'No way, Josie. I'm sure you'll make it through,' Tori says, slightly too helpfully. I've been avoiding her well-meaning William reassurances all week.

'We won't.'

'You will.'

'No. We won't.'

'You will. They totally will, won't they?'

I can't argue any more. I'm too busy basking in the reassuring noises. Even Chelsea gives a sympathetic cluck or two. It feels wonderful. I sniffle and let them fuss until it's time for class.

At lunch I finally meet Jake Matthews. There's a

buzz as he walks towards our table. The girls whisper his name and stare.

'Hey,' he says, leaning towards Chelsea with a smooth bicep-flexing movement.

I think all the girls stifle gasps.

'How ya doin', Cookie?'

I give Tori a meaningful look and mouth, 'Cookie?' I thought Chelsea was with Bryce.

'Just his nickname for her. Her last name's Cook,' Tori whispers to me, without taking her eyes off Jake Matthews. 'She and Jake have known each other like for ever.'

I soon stop thinking they might be an item. Because I can't help noticing that, all the time he talks to Chelsea, Jake Matthews is looking over at me.

At ME!

I keep looking down or around because I don't know what to do. Should I smile at him? Should I just gaze into his eyes? His eyes are amazing. They're different colours. One is blue and one is brown. And he keeps looking at me. Those EYES!

Then he smiles at me. Wow, what a smile. I can see why Chelsea and Kristy and the gang all fancy him. He's the male equivalent of them, really. He's blond and perfect. More than perfect.

He gives me one more look and says, 'Later.'

There's a silence as we watch him go. He has an amazing body. His muscles actually ripple as he walks. He's fit in every sense of the word.

Wow. It's nearly the end of my first week in US high school, and not only have I survived, but I'm friends with the coolest girls in the school, the hottest boy in the school is acting like maybe he fancies me, and I'm about to go to an exclusive party with all of them. It's more than any Batgirl could have hoped for.

As we walk to class, Tori describes the outfit she's decided to wear for her party. I used to find this kind of talk boring, and part of me still does, but I'm also fascinated by some of the details. There are types of neckline I've never heard of, and even the colours Tori lists sound exotic. Like, what's 'deep plum'? And 'smoked cerise'? There's a whole rainbow of hues I've never heard of, here in cool-girl land.

We all stop by Chelsea's locker.

Chelsea frowns at me. I realize I've been smiling at nothing in particular. I push my face into a matching frown. I forgot – cool girls aren't supposed to smile, not without prior authorization.

We stand around in non-smiley silence for a minute while Chelsea gets some books out of her locker. A group of younger girls walk past and give Chelsea admiring looks. Actually they're giving me those looks too. Wow. I've never been looked up to before. I could get used to this.

Kristy gasps. 'Oh God, Chelsea. Witchy losers at ten o'clock.'

Chelsea yawns. 'Kristy, no one does the o'clock thing any more.' But she turns, and the rest of us copy her.

There's no one at ten o'clock, but somewhere around half past eleven I see that sleek-black-hair girl again – Rachel. She's with the supermodel and the wild-looking boy I saw her with on my first day. I think all three of them are in lessons with me, but I usually spend all my time planning what to say to the cool girls at lunch. I haven't really noticed the other honour student nerds.

The wild boy gives me an infectious sort of grin, complete with eye-twinkling. He looks like fun. I grin back.

'Omigod, Josie smiled at psycho boy!' Kristy declares.

I wipe the smile off my face again.

Rachel's seen me too. 'Limey!' she calls. 'Look at you! Nice clone job!'

Wild boy says something and puts his arm on Rachel's shoulder. She shrugs it off.

Their tall friend walks up to me. 'Hey, newbie.' Her voice is clear and proud. 'You don't want to be friends with them.' She looks genuine and friendly. 'Believe me.'

What does she mean? The cool girls have adopted me since my first day. I DO want to be friends with them. And anyway, what's the alternative? Not tall girl and her friends – Rachel made it pretty clear what she thought of me.

'Oh MY God,' Kristy says, putting her hands on her hips.

'Kendis, you're so not welcome here. Stick with the freaks where you belong,' Chelsea says. She waves her away with one hand.

The tall girl – Kendis – narrows her eyes. 'They're much better friends to me than you ever were, Chelsea, honey,' she says.

Rachel adds, 'And I'd watch out for that so-called boyfriend of yours. Heard he was hanging round the freshmen again, looking for fresh meat.'

Rachel and Chelsea stare at each other for a long moment, and I wonder what Chelsea's going to say next, but a boy appears behind her and puts his arms around her waist.

'Bryce!' Chelsea squeals. She squirms as her boyfriend kisses her neck.

Rachel and the wild boy kind of whisk Kendis away, but not before I hear Rachel hiss, 'You'll be so sorry, Limey.'

I feel a bit shaky. I say quietly, 'What was all that about?'

'You don't even want to know, Josie,' Kristy says importantly. She's definitely about to tell me, but she freezes. I smell a minty, smoky fragrance. I turn sharply towards it.

Jake Matthews is standing really close to me. I can barely breathe. All the other girls stare at me, except Chelsea, who's mid-kiss with Bryce.

'Hey,' he says casually, as if he hasn't noticed the effect he's had on me. On all of us.

'Hey,' I squeak.

'You going to the party on Sunday?'

I nod.

'Cool. See you there.'

He swaggers away. Kristy's mouth is hanging open.

Tori tugs at my arm. 'Oh, God, Josie, he likes you, he likes you!'

Bryce is chewing on Chelsea's ear. He whispers something and Chelsea laughs. Then he shouts, 'Wait up!' and bounds after Jake Matthews.

'Class,' Chelsea announces, and we all trot off behind her.

I spend the time between then and the party in a dream-world, constantly thinking: He likes me, he likes me.

Taking a Rain Check

It's Sunday, the day of my first ever American party.

We're in the basement at Tori's house, but it's not like any basement I've ever been in before. It's not dank or dark and I can't see a single cobweb. There are no spiders – they've probably all died of starvation because it's too nice for bugs to live here. It's all glitzy and glam, like most of Tori's house, and there's a bar, and plush sofas and soft lighting. I can see why the cool gang use this as a party venue.

Tori's parents are upstairs having their dinner party, and they haven't poked their heads down once to see if we're OK, or even to ask me any more questions about the royal family. There's a separate entrance to this basement, so it's really like we've got our own club.

At the beginning of the night, Tori's brother Albie comes over to say hello. He gets me a drink and we sit on a sofa. He laughs softly with me about his dad. He asks me loads of questions about how I'm settling in. I start telling him about Mum and hotels and doughnuts, but I trail off when Jake Matthews yawns and stretches by the bar, his muscles rippling. I catch Jake Matthews's eye and he smiles at me.

'You know Jake Matthews?' Albie asks.

'Uh-huh.' I don't manage to steer my gaze away from the bar area. There's a silence. I can't help it. Jake Matthews has cast some kind of spell on me and I can't look away.

'I gotta go. We're playing in a few minutes. My band, I mean. We need the practice,' Albie says.

'Uh-huh.'

Jake Matthews chugs a beer. Such manly chugging.

'Hey, maybe later you can tell me what you think of us.'

'Uh-huh.'

Jake Matthews throws his head back and laughs at something Bryce says. Even his laugh is sexy.

'Well, I guess I should go,' Albie says.

'Uh-h—' Oh God! He's coming over. Jake Matthews is coming over here.

'Hey,' Jake Matthews says, beaming that amazing smile. At me.

'Hi,' I breathe.

'So see you later,' says Albie, getting up.

'The Red Sox,' Jake says, sitting in the space Albie has left. He stretches out and rests his arm on the back of the sofa. 'This season against the Yankees . . .' He keeps talking.

I watch his beautiful mouth move, and wonder what it would be like to kiss him. I put my arms by my sides to steady myself. I feel slightly faint.

After a few minutes some music strikes up, guitars jangling an indie rock sound. It's good enough for me to tear my eyes away from Jake. I look over to where Albie's singing, his face full of concentration and passion.

But Jake's arm creeps closer to my shoulder and the sudden whoosh-whoosh of my heartbeat in my ears drowns the music out.

'. . . Red Sox. Don't you think?' Jake looks straight at me again with those eyes. My stomach does a somersault.

I nod and giggle, all Josie the Cool.

And then he throws me with, 'You don't know what I'm talking about, do you?'

'Um, not really,' I say in my Jo voice. I add another Josie giggle to make it OK.

He laughs a deep laugh. He touches my shoulder. I shiver. Could this guy BE any sexier?

Yes. He could.

He leans closer and says, 'Listen. Let me tell you about baseball. It's all about getting to the bases. First base. Second base. Third base.' He takes a long swig of his beer. 'Home run,' he says meaningfully, piercing me with those eyes.

If I was in a cartoon right now, the caption would read: 'Gulp!'

'Not like you guys with your soccer,' Jake Matthews continues in a throaty voice. 'Straight to the goal. You know, in one smooth move. Wham, bam, thank you, ma'am.' He punches his arm forwards.

Double gulp!

OK, we're nearly there. The kiss.

So. Albie's band takes a break and the room goes quiet.

Then Tori says, 'So, hey, guys, should we play Seven Minutes in Heaven?'

There are a lot of loud groans and comments about not being in seventh grade, which doesn't mean a lot to

35

me but I understand that they think kissing games are for babies.

Then Chelsea cuts through the protests with, 'Tori wants to play. It's her party. We're playing,' and everyone stops moaning.

I can't believe they really do play those kissing games at parties, like in films. In England, all the boys who've ever tried to snog me (OK, only two boys, mentioning no names, Leechy Lewis and Slug-kiss Steven, urgh) got drunk first. Nothing as nice and polite as a game.

Chelsea tells us we're playing Guy Rules – some simple version of the game. We won't be spinning a bottle or anything because that's way too seventh grade. Each boy just picks a girl and they go in the closet for seven minutes.

Bryce shouts, 'Matthews, you go first! Go get some of that accent action!'

Jake Matthews takes my hand and stands up. I manage to stand on my wobbly legs. Jake Matthews. Is. Holding my hand.

'Come on,' he says, heading for the closet.

He chose me. Jake Matthews chose ME!

I let him pull me into the closet.

He doesn't exactly click his fingers. I don't exactly come running. But, you know. Jake Matthews . . . and me. I'm definitely not Batgirl now.

I go into the closet with Jake Matthews.

He shuts the door, turns and presses his lips on mine.

And now.

Here I am:

Kissing Jake Matthews.

I can't believe this is happening to me! I'm the luckiest girl in the world.

His lips are soft and his tongue is, um, wet. Not sluggy, like Steven. He tastes of sweet mint with an underlying smokiness, but just a hint. Nothing too disgusting.

I don't feel like throwing up or anything.

Wait though.

Isn't a real kiss with a mega-fit guy supposed to lift me off my feet?

Why am I even thinking about Sluggy Steven or being sick?

I know why. It's because I'm being Jo the Nerd. And I'm thinking, Jake didn't ask me anything about myself. What does he know about me? I could be any girl.

My Josie the Cool side, though, is thinking about what the girls must be saying outside. I bet they wish they were me.

My mind keeps wandering.

So do Jake Matthews' hands. They're sweeping over my clothes, they're creeping under my clothes. They are everywhere. There's one reaching up my top, there's one pulling at the belt loops on my cool jeans (well, Tori's jeans), there's one up my back on my bra strap, and another one at the top of my left leg. He must have about eight hands. I pull them away but they keep coming back.

A few more minutes of this and he says, 'Baby, please, let me touch you,' in a low, husky voice. A melty voice that makes me think maybe I should let him. I've never been called 'baby' before – well, not that I can remember. I was probably a baby the last time. And what's the harm? It certainly feels . . OK. Sort of nice, I suppose.

But there's Jo the Nerd in my head, blaring, *No, no, get off!* All I actually say is, 'No.'

'Come on, baby,' the husky man-voice pleads.

'Let's just do *this*.' I move his hands and kiss him.

This is fine for another three seconds and then his hands are back again.

I nudge them away politely.

'Please, baby.'

'No.' This is muffled because his lips are clamped to me.

The hands keep reaching.

'No.'

The hands move and push.

'No!'

Ugh! I pull back suddenly.

This doesn't feel so great any more. This kissing-

Jake-Matthews-in-a-closet thing. The closet smells damp. The kisses feel cold.

I laugh nervously. 'It's just that I have this boyfriend at home,' I say. 'I mean, it's not serious, and I want to kiss you and all, but . . .'

I put my mouth back where it was, setting my body firmly to 'kissing only', hoping that will be OK.

But Jake Matthews pulls the light on – and I'm too nervous to be impressed that they have lights in their cupboards here.

I blink for a second or two and then I see that he isn't smiling. Those beautiful eyes are on fire, especially the blue one. I don't like them like this.

'You should have told me before,' he says.

Yeah, like when? When he was leaning over and talking to me about baseball and soccer? I didn't want my imaginary boyfriend then. I wanted Jake.

'I just like you so much,' I say. It's my Josie voice, all whiny and girly.

'Everyone does,' Jake says without a trace of irony. 'You should dump that Brit guy and hook up with me again. And let's at least get to second base here.' He sinks his mouth onto my neck.

Look, I know what you're thinking. But this is Jake Matthews, the greatest catch in the school. And he wants to 'hook up' with me.

Plus, what he's doing to my neck? Tingly much? Wow.

Wait a second though. Hook up? Second base? What exactly does that involve? That was my Jo the Nerd voice, asking that. Yeah, she's still here.

My Josie the Cool side says out loud, 'You know, maybe next time . . .'

The butterflies in my stomach do an Irish dance and, in my head, Jo the Nerd shouts, *No way, Josie-José! No next time!*

Split by a Kiss

'OK,' says Jake Matthews. 'You're kinda different. I sorta like you.'

He gives me a hard slap on my bum. He puts his hand on the closet door knob.

He says, 'Next time.'

My Josie the Cool side giggles.

My Jo the Nerd side gasps.

I feel woozy. The closet's spinning.

I try to steady my head by focusing on a boyishly stylish padded jacket hanging in the corner, but everything still whirls around me. The whooshing in my ears is deafening.

Josie the Cool feels nearly sick with passion and the minty manly smell of Jake Matthews.

Jo the Nerd feels nearly sick at the stale cigarette-smelling arrogance of Jake Matthews.

My mind pulls in different directions.

I'm splitting, tearing in two.

I'm two different people.

Literally.

Two.

I'm split.

How will I ever be ME again?

Who am I, anyway?

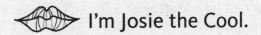 I'm Jo the NeRd.

I'm Josie the Cool.

I'm Jo the NeRd.
I push away my Josie the Cool side, and just like that, she's gone. Who was she anyway, giggling at this total letch?

Jake Matthews doesn't like me. He doesn't even know me. I could be any girl.

Who cares what the girls out there think? They're not real friends.

As Jake Matthews opens the closet door, I slap him.

I shout, 'You need to learn to . . . to respect women!' and I storm into Tori's basement with my whole body trembling, shaking in a totally different way than on the way in.

I can't believe I just did that.

I really am Jo the Nerd.

41

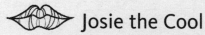 Josie the Cool

I push away my Jo the Nerd side, and just like that, she's gone. Who was she anyway, turning away this perfect catch?

Jake Matthews likes me. Who cares about anything else?

All my new friends must be wishing they were me.

I follow Jake Matthews out of the closet. I pull at my clothes, not realizing at first that everyone is staring at me, until one of Jake Matthews's friends shouts, 'Way to go, Matthews!'

I'm the girl Jake Matthews wants to hook up with! I'm so lucky! I'm Josie the Cool!

SECOND BASE

Jo the Nerd

There's a roomful of people staring at me.

Did I really say that 'respect women' thing? Out LOUD? Did I just SLAP Jake Matthews?

Although he slapped me first. On my bum. I HATE that. Why do boys do that? It's so 'I-own-you'. They deserve to know how horrible it is. They deserve to be slapped back.

The room is quiet except for a couple of talk-show-audience whooping noises. Jake Matthews smiles calmly and says, 'Whatever, man. That chick has issues.'

Chelsea has a smirk on her face and I feel like slapping her too. Now I've started, I can't stop. I'm a slapper. I take a big breath, and then another one.

'What's the problem, Josie?' Chelsea asks, with that sickly sweet smile.

'Your friend Jake Matthews is the problem,' I say. My voice is shaking. 'I think he should leave. Now.'

This might be overkill. But I'm so angry! And the more people stare at me with those stupid expressions the angrier I feel.

There's more whooping and some boy says something about ice and needing to melt it. Jake Matthews shrugs but Bryce suggests the other boys might help, and a few of them laugh and do high-fives.

Chelsea isn't smiling any more. 'Josie, chill out,' she says.

'She couldn't get much COLDER,' a boy calls. I think it's Chris's boyfriend. I've never even spoken to him.

'My name is Jo, not Josie,' I tell Chelsea. I look at Jake. He's gulping a beer. 'If he's not going to leave, then I will!'

'Suit yourself,' says Chelsea.

Chris adds, 'Loser.'

'Yeah, Josie, Jo, whatever your name is,' says Kristy. 'Maybe now you can stop trying to look like us and get some clothes that fit you.'

I pull at the clothes I'm wearing, all Tori's clothes. Suddenly they seem too tight and I feel squeezed and ugly.

'Maybe she can wear some of that baggy thrift store garbage like she was wearing the first day of school,' says Ana.

'Told you she wasn't cool,' says Kristy. She looks at Tori, but Tori's looking at the floor.

'But Ana, that's what they WEAR in EUROPE,' Chris sing-songs. 'I'll bet Will-YUM-YUM loves dating a girl who looks like a BUM!'

'Watch it, Chris,' says Chelsea. 'She's British. I think you just said Jo looks like a BUTT.'

Now they're all laughing, except maybe Tori, but I can't tell because Tori is still studying her feet.

'Watch out or she'll send William over to get us,' Kristy says, smirking. 'IF he even exists, that is.' She looks me up and down, full of catty challenge.

I'm too shaken up to think straight. I just stare.

'Yeah, what colour are William's eyes? You've told us at least three different colours so far. How many eyes does he have anyway?' Kristy asks.

'Maybe he's from another planet,' Chris says seriously.

'I don't buy it,' Kristy continues. 'But what kind of uber-loser would invent a boyfriend?'

Everyone's eyes are on me. Tori looks worried. Jake's still got his 'whatever' face on, but I think I see a flicker of interest there too. I wish I could disappear.

I probably did change William's eye colour a few times. How was I to know Kristy would listen to me so carefully?

Tori speaks softly. 'William's real, isn't he, Josie? Waiting for you back in Britain?'

There's no point. 'No,' I mumble.

There are new rumbles of laughter. People who didn't even know I ever said I had a boyfriend called William are joining in. Haven't they got anything better to do? I've had enough of entertaining everyone with my humiliation.

'I don't care what you think of me. I'm leaving,' I say, and I head for the door. Behind me, Kristy's talking in a fake British accent, with added extra-whiny tones. *'I'm special. I'm Jo! I date invisible guys. Oh, Jake, don't kiss me THERE, it wouldn't be PROPER!'*

The rumbles turn into roars. Laughter rocks the room.

A male voice from the back of the room says, 'Hey, wait!' I don't stop to see whose it is.

I hear it again, louder, but then Chelsea says, 'Just leave her, Albie. She wants to be ALONE!'

I shut the door on the laughter and run out, my steps thudding in my ears. I blink back tears. So much for being cool. They can keep their cool. I wish I could go back to Boringtown tomorrow. I wouldn't mind being Batgirl again. How am I going to face school now?

Josie the Cool

There's a roomful of people staring at me.
I adjust my clothes and smile.
Jake Matthews high-fives a friend and grins.

'How far did you get?' a male voice shouts.

I giggle and say, 'Shut up!' to Jake Matthews, even though he didn't say anything.

The room dissolves back into conversation and the girls surround me.

'What was he like?' asks Chris.

'Dumb question, Chris – just look at her face,' Ana replies.

'Jake Matthews is so hot,' sighs Kristy, checking quickly that her boyfriend Carl, who is two steps away, hasn't heard.

It doesn't look like I have to do any of the talking here. Phew. I give what I hope is a Mona Lisa smile. I am an enigma! An enigma who has just snogged the hottest boy in the school and is pretty confused about it but wouldn't dream of letting on.

'So are you two an item now?' asks Chris.

'Will he take you to the Winter Dance?' asks Ana. 'Oh, I bet he will. What will you wear?'

'It's over two months away, Ana,' says Kristy with a sniff. 'There's no way they'll last that long.'

'I'll lend you a dress, Josie,' says Tori.

I notice that Chelsea hasn't said anything. In fact, she's looking at me like she wants to squash me flat with her spiky-heeled shoe and scrape me off on the pavement.

'Who's going in next?' says Chelsea. 'There are hotter guys than Jake Matthews.'

'There are?' Ana asks.

'Hey! Who's next? When's it my turn for some?' Bryce yells. 'Oh yeah, Jonny boy, you need it more than I do. Go get your chick.' He shoves a shy-looking boy towards us.

'Want to?' Jonny mumbles at Ana.

'OK,' Ana mumbles back.

They disappear into the closet.

'So anyway, Josie, tell us how far he got in there,' says Chris, and our group closes the gap that Ana's left, more or less leaving Chelsea out. Out of the corner of my eye, I see her glowering. But I don't care. I'm cosy in this circle of admiration, with me at the centre. I think I've really made it here. I love this feeling.

I don't live far from Tori's house, but the walk takes me away from the large houses with lawns and fences, across Winter Street and into a whole different area, where the houses are clustered together and are mostly three-families like mine. Through my blurry eyes, I keep seeing things I love about living here. Everything looks foreign and yet weirdly familiar. Little bars and convenience shops are dotted among the houses. There's a faint smell of fried chicken in the air. There are different road signs – bizarre yellow rectangular ones (why are those SLOW CHILDREN all running?), and exotic red-and-white ones (NO RIGHT TURN ON RED, when red surely means 'stop' anyway?). The traffic lights hang from cables in the middle of the street, like I've seen on television for years before coming here.

I love seeing all this, but I've had my adventure. I want to walk into Boringtown Sixth Form College tomorrow and sit with Hailey and talk about what we watched on television last night, because we don't have boyfriends, and though we moan about it, we have each other and we're happy. I don't worry about who my friends are. No one stares at me when I speak. It's my world and I can hide if I want to.

I hear footsteps somewhere behind me and I break into a run without looking back. I didn't worry at all about getting home. I was sure someone from the party would drive me. How was I to know they'd never even talk to me again?

Even though I'm wearing Tori's shoes, I manage to run pretty fast, probably thanks to all the times Hailey talked me into training with her when I didn't have running shoes on. Then I stop for a minute to get my breath back, looking round nervously. Silence. Nothing. I must have imagined it. All the stress is sending me loopy. I walk again, ignoring my pounding broken heart.

I'm going to tell Mum I want to go home. She's been so understanding, constantly checking whether I like it here, reminding me that it might take a while to settle in. But she's settling in just fine. We had to rent or buy everything when we moved here, away from 'the drabness of Britain' (I think she meant 'away from Dad'). She pretended it was all a headache, but I think she loved it. She kept going on about our 'new start' and she relished bargain-shopping for all these American things like 'fry pans' and 'toaster ovens' and 'take-out sporks'. Even the kitchen stuff is cooler here. But no amount of cool sporkitude can save me from the horror of facing The Mill tomorrow.

When I get back to the house, Mum is still up. She is watching the cable television we got hooked up as soon as we moved in. Everyone at Mum's work told her that even if she couldn't afford a bed yet, she'd have to get cable. And they were right because we have this channel called Lifetime, which shows all our favourite TV movies on some kind of blissful continuous loop. But right now even the thought of Lifetime doesn't cheer me up.

Mum's feet are up on our rented coffee table, a big bowl of buttered popcorn in her lap. She almost chokes when she sees me.

'You're home early!'

I sort of nod. If I speak, I'm going to cry.

'Everything OK?'

I make an uh-huh sound, but it turns into a sob.

'Oh, Jo-Jo! What happened?'

I sniff and shove a big handful of Mum's popcorn into my mouth. It looks so tempting, I can't help myself.

Mum looks relieved. 'Oh. Bad party?'

'Stop asking questions! Leave me alone!' I pull at my clothes. Tori's clothes.

I run to my room, kick off Tori's shoes, tug off her clothes and throw them on the floor. At some point I'll have to give them back to her, if I can ever face her again. She looked so let-down about the William thing. I can't even think about it. I pull on fleecy purple Jo-style pyjamas, throw myself on the bed and give in to crying.

'Jo-Jo!' Mum calls after a few minutes.

'What?' I mumble into my tear-soaked king-sized duvet.

'Come here! Quick!'

I can still smell the warm butter on the popcorn. I may as well see what she wants. I shove my feet into my slippers and shuffle back into the lounge, sniffing.

Mum points to the television. 'It's your favourite.'

It's an advert. A man with a heavy Boston accent is talking about the CA-ARS in his showroom and telling us to TRUST him, Kingly Cars are the WICKED BEST, they beat all the rest. Then he bursts into a song-and-dance routine, all twenty stone of him, and he leaps onto the bonnet of this huge brown car. I swear I can see a dent where he landed. This usually makes me howl with laughter.

Tonight I manage a small smile.

'Oh, Jo, can't you tell me what happened?' Mum holds her bowl of popcorn out to me.

'No! Nothing.' Just total humiliation, that's all. I take a handful of popcorn and slump down next to her. 'Mum, I want to go home. I mean, for good.'

'Really?' She stares at the telly. We watch another couple of glitzy American adverts. 'I thought you were enjoying it here.' She points around the room. 'You know, the electrical sockets are dainty.'

It's true. We both raved about those little cuties when we moved in.

'And we have screens on the windows,' I say quietly.

Mum nods. 'And that charmingly infuriating lock on the bathroom door,' she adds. The bathroom door mysteriously unlocks itself if you turn the handle from the inside, causing me and Mum to spend hours opening the door when we want to check it's locked.

I know Mum has a point. I am in the United States of America. Even the boring stuff is interesting and new. Everything here is better than I imagined. I've just embarrassed myself beyond belief in front of the coolest people in the school. But I haven't seen a New England snowstorm yet. Or tried to skate at an ice-hockey rink.

'I can't go to school tomorrow! I'm not . . .' I look down at my *Buffy* slippers. 'I'm not cool!'

'Oh, I see.' Mum shakes the bowl at me. 'Cool. Who's cool? I bet none of the people I work with were called cool at school, but they are the most interesting people in the world to talk to. Some of them have maybe even met Tim Berners-Lee. You know, at MIT.'

I don't have a clue what Mum is on about, but I nod and delve into the popcorn. 'So if I'm not cool, do I have to be a computer geek like you?'

'No, you can be another sort of geek,' Mum laughs. 'There are lots to choose from.' She absentmindedly smoothes my hair. 'Anyway, Jo, you've still got your friends in England. Send Hailey an email right now! You haven't been in touch yet, have you? It can be hard for the one left behind, you know.'

'I know. You've said that before.' But she's right. I've been so caught up in the party preparation with Tori, I've ignored my real friend.

'Hey, you could invite her here. Maybe she could travel with your father, before Christmas. She can sleep on your floor. And if you really wanted to, I suppose you could go home with your father afterwards. We'd have to talk to him about it.' She grimaces.

'But Christmas is years away,' I moan. How am I going to survive in the meantime?

'Your father and Kelly can go to a hotel, of course. There's no way I'm having him here. There's no way

I'm having HER here, pointing out dust particles.'

I'm always impressed by how casual Mum is about all the pain Dad caused her. He left over three years ago now, but I still feel hot and panicky in the pit of my stomach when I think about it.

I do my best exaggerated Kelly voice to block the feeling. *'Oh! Calamity! There's a speck of dust and my weeny wittle Lau-wen-wen might breathe it in!'*

'Jo!' says Mum, pretending to be shocked. Then she adds, in her newly developed American accent, 'It's a cleaning emergency! Call 1-800-CLEANER!'

Even through my laughter, I can't stop thinking about school. If I hadn't reacted so Jo-the-Nerdishly, I'd still be at that party now, and I'd still have friends. Kristy might not have said anything about William. In fact, they'd probably be congratulating me for kissing the hottest boy in the school. I have blown my one chance of being cool.

But I was just being myself. How could I have done anything else?

Mum nudges me. 'Jo, don't worry so much. I can't believe you haven't noticed what I'm watching.'

On the screen, a trashy-looking girl is holding a gun. Her bottom lip quivers spectacularly. I recognize the TV movie instantly. I've seen it thousands of times.

'Oh Mum! Of course! It's the superior version!'
Mum nods.

This remake was less famous, less cool. I think it was better.

'Don't do it for him!' I shout at the television.

'He's not worth it!' Mum joins in.

'No man is!'

Mum laughs. 'Oh, Jo,' she says. 'Talking of men, but nice men, I need to ask you. Do you want to come to this international party thing my work are having on Friday? It's at a posh hotel.'

My first thought is: Hotel? Will there be doughnuts? But then I roll my eyes and rest my head in my hands. I mean, I have no friends, and I'm considering socializing with my mother. How low can I sink?

What did Mum just say though?

'What do you mean, *talking of nice men*?' I've never heard Mum show any interest in men.

'Well, OK, nice boys. One of my colleagues has a boy at your school. Apparently his son asked if you were going to the party.' Mum nudges me. 'See, I don't know why you worry.'

'Mum!' I roll my eyes again but now I'm totally intrigued. 'What's his name?' I don't know why I'm asking, really. Mum's always been rubbish at names.

'Frederick McSomething. We all call him Frap because he's always drinking those frappuccino thingies at work.'

I give her a look.

'Oh, you mean the boy. I don't remember. Frederick

McSomething Junior?'

I sigh. 'No distinguishing characteristics?'

'Frap didn't mention any. They're originally from Manchester, if that helps.'

I can't think of anyone with a Manchester accent at school, let alone anyone who might have noticed me.

Then again, I haven't exactly been approachable at school since I started. I've always been surrounded by the in-crowd, wrapped in a thick layer of popularity. And look how that turned out.

McNiceBoy might be just the friend I need.

'OK, Mum, I'll go. Being seen with you in public can't make things any worse right now.'

Mum smirks and pretends to throw popcorn at me, until I take the whole bowl off her lap.

I settle down and shout at the screen. 'NO! Don't kiss him! He'll only let you down!'

'Typical man!' shouts Mum.

I laugh hard to cover the scary feelings about surviving in this country till after Christmas, when tomorrow at school I will be so socially dead.

 For the rest of the evening, girls ask me about Jake Matthews. I feel sparkly and popular.

As everyone starts to leave, Jake Matthews catches my arm and says, 'So it's Josie, right?'

'Yeah, um, Jake Ma— Jake,' I say. It feels strange not

calling him 'Jake Matthews' – no one ever calls him by just his first name. I wonder if even his parents do. I imagine his mum calling, 'Jake Matthews! Your dinner's ready.'

My arm burns where Jake Matthews – sorry, Jake – is holding it. I think I'm smouldering with passion. Or maybe it's pain because he's gripping me too tightly. One or the other. I giggle at him.

'So, Friday night. Me and you.'

It's not a question, but I chirp, 'OK,' as Jake casually walks off with his muscle-bound friends.

'Want a ride home?' Kristy asks me. I can't believe she drives! We're only sixteen. I nod and follow Chris and Ana to Kristy's car. I nearly climb in behind the steering wheel, but I realize my mistake and laugh. Then when I do get in the right side, I have to climb under a seatbelt that's already done up and I get all tangled, and I laugh even more. Kristy stares at me. Chris and Ana get in the back and whisper.

'So you're seeing Jake?' Kristy asks me as she pulls away.

'Yeah.' I try to keep my voice casual, but I don't manage it for long. 'I think he asked me out!'

'Uh-huh,' says Kristy. 'Anyway, where do you live?'

I'm slightly embarrassed about the girls seeing my house – it's not in the swimming pooled, we-have-a-gardener neighbourhood they live in. On the other hand, I can't wait to tell Kristy my address. It's wonderfully American-sounding.

I live on Main and Lexington,' I say. Soon I see the two green street signs, one crossed over the other in that American way, right by my house. It gives me a kick every time I see them. But Kristy just says, 'Here? That's so – adorable.'

I haven't yet managed to work out sarcasm here. So far I get the impression Americans are not sarcastic at all. Like when they say 'Have a nice day', they really seem to mean it.

So I mutter, 'Thanks, Kristy,' and I get out of the car. And she says, 'Sure.'

Chris says, 'That explains a lot,' and laughs, but I'm sure it's not about me. She's been talking to Ana all the way here.

The house is silent. Mum must be asleep. She's left me a note that says, *Hope you had a nice night. I did! Good one on Lifetime! Forgot to tell you – big work party on Friday – want to come?* And she's drawn tick boxes for 'yes' and 'no'. Mum is enjoying herself, I can tell. She's thrown herself into our 'new start'. This last week I've been out at Tori's a lot and I haven't seen her much, but every time I come home she's bought a new American-sounding thing for the kitchen, and when she talks about living here, her eyes go all bright. I bet she'd love me to go to this thing with her on Friday.

I hesitate, but of course I'm seeing Jake Matthews on Friday. And he's just 'Jake' to me!

I pick up a pen and tick 'no'. I can't be going to social events at Mum's work – that's such a Jo thing to do. Besides, how could I break a date with Jake?

I put down Mum's note and that's when I notice that the laptop we brought from England is switched on. Mum's left it open on our web mail page. I bet she's hinting that I should email Hailey. The other day she said, 'Have you phoned Hailey yet? It's always harder for the one left behind, you know.' I was on my way out to Tori's, so I mumbled something about phone bills and ran, but she called after me, 'Email her! Tell her about Voice over Internet Protocol!'

Even Mum's nagging is nerdy.

I know Mum likes Hailey, but I bet she wouldn't like Chelsea's crowd. Mum's got short hair and wears comfy, hippie-style clothes and chunky shoes and no makeup. I bet Chelsea's parents are drop-dead glamorous. Mum doesn't care about that stuff. She's a grown-up version of Jo the Nerd.

I sit down and log in to my mail. There are five new messages from Hailey, full of gossip about people who seem a lifetime away. There's a guy called Jonathan at her running club and he might be about to ask her out. I thought I'd feel upset if she got a boyfriend when I wasn't around to approve, but now I've got Jake and I think she deserves someone too.

I wonder what Hailey would make of Chelsea's crowd? She'd probably have a go at me, tell me I was turning into a Delicate. I don't know how I'd explain that the girls I hang around with here aren't like that. They hold more power in their perfectly manicured fingernails than Boringtown's most muscle-bound Delicate-girl-rescuing boy. I'm not giving myself up to be a part of Chelsea's gang – I'm making myself more. Tonight proved that to me.

I write Hailey a message telling her I'm fine, but I don't go into detail. I invite her to visit at Christmas – maybe she could even travel with Dad. Besides, December's miles away – it should give me some time to explain my cool friends.

I go to my room and take off my clothes and shoes. Well, Tori's clothes and shoes. She's the best friend ever. Like Hailey, but cooler.

I lie on my rented bed and pull back my king-sized comforter. (I love the name 'comforter'. It's so much cosier than a duvet.) I wrap it around me and, comforted, I replay the evening. Jake chose ME. And I think Chelsea was weird with me because she's jealous. What a rush to have Chelsea jealous of me! I think, as long as Jake Matthews is interested in me, I can easily stay in with Chelsea and her friends. And I definitely want that. I could never go back, not now I know how it feels to be the centre of attention, the girl everyone wants to be.

I must ask Tori exactly what second base means. I need to be ready for Friday.

As soon as I get to school on Monday, I have a brief encounter with the Ugly Sisters in the corridor, and it's exactly the kind of thing I was dreading. I hear Kristy hiss, 'Oh, isn't it suddenly so COLD in here,' to Chris, who laughs and says 'Brrr' and hugs herself in a stupid mock-shiver.

'Quiet, Chris, you'll upset her imaginary boyfriend,' Kristy laughs.

I pretend I haven't heard them and I put my head down and walk round the corner. How am I going to get through the day? Especially lunch? And there, right in front of me, is the perfect escape. A sign-up sheet for a lunch-time class. It's called 'Personal Relationships', and it's every Monday and Thursday for the whole semester (and semesters are even longer than terms, of course!). I'll figure out what to do with the other three lunch hours some other time.

The first thing I notice when I get to Personal Relationships is some kind of counsellor with wild red hair. She has to be a counsellor because when I go in, she gives me a serious and sincere smile, and says, 'Hi, I'm Karen! Welcome to our kooky group. Feel free to eat your bagged lunch if you have one, and chill out with the others for a few minutes before we begin.'

Our kooky group? Eek! Is this a cult?

There are some others here. I don't look closely at them, but they give off a general moody slouching vibe. No one's eating. The chairs are arranged in a circle. I feel lots of eyes on me as I slump into the nearest empty seat.

The boy sitting on my left asks me, 'What are you in detention for, dude? Did they catch you with dope too?'

What? Dope? Detention? It didn't mention that on the sign-up sheet.

I shake my head and shrug. I think I can blend in OK if I don't spoil it by opening my mouth and being all British and standy-outy.

I look to my right and notice that Rachel's friend, the wild-looking boy with the infectious smile, is sitting next to me. He's concentrating on tying the laces of his leather boots.

I scan the room for his friends, and sure enough, Kendis and Rachel are here too. I wonder why they're in detention, if that's what this is. Maybe they're escaping lunchroom taunts, like me. I seriously doubt any amount of insults would trouble Rachel though. Her black hair is covering her face and everything about her says Back Off. I hope she's not going to notice me and start up the 'Limey' thing again.

Kooky Karen looks at her watch. She seems to be counting.

'Hi, I'm Karen!' Kooky Karen says at last. I think she

cued herself in. 'As most of you know. But it's nice to see a new face here today.' She looks at me and so does everybody else. I shrink into my chair.

'So, let's introduce ourselves. I want you to say your name and something about yourself – one feature will do. See how much you can remember on the way around. It's a good way to connect. I'll start. My name is Karen and I have red hair. OK? Lenny.'

'Er,' mumbles a boy with long greasy hair. He hesitates, but he's obviously done this before, because he starts to recite, in a monotone, 'Her name is Karen and she has red hair. My name is Lenny and I have brown eyes.'

The person next to Lenny, the druggie boy who spoke to me earlier, comes to life again for a few seconds. 'Her name is Karen and she has red hair. His name is Lenny and he has brown eyes. My name is Daniel and I have dark hair.'

Is this for real? Oh no, I'm next!

'Karen, red hair,' I say. Everyone sits up a bit and stares at me. Yes! I have a funny accent. And a bit of an attitude in my voice, because I can't quite believe I'm here. 'Lenny, brown eyes. Daniel, dark hair.' And then – I really don't know why, except that I'm slightly worried that all the hair and eye colours will be used up pretty soon – I say, 'My name is Jo and I've got a big nose.'

There's a slight rumble of laughter but it dies down

quickly and it's wild boy's turn to recite the list. His accent is different – maybe he's British, but he also sounds American. I'm concentrating so hard on placing his accent I almost forget what he's about to say. Until he says it. Loudly. 'And she's JO and she has a BIG NOSE!'

Everyone laughs.

Karen looks disapproving. 'David, Jo has chosen to share something with us and we need to respect that. We can ask her to share her feelings about her body with us later.'

Noooooo! You canNOT do that later! Or ever! What feelings about my body? Why doesn't Lenny have to share his feelings about having brown eyes?

'But by the way, Jo,' Karen says gently, 'you don't have a big nose.' She holds my gaze with a sincere smile.

Well, thanks. I think. But it IS quite large. It's just never worried me. Before.

Karen says, 'David, please continue.'

David has a gleam in his eye. 'She's Jo and she has a big nose,' he repeats, obviously enjoying himself. 'Jo, big nose. Big nose Jo. And I'm David, and I've got grey-green eyes.' He gives me a cheeky smile. I'm still trying to shrink into my chair. But not so much that I don't notice his grey-green eyes sparkling at me. 'And a normal-sized nose and normal-sized ears. But you should see the size of my—'

'That's enough, David,' Karen says. She doesn't look happy.

'I was going to say toes—'

'Kendis, your turn.'

Kendis smiles at David and tells the class proudly that blah, blah, blah, Jo has a big nose, blah blah, and she has African-American hair. And then it's someone else's turn, and he says Jo has a big nose and he has brown eyes. We've already had brown eyes, but Karen lets him off. So much for originality. I wish I'd kept my nose-size to myself and stuck to having brown hair. I could've even said curly. That might have been better than listening as each person in turn tells me I have a big nose. I couldn't possibly shrink any further into my seat.

Rachel goes last, and she forgets some of the details. But she doesn't forget my nose size. She shakes slightly as she's saying it, as if she's fighting the giggles. It makes her look a lot less scary and mean.

I manage to hide for most of the rest of the session, which concentrates on Lenny and some boring problem he has respecting his teachers and Kooky Karen thinks it might be because his dad once made him angry. Right at the end of lunch hour, KK says, 'Jo, we'll discuss your body issues next session. Sorry we didn't have time today. Thanks, everybody, for sharing, and remember to express yourselves, externalize your feelings. See you on Thursday.'

I leave the room, wondering how I can get out of the session on Thursday – even Kristy's Big Freeze has to be better than this.

'Hey, Limey, wait up,' says Rachel. She and her friends surround me. 'You met Kendis, right?'

'Hi,' says Kendis.

'And this is David.'

David smiles that twinkly smile at me.

'He's another Limey, of course. He's been wanting to talk to you, but you've been too busy being oh-so-POPular.'

'Hey, Jo,' David says in his funny accent. 'My dad works with your mum. Did she mention him? Frederick McCourt?'

Aha!

'Frap, the Frappuccino King?'

'Who the what?'

'Never mind. Yeah, she did say something.' So David talked to his dad about me? Interesting.

He's not bad-looking. Not at all. Especially when he smiles. And I like the way his hair falls messily over his eyes.

'Less boring talk, more action,' Rachel says.

'Rachel, honestly, you are so rude,' David says. 'Jo, what Rachel meant to say was: do you want to walk with us to class?'

'No,' says Rachel, 'I meant to say: do you want to walk with us to class, Big Nose?'

I tag along next to them as they stroll down the corridor, laughing and nudging each other.

On Monday at school, I'm at my locker talking to Tori before my first class when I see Jake absentmindedly kicking his locker shut. He's got that slouchy yet confident, sporty-guy look, like he's so in control of his every movement there's no point in putting any effort in. The way he kicks his locker is precise and effective. He is fitness on legs. On fit legs. So what if his kisses didn't lift me off my feet? When I look at those amazing, differently coloured eyes – eyes that are fixed on ME – my knees feel weak. I clutch Tori's arm and lean against my locker. Jake walks over.

This is it. This is where I find out whether what happened in the closet, and afterwards, was all a dream. I can barely breathe.

'Hey,' he says. He rests his arms on my locker, one on either side of me. I'm framed by his strong arms, held in thrall by his fit body.

So I wasn't dreaming. Maybe I'm dreaming now.

'About Friday?' he says.

'It's OK,' I simper.

I'm not quite sure what I mean. I think I mean, It's OK to cancel. But maybe I mean, Whatever you want to do on Friday, it's OK by me. I think I would agree to anything.

I giggle.

'Good, 'cos I have tickets to the hocky game at Harvard. It's a pre-season game. Should be good.'

He leans slightly closer to me.

I hold my breath.

'You like hockey?'

I nod, because I can't speak. I don't really know what he's talking about. What's a pre-season game? And hockey? The girls at the posh private school in Boringtown play that, and I've heard it's all about who can bash their opponents' ankles the most.

Then I realize that I'm in Boston now, and of course he's not talking about schoolgirls in gym skirts. He's talking about ice hockey.

Cool, I've always loved skating. Or rather, the idea of skating, and watching skaters. It hadn't really occurred to me that I could ever watch a roomful of men skating, live. It sounds great.

Although, if I'm going with Jake, I probably won't be able to think about anything except him and his wonderful sporty-guy-itude.

'I'll pick you up at eight. Main and Lexington, right?'

I nod again. I never told him my address. He must have asked Kristy! Oh WOW!

'OK. Friday.' He moves in even closer and for a second I think he's going to kiss me. If I hold my breath any longer I'll faint. But I'm saved by Chelsea in the distance, calling, 'Jake! Bryce is looking for you.'

'Sure,' he calls out and then, quietly to me, 'Later.'

Tori's bursting with an I-told-you-so smile.

Neither of us speak for a long time, and then she says, 'So how about Wednesday after school? I'll pick out an outfit for you.'

I nod gratefully.

This hockey date sounds perfect. Plus he can't expect to get to second base while watching a game, can he?

I wish I wasn't an honour student – I can't talk to any of those nerds in my lessons. I wish I shared classes with Tori so that I could talk to her about Jake Matthews all day long.

It turns out that Kendis and Rachel are in nearly all of my lessons. So is David, who I'm finding more seriously gorgeous by the second, though I'm managing to hide my feelings. At least, I hope I am.

I rush at the ends of lessons so that I'm ready to tag along with Kendis, Rachel and David to the next classroom, but by Wednesday I'm starting to notice that they're waiting for me anyway, like they're expecting me to hang around with them. They're full of out-there jokes I don't understand, but by sticking close to them, at least I avoid the in-crowd taunts. And no one else in the school even knows I exist.

That's what I think until Thursday morning before my first class.

I'm in the girls' toilets, in a stall. I would have left by now, only I've stopped to look at a brilliant caricature of one of Jake Matthews's friends, drawn on the wall. It's Bryce, with whiskers and mousy ears. Underneath it says, *Avoid this rat*, and another couple of scribbled comments. Above all this is a printed sign that says, THESE WALLS HAVE BEEN TREATED WITH ANTI-GRAFFITI PAINT. RESPECT YOUR SCHOOL. THE ADMINISTRATION. I smile – the Bryce-rat artist obviously doesn't care about respecting the school.

Then I hear some voices from outside the stall. I freeze. They're talking about me.

'So did you hear about the new girl? She threw her-self at Jake Matthews, even though where she comes from kissing is, like, deeply wrong.'

'Really? Deeply wrong? Where's she from?'

'Europe or Australasia or somewhere, you know, WEIRD. But anyway, then she, like, remembers her Australasian beliefs, and she goes all wild, and hits Jake Matthews.'

'That's cold.'

'Isn't it? And she says her boyfriend will hit him too. Only it turns out – get this ...' The voice is slightly muffled. I imagine its owner standing with her hand clasped to her mouth. 'This boyfriend? She totally made him up.' I hear giggles and a sing-song 'Lose-errr'.

I try to think of something cool and cutting to burst out of the stall and say, but my mind's blank.

'So Chelsea's all, *Please would you leave, freak*, but the weird girl is all, *No, Jake Matthews should leave*. But he doesn't, of course. He stays and hooks up with Chelsea.'

'I knew that part! I saw Jake Matthews and Chelsea making out in the hall. Jake Matthews is hot! Chelsea was so right to ditch Bryce for him. Did you see those rat pictures of Bryce? He's a total sleaze.'

I think for too long and the voices fade out of the door and down the corridor.

After that I hear 'cold' comments around me all day – not just from Chelsea's gang, but from people I've never spoken to. Even the ones who are obviously mega-uncool. 'There goes the ice queen.' 'Who brought the cooler?' 'Brrrr.' Ha-ha de ha-ha-ha, not. I don't say anything.

At least I can hide in Personal Relationships at lunch. I can swap the freezer jokes for a roomful of people who think I have a big nose and a counsellor who wants to discuss my body issues. Although maybe Kooky Karen senses I don't want to talk. She spends the session talking about competitiveness, and how girls frantically try to outdo each other, even if it's just to see who can put themselves down the most.

It could be interesting, but David catches my eye a couple of times when Karen's back is turned and makes

crazy faces at me. I have to turn my laughs into cough-
ing fits. Rachel spends the session sketching in a
notebook. Only Kendis looks like she's paying
attention. She sits upright with an intense, determined
look on her face.

As we leave Personal Relationships, I hear someone
say, 'Who turned up the air con?' It's Chelsea, looking
right at me with steely blue eyes and a lopsided, calm
smile. Kristy stands next to her with a matching
expression. Oh no, not again – and not in front of David!

Also, I can't believe I STILL haven't thought of any
clever responses. Never mind Personal Relationships, I
need to take Advanced Comeback lessons.

Behind Chelsea is Jake Matthews – her new
boyfriend, I remind myself. Kristy has her boyfriend,
Carl Earlwood, behind her too. Jake and Carl are like a
pair of pumped-up bodyguards. They have stupid
grins on their faces, like they're thinking 'Ooh – cat
fight' or something naff like that. Actually, Jake is
mostly staring at my chest, what there is of it, even
though his perfectly proportioned girlfriend is right
there. I'd slap him again, but I've lost all my nerve since
that party – these taunts have worn me out. I put my
head down, my cheeks burning. Luckily David has
walked on with Kendis – he seems to have missed
Chelsea's razor-sharp wit altogether. But Rachel hasn't.
She stops and shouts, 'Ooh, Chelsea, you are so HOT –
when can we get together again?'

Carl lets out a long whistle.

'Get lost, lesbian freak,' Chelsea says. 'As IF!'

Rachel makes pretend kissy noises.

'Rachel, you are a WITCH,' Kristy hisses.

'I AM a witch, and I have a voodoo doll of you, Kristy,' Rachel says. She mimes sticking pins in a doll, with a vicious stabbing action.

'Oh, I'm so freakin' SCARED. You're all freaks.' Kristy shoots killing glances at us and leaves. Carl hurries after her.

Chelsea doesn't look so calm any more, but she still gives Rachel a withering look before wrapping herself round Jake Matthews. She whispers in his ear.

'Cookie, chill out,' he says. He smiles at me. Then he links arms with Chelsea and they walk away.

How dare he smile? I hate him.

'Thanks, Rachel,' I mumble.

Rachel doesn't look at me. Her usually pale skin looks almost grey-blue right now.

David and Kendis are waiting for us round the corner.

'Had to stop and use my Cookie cutter,' Rachel steams. 'For Jo, not Kendis. So at least they've moved on, huh?'

Kendis rolls her eyes upwards. 'God, it's all gotten so old.'

David's fists are clenched at his side.

Kendis sighs. 'You know what? I need to move on too.'

'Chelsea would be no one without the guys,' Rachel says. 'I hate guys.'

David mock-coughs.

'No, I mean it. Guys all think with their dicks.'

David shrugs. 'You're probably right.'

I try to smile reassuringly at him – I'm sure he's not like that – but he's not looking at me.

Rachel says, 'I know I'm right.'

'Don't be like that, Rachel,' Kendis says. 'Some guys are OK and you know it.'

David smiles at Kendis. 'See, Rachel? Kendis likes me.'

'Not you.' Kendis hits him lightly on the arm. 'I mean, yeah, you're OK, but you know what I mean.'

Rachel glares at Kendis. 'I know what you mean. You mean the king of basketball finally asked you on a date.'

Kendis smiles sheepishly. 'Yeah, maybe he did.'

'You're not seriously going out with him, are you?'

'Yeah, Rachel, maybe I am. Trey is nothing like Bryce, you know. Anyway, I'm not a victim. You heard what Karen said.'

'I tried not to. I wouldn't even have to tune out Karen's boring self-righteous garbage if we hadn't all gotten detention because of that Bryce creep! So what?'

Rachel gets air-quotes ready. 'So you "forgive" him now?'

'It's not detention. It's supposed to help us.' Kendis looks Rachel straight in the eye. 'And I didn't say I'd forgive him.'

'No, that's peachy, Kendis. You go off with Trey, happy ever after. Believe he's not just another asshole.'

'Rachel, please—'

Rachel holds a hand up to Kendis. Then she turns to me. 'Come on, I need to Stone. Right now. Kendis isn't going to help me, so you can be my new lookout.'

Oh no. She needs to what? Stone? She has to be talking about drugs. It figures – they chat to Druggie Daniel in Personal Relationships sometimes. And Rachel expects me to be her lookout? How many difficult peer-pressure situations can I get myself into in such a short time? Hailey and I never got anywhere near this kind of stuff back in England. It was like we had post-it notes on our heads that said, *We're clean and you know we are.*

'Rachel, you know, I think you should stop the Stone thing now,' Kendis says.

I pluck up some courage. 'Look,' I say, 'I don't think I want to get involved in . . . drugs.'

There's a silence.

Great. Now I've probably lost the only friends I have. Again.

'Sorry,' I say. I sound pathetic.

Everyone looks at me. David laughs, but kindly, and his gorgeous dimple distracts me momentarily from my shame.

Kendis says, 'Ri-ight. You don't know what we're talking about.'

I give a wary shake of my head. Maybe I don't want to know.

Rachel looks at Kendis. 'Listen, Jo, I'll tell you later.'

Kendis says, 'It's OK, I can talk about it. It's just . . . Jo, there's this guy called Bryce, and last semester, well . . . he kind of got out of control at a school dance. With me. You know what I mean. I mean, he didn't exactly . . . but he almost . . .'

'He's a jerk pig asshole date rapist,' Rachel states.

'Kendis, are you sure you're OK?' David asks.

Kendis nods. 'I told you, I'm over it. You should try listening to Karen sometime.'

Rachel says, 'Huh!'

'Rachel and David are in those sessions because of me,' Kendis tells me in a soft voice. 'David got into a fight with Bryce that night—'

'I would've won too, if Coach Harrison hadn't come along, siding with that tosser.' David clenches his fists again.

'And Rachel got caught drawing pictures of Bryce on the restroom walls – warnings,' says Kendis. 'She calls them "Stones", named for this author called Tanya

Lee Stone, who wrote a novel where girls give warnings to each other in a book – warnings about boys like Bryce.'

'I write mine on the walls,' Rachel says with pride. 'Chelsea's never going to look at a book. And anyway, it's not just Stone like the writer, it's also like Stonewall. You know, equality and justice for lesbians, gay men and bisexuals worldwide. Fighting for the rights of the oppressed. We're oppressed as women.' She looks at David. 'You wouldn't understand.'

'Whatever.' David shrugs. 'It's one of Rachel's phases, like the witchcraft and the—'

'Shut up, David! I am helping people! I don't believe you – you total GUY! You are unreal!'

'Guys, guys. Don't, please.' Kendis puts her hands on her hips. 'Rachel, honey, I've told you before, I love where you're coming from' – she pauses and looks at David – 'but school's not the place for it. It's not worth getting into constant detention for this. Chelsea wipes it off every time, anyway – or rather, she asks one of her sheep to do it. And anyway, don't you think you're getting more at Chelsea than at the real problem? You know, like . . . Bryce?' Kendis's lips tighten as she says his name.

'I AM getting at Bryce,' Rachel says. 'Chelsea dumped him, and I bet it wasn't just because she hooked herself Jake Matthews. My Public Service Announcements helped. Anyway, she's part of the problem. Her and those guys – they feed off each other.'

'Honey, Rachel? I appreciate what you're doing for me.'

'And the administration doesn't care any more.'

'But, really, please stop. For me.' Kendis looks at David, but David just shrugs again.

Rachel scowls. 'No, Kendis. You go out with your cutie Trey if you like. You forget all about what happened, like Coach Harrison and the whole school want you to—'

'Nothing did happen, Rachel. Not exactly.'

'Whatever, Kendis. I guess I can be happy for you. But I don't have to follow you.' Rachel turns to me. 'Limey, like I said, you're my lookout.'

'Rachel, leave her out of this. It's not her problem,' Kendis says.

'Come on, Limey.'

'I don't know if I—' I nearly add 'approve'. But, to be honest, I liked the cartoon I saw earlier. And maybe Rachel has a point about annoying Chelsea. I think back to the day I cried all over the in-crowd about William. There must have been a Stone on the wall that day. Chelsea was obviously bothered by it. Isn't it time so-called uncool girls had some power over someone like her?

Plus, anyway, *I don't approve*? What is THAT? I sound like a teacher. I'm so glad I didn't say it out loud.

And at least she wasn't talking about drugs.

Rachel marches me away from Kendis and David.

I stand outside the main door to the toilets listening to the distant squeak of Rachel's pen inside.

'Hey, Jo,' Rachel calls. 'You want me to draw that Jake Matthews asshole for you?'

I don't reply. I want to say no, but I don't know why. I'm not sure what exactly went on between me and Jake Matthews. All I know is that, since then, I haven't felt like myself. It's changed everything. Not for him, though, obviously.

I shift from foot to foot, staring down the corridor. I'm so pleased no one has tried to get past me.

Tori's brother Albie is walking towards me. I haven't seen him since the night of the party. I put my head down – I hope he doesn't see me. He was always so nice to me, I couldn't stand it if he started with the 'cold' jokes too.

He slows down. 'Josie?'

'Jo,' I say. I don't look at him.

'Jo, are you OK?'

'I'm fine.' I check the other end of the corridor.

'Really?'

No.

I feel like telling him everything.

Instead, I nod at the wall. 'Yeah.'

'Well . . . Good. I guess.'

I study the empty corridor carefully.

'So . . .'

The door swings open behind me. 'Let's go, Limey,' Rachel says. 'We're late.' She links arms with me, ignoring Albie, and we walk to class.

The next time I use the toilets, the walls are blank. Chelsea must have wiped Rachel's latest Stone off the wall already.

I'm desperate to talk to Tori about second base. I count the days and hours till my after-school pre-Jake-Matthews-date makeover session.

Finally it's Wednesday, and I'm in Tori's bedroom trying on her clothes. I'm wearing a revealing top that probably cost more than my entire wardrobe put together. I would never normally wear anything so low-cut because I haven't got any boobs. But this top has a special bra-thingy inside it, and there it is – cleavage.

I've never had cleavage before. I pout a bit for the mirror and stick out my boobs.

Boob-popping! Me! Who'd have thought it? I'm a whole new Josie.

I find myself wondering if Tori will call Albie in to get a guy's point of view, like she did that time before the great Jake Matthews kiss.

But that's an odd thought. Where did that come from? Albie's great, but just in a friend's-big-brother kind of way. Has it taken one not-so-brilliant kiss from Jake to turn me into some boy-crazy girl who looks at every male as a potential boyfriend?

I need to concentrate on Jake. Who could want anyone else?

Behind me, Tori is wibbling her lips about because she's just tried a new shade of lipstick. She has unusual looks for a cool girl – she's not all perfect-featured like Chelsea is, or ordinary and even-looking like the others. In fact, it's like all Tori's features have said 'Yes' to the supersize option at the McFeatures restaurant. Large eyes, large nose, large mouth, large face.

But she's in proportion and I think it makes her look striking. Especially her huge eyes, which I've only ever seen enhanced by perfect barely-there makeup and extended spider eyelashes, which I think are false, but maybe not.

And her nose. I've always been annoyed about the way cartoon pictures of girls rarely have noses. Why shouldn't girls have noses? I have a nose and I'm proud of it. And Tori has a nose too. Noses of the world unite! Be large and proud!

Urgh, I'm still thinking those geeky Jo thoughts! I need to concentrate. There are more pressing things I need to discuss with Tori.

'Tori, can I ask you a personal question?' I start.

'Sure, Josie, what?'

'OK, it's like this. Um . . .'

'Yes?'

'Um . . . What's second base?'

'Oh, Josie. Maybe you should ask someone else, someone like Kristy or Ana. They're better at explaining stuff.'

'No, I want to ask you. I can talk to you.'

'You're so cute and British,' Tori says. 'Huh, well, let's see. It's more than kissing. It's like if you let him touch your boobs, I guess, or maybe get under your clothes. You know?'

Touch my boobs? Eek! I didn't even have any until a few minutes ago. And UNDER MY CLOTHES?!

'So, um, have you been . . . to second base, Tori?' I can't quite look her in the eye now.

'Yeah, sure,' she replies easily.

If she's so comfortable, I may as well carry on. 'So what's, er, third base?' I glance at her sideways. She doesn't look at all embarrassed.

'It's more than that, but less than, you know, full sex.'

I go a bit red when she says that last word. Oh, honestly. Tori must think I'm a total baby. I mean, all sixteen-year-olds know this stuff, even if they haven't actually done it.

What am I saying? All sixteen-year-olds have probably done it. They haven't spent their lives being Jo the Nerd and repelling boys.

I need more facts. I've got some catching up to do.

'And when are you supposed to . . . do it all? What kind of timescale, if you know what I mean?'

Tori sits down on the bed and pats the spot next to her.

'Sit, Josie.'

I sit.

'Don't let Jake pressure you. Because if you're not ready, he should respect that.'

'I know.' I do know. 'But he could easily . . . find someone else, couldn't he?'

'Why would he want to, if he has you? Don't worry about it. I mean it, Josie. Only do what you're ready to do. It's supposed to be fun, you know.'

'I know.' I take the top off and quickly pull on my own baggy shirt. 'Tori? Is it? You know. Fun?'

'Yeah.' She smiles.

'So have you reached, you know, third base with Greg?'

'Um, yeah.'

'Have you been all the way?'

I can't quite believe I'm asking her this. Oh, Hailey and I used to talk about this kind of thing all the time, but I practically grew up with her so it's different. Plus neither of us had boyfriends so we didn't have a clue what we were talking about.

Tori is a cool girl – I think she's the lowest-ranking cool girl, but she's still way cooler than me and Hailey.

And I barely know her. I'm sure I shouldn't be asking things like this.

'You don't need to answer that,' I add quickly.

But Tori looks perfectly relaxed. 'It's OK. Yeah, Greg and I have done it. It's no big deal.'

'When did you first . . . you know? How many dates, or . . . ?'

'Well, Josie, don't feel any pressure if I tell you this. We hadn't been together all that long. I was ready, you know. But everyone's different.' She pauses. 'It wasn't my first time.'

'With Greg?'

'No. A couple of years ago' – she hesitates, biting her lip – 'I hooked up with Carl Earlwood.'

I try not to look shocked. 'KRISTY's Carl?'

'Yeah, that Carl. It was before he got with Kristy, although Kristy already had a thing for him. But no one knew about me and Carl, it was kind of a private thing. There's no way Carl would ever tell Kristy – he knows she'd dump him for sure.'

'Really?' I feel for Carl. I wouldn't like to be on the wrong side of Kristy.

Tori looks thoughtful. 'Listen, don't tell the others, all right? I trust you, Josie, but you've heard how they can be. They twist things. Sometimes I wonder if they're my friends at all.'

'Of course they are,' I reassure her. I don't know why she's worried. They reserve any serious bitchiness for people outside their circle. That's part of the reason I'm so happy I'm in with them. Me and Tori are safe.

'Yeah, I guess.' She nudges me. 'Anyway, what about you and William? You've been with him for, like, a year? And you didn't get to second base in all that time?'

I'm quiet, and Tori adds, 'Even though I know you're kind of cheating if you go on this date with Jake, but I guess that's OK if William's cool with it. Does William know about Jake?'

'Let me tell you a secret too.'

'What, Josie? Did you and William break up?' Her face clouds with sympathy.

'No.'

I take a deep breath. Maybe I shouldn't say this. But she's been so honest with me. I want to tell her.

'There's no William. I made him up.'

Tori looks confused, as if she's not quite sure if I'm kidding or not. Then she laughs. 'Oh, Josie, you're too much! Aw, I felt so sorry for him too. I thought about calling him and telling him about Jake.'

'You wouldn't have!'

'No, of course not. I wouldn't break the girl code.' She punches my knuckles with hers. 'But I didn't think it was right to cheat on him. I thought you two had kind of a strange relationship.'

'We have a strange relationship all right. He's Mr Invisible!'

'Ooh, can you imagine that?' Tori puckers up and reaches for an invisible boy in mid-air.

'Oi! Hands off my William!'

Tori falls off the bed with laughter and rolls around shouting, 'William, where ARE you?'

Albie shouts, 'I can't hear my music!' and that makes us laugh harder.

I really wish Hailey could have come with me to Mum's work party. I'm trying to take in every detail so that I can describe it to her later.

Mum wasn't joking when she said it was at a luxury hotel. We're in downtown Boston, and the hotel is so grand it has a shopping mall attached to it and escalators leading in, with some kind of trailing jungle plant-life and a waterfall. I'm in the ballroom and there are fancy chandeliers hanging from the ceiling and grand decorations everywhere. Odd decorations. For example, I've no idea why there's an ice sculpture of a horse on the snack table in the middle of the room. This is a party for the international staff of Brain Drain, Inc. Maybe the horse is an international symbol of friendship? Or work? Or friendship at work? No one pays much attention to it except me. I've been staring at it for half an hour trying to work out how they chisel all that detail in. OK, I admit it, I'm bored. I'm also nervous, and I'm trying to look like I'm supposed to be here.

I'm wearing a calf-length, dark-green ball gown that I bought last weekend at the Walnut Street thrift store. It didn't take long to alter the dress to fit perfectly, and Mum added some antique jewellery. My hair's gone back to the mop look, now that it's not being fashionably straightened by Tori, but tonight it's falling in slightly less unruly tendrils around my shoulders. I might not look good by Chelsea's standards, but Mum said I look like a million dollars, and at least I feel like myself.

I leave the ice sculpture and find Mum. She's with a mixed bunch of people. They have accents that I think must represent most of the countries in the world. They have one thing in common, though – they all seem to love their work. And talking about it.

I stand with Mum for about a year, picking up odd words I recognize here and there – 'firewall', 'burning', 'going gold'. Or something. I've got this big smile when I'm introduced to people, but little yawns keep trying to creep out of the edges of my wide mouth. I can't think of a single intelligent thing to say, but I feel like I should say something. I start talking about the horse ice sculpture. And I don't seem to be able to stop. I bet they think I inherited none of my mother's brain-drainable tendencies.

One by one, Mum's smart colleagues excuse themselves, and then even Mum wanders off (traitor!) and

I'm left talking to just one person. He's a tall man with a moustache. He raises a polite eyebrow as I waffle, 'I wonder if a horse is harder to sculpt than another animal, like, say, a pig.'

'Horse or pig,' says Moustache Man, only he says 'orse' and 'or' with an amazingly French-sounding 'r', and he says 'peeg'. 'What makes you compare ze orse and ze peeg?'

I'm about to try and explain how much harder horses are to draw than pigs, in my limited experience, but I catch myself nearly saying 'peeg' and I have to stop talking because I don't want to sound like I'm mocking him. I can't help it – I always catch accents off people within minutes of meeting them. I bet Hailey would tell me I already have an American accent, even if no one here can detect it and everyone still thinks I'm quaint and British.

I take a deep breath and try the speaking thing again. 'Well, pee— Uh – PIGS . . .' I say loudly. And that's the moment when David appears at my side.

He has turned up to this formal ball wearing his leather jacket and boots. Not just any boots, either – they have silvery-white illustrations on the side, cartoon pictures of himself. It looks like Rachel's artwork, from what I know of her Stones.

He's wearing a posh shirt and black trousers too. It gives a strange effect. It sort of matches my thrift shop ball gown, I think.

'Hey, Jo with the big nose!' He notices Moustache Man. 'Uh, hi, I'm David McCourt, Frederick's son.'

Moustache Man says a French-sounding name I don't catch, and shakes David's hand solemnly. Then he excuses himself and walks away. I bet he's glad to get away from the Mad Peeg Girl at last.

David twinkles his eyes at me. He's got an uncombed, unconventional but extremely good-looking thing going on. He looks like trouble, but fun trouble.

'Got the drinks in, then? Where's my pint?'

'You must be joking,' I groan. I still can't believe I'm not allowed a drink. I look younger than sixteen, but I'm sure I'd get served in a place like this if I was in England, especially if I was surrounded by ancient parent-types. I drank wine at Dad's stupid wedding, and that was three years ago.

'I know! They are so annoyingly big on the ID thing here. But the A-list have automatic access to booze, don't they?' Twinkle twinkle go his eyes. 'Ah, at last I can ask you without Rachel snarking at me. What was it really like to be A-list? Was it totally wonderful? Should I try out for the team and ask Chelsea Cook for a date? I bet I could take Jake Matthews on.' He laughs.

I laugh too, though for a second I miss being part of that group. Well, I miss Tori, anyway. But then I remember that she and her friends think I am a block of ice. An ice sculpture of a person. The international symbol of loser-dom.

David says, 'I heard this rumour you were dating an invisible snowman.'

'What?' This is awful! How does this stuff spread so far around the school? I try to think quickly. 'Snow I wasn't. Snow way! Er . . . so have you seen that horse sculpture?'

'Cool.' David moves closer to the sculpture and so do I. It gives us an excuse for a comfortable silence. At least, I hope this silence is comfortable, because it's certainly long. A band on the stage starts playing old eighties songs and a load of Mum's new friends start doing gawky middle-aged dances. David stares at the ice sculpture.

'You don't often get those back home in England, huh?' he says at last. I can't get used to his odd accent. He sounds all American with this strange British undertone.

'Um, so you're really from England? Are your parents English?' I ask. Even though I've been hanging round with David all week, I don't know any of this stuff.

'No, Dad's from Manchester, but Mum's Bostonian,' he says. 'I'm a Yank Manc. We've moved around, lived a bit there and a bit here.'

'Two-parent family?' I ask. I absentmindedly touch the base of the ice sculpture and make a little finger-shaped melty dent.

'Uh-huh,' he says.

'My friend from home's like that. Hailey. We go running together.' Oh no – my mouth's taken off again. Why would David care about Hailey? 'Tori's parents are together too.' Why can't I stop speaking? 'Mine aren't.'

'Don't worry,' David says. 'It's not all it's cracked up to be. I'm not very, um, what Karen calls "well-adjusted". You know, like the way I fight idiots who deserve it.' His face is set in a hard scowl. 'Unfortunately, the whole of The Mill sides with the A-listers. Even the principal. That Kendis stuff last term . . .'

I'm not sure what to say. I put on a Kooky Karen voice. '*Well, it's important to EXTERNALIZE your FEEL-INGS.*' Then I add in my normal voice, 'I can't believe I'm voluntary in Personal Relationships. You must think I'm crazy.'

'Yep.' David's face relaxes again. 'I do.'

I pull at the neckline of my green dress. The velvet's feeling hot against my skin.

'Great dress,' David says.

'Thanks, and you look good too. I mean, uh, your boots are really cool. Did Rachel draw those?' I point to the pictures on his boots and hope he doesn't notice me blushing. Did I just tell him he *looked good*?

'Aw, shucks!' says David. 'Yeah, Rachel. She doesn't only draw on walls.'

'Hey, do people actually say "shucks" in America?'

'Nope, never heard anyone say it.'

I laugh. 'So do people still think your accent's cool or are you too American now?'

'Are you kidding? They think I'm a total Brit. I can get away with murder. Uh, mostly. But in England I get the loud Yankee tourist jokes.' He motions around the room at the international employees of Brain Drain, Inc., as if they would ever say anything like that. They'd be more likely to joke about the fall of Silicon Valley. Or peegs.

'People want you to be different, but it's got to be the right sort of different,' I say.

'That's exactly it.' David laughs. 'I'm just the same. I like the right sort of different.'

I laugh too, though I'm not quite sure why. 'But no one at school seems to understand a word I say. The teachers keep making me repeat myself.'

'Pardon?'

'I said the teachers— Oh, ha ha!'

I can't believe I fell for that! I talk quickly to cover it up. 'And Rachel still calls me a Limey. She was quite rude to me on my first day of school.'

'Oh, you really shouldn't worry about Rachel. I thought you'd got that by now. I think I taught her that word. I'm sure she means it as a compliment. She's a weirdo. But she's great, you know. She's a great weirdo.'

I almost tell him that she scares me sometimes, but I stop myself. I don't know either of them well enough.

'So how do you like maaaa motherland, Jo?' David puts on a drawl in his unusual accent, so now he sounds like he's doing a George Bush impression.

'It's better than staying in English-land.' My speaking problem is getting worse. 'I mean, England.'

'Don't you miss your friends? And your boyfriend? Apart from that invisible one everyone's talking about.'

Not that again! Wait, is he asking me if I have a boyfriend? Could he be . . . flirting with me? Quick, Jo, THINK! 'I don't miss him. He's here.' I put my arm around thin air beside me. 'William, meet David.'

David doesn't miss a beat. 'Pleased to meet you,' he tells the air to my right.

I look at him. He's not flirting – he's just being friendly.

'You're very quiet,' he says.

I'm not sure if he means William or me. I put my arm down. 'He's gone to the bar.'

'Good luck to him. Hope he's got fake ID.'

'He's over twenty-one.'

'Ah, you like older men?'

'Not really.'

There's another long silence. The beat of the music changes.

'Bowie,' says David. I look towards the stage. Aargh – is that Mum up there? It is! She's dancing with

Moustache Man, he of the 'peeg' fame, and they are mouthing the words of the song at each other and shaking their heads a lot. I will SO tease her later.

'Let's dance,' says David.

'Yes, Bowie,' I say. 'Mum loves his early stuff.'

'No, let's DANCE!' He gives me another of those twinkling killer smiles, then grabs my hand and drags me onto the dance floor.

Oh, right.

David dances! A boy who dances with me!

Well. Now I know I'm in love.

Friday night comes round far too quickly. Even though I've been working up to this all week, with Tori giving me advice every chance she gets, I don't feel ready for it.

I'm wearing Tori's clothes again – some very expensive designer jeans coupled with the Cleavage Top. I'm in Mum's room, watching her getting ready for her work party. She's totally dolling herself up, by her standards. I even saw her reach for a lipstick a second ago, although I think she's eaten it off already. My old makeup-eating habits were inherited from her.

She changes her outfit for the third time, pulling on a dress I've never seen before. The outfit is totally her style – tie-dyed all the colours of the rainbow in long, hippyish layers.

Tori would not approve.

'Walnut Street thrift shop,' she says, noticing me staring.

I would never shop there any more. Although I did see a handbag in there the other day that looked a lot like Chelsea's. It had a Louis Vuitton label, and I would have bought it except it's probably a fake and all the girls will laugh at me.

'Mum, are you sure you don't want to change your look a bit?' I say. 'Tori says—'

Mum makes a face. 'Do you think? I'm comfortable like this.' She pulls on a set of multi-coloured beads. 'Do you like these? They're new.'

Jo the Nerd would have loved them.

I'd never get away with wearing anything like that around Chelsea and her friends. I shrug.

'Well, I like them,' Mum says. 'Aren't you going to get ready? I thought you were going out? You need to wear something over that vest. You're a bit . . . exposed.'

I pull the two sides of Tori's top together near my neck. Of course, Mum's never seen my cleavage before either.

I won't bother telling her this isn't a vest, or that this is what I'm wearing to go out.

I don't lie though. 'This is Tori's,' I say.

Mum goes back to fussing over herself. 'I'm glad you've found a friend here, Jo-Jo. She sounds nice. Generous. Even lending you her underwear.' She stares into the mirror and fiddles with her beads. 'Did you say you were going to Victoria's house again tonight?'

'Everyone calls her Tori.' Again, not a lie.

Outside, an engine roars arrogantly and a horn beeps.

Jake!

I run towards the door.

'Bye, Mum, have fun!' I call, and then, just before I shut the door, I feel a twinge of meanness about not going to Mum's party, and sort-of-almost lying to her, and going out in a push-up vest.

I open the door again and shout, 'The school bus is here!'

I hope it makes Mum smile.

Jake's waiting outside, leaning against his car. And he's not alone. The car has people in it already – boys, in the back. I recognize Bryce, and I think the other one is Chris's boyfriend. I can't remember his name.

'School bus?' Jake frowns. 'It's just the guys.'

Oh, no, he heard!

Oh, no, the guys! I thought this was supposed to be a date. Why are they here? Or is that a good thing? For me, I mean. He won't expect to get to second base with them around, will he?

And yet, I don't want him treating me like one of the guys, do I? Not if I want to be the envy of the girls. Why are they here? Should I say something?

'School bus. Yes. It's, um, British humour,' I say quietly.

'Right,' he says, as if that's what he suspected all along. '*Monty Python*. Let's go.'

Jake gets in the car and waits for me. Luckily I pick the right side, unlike that time in Kristy's car. Of course, if I got it wrong I'd be sitting on his lap.

I shiver at the thought. It must be Jake's effect on me. My shivers don't seem to stop though. That's when I realize my mistake – I'm not shivering with passion. I'm cold. And we're going to an ice rink. I don't imagine they have their central heating set very high there.

'Hi, Br-Bryce. H-hi, um,' I say, nodding to the boys in the back seat.

'Anthony.' The boy who isn't Bryce gives me an evil look. Well, pardon me for not etching your name on my brain. Anyway, pop quiz, as they say here. What's MY name, eh, Mr Anthony-Uppity?

'How you doing, Josie?' Anthony adds.

'OK,' I mumble. Yeah, yeah. Lucky guess. I turn to face forwards, wondering why I'm on a date with three guys instead of one. And why I didn't bring a coat.

'So I'm psyched to get these tickets,' Jake says. 'Aren't you, guys?'

'Yeah, man. Thanks for bringing us!' Bryce says in a jokey over-loud voice.

Should I say something too? Am I included in

'guys'? Yeah, MAN, thanks for letting them crash my date?

'Yeah,' I say, only it comes out, 'Ye-ee-eah,' because I'm shivering.

There's a long silence. Jake's probably wondering if acting weird is British humour too.

I adjust my Cleavage Top. Feeling cold makes me even more conscious of my boobs. When we stop at some lights, Jake takes his eyes off the road for a second and glances at my chest. Then he looks at a pack of cigarettes on the dashboard in front of me.

'Want a smoke?' he asks my Cleavage Top.

'No thanks, I don't sm— feel like one,' I say. Good save – sounding prim wouldn't go with the boob-popping effect at all. 'You?' I pick up the pack and offer it to him, trying not to panic. I hope he doesn't want me to light a cigarette for him or anything cool-girl-ish like that. I wouldn't have a clue.

'Matthews, Coach says shoot the death sticks!' shouts Bryce from behind me. 'We got GAME, man.' His laugh scrapes my ears.

'Who brought Coach along?' Anthony grumbles.

Jake stares at the cigarettes in my hand, then quickly back to my chest, then back to my hand. The hand:chest ratio is around 2:1.

'Coach says I have to give up,' he tells my hand. 'But that's OK. Smoking's for losers.'

Oh. Then why can't my boobs compete with the

cigarettes? Isn't tonight supposed to be second base night? I wiggle, trying to work the Cleavage Top, but his eyes follow the cigarettes as I put them back.

It takes us about an hour to park, and every time I point out a parking space, one of the guys tells me loudly why it's the worst spot in the world. I'm sure they nudge each other at one point, as if to say, *Who's this loser who couldn't find a parking space in a desert?*

'There's one, Jake,' I try again.

'Who brought HER?' Bryce shouts. I don't think he can speak at normal volume. *Who brought YOU?* I want to shout back. *This is MY date.* But I manage to keep quiet, except for a suitably Josie-like giggle.

'Fire hydrant,' says Anthony. 'Duh.'

Even Bryce's sniggers are loud. It's going to be a long night.

Things start looking up once we're inside the ground, or rink, or whatever an ice-hockey place is called. I can feel the buzz of excitement. Our seats are right at the front, behind a low scratched plastic wall, and I'm happy that I'm going to get such a good view of the muscley skating men at my first ever hockey match.

There's a band playing in the corner, a real-life brass band full of kids about my age. They're wearing bright-blue uniforms and looking very serious as they concentrate on their instruments. They're playing

God Bless America. I know this because a few people are singing along, hands clasped to hearts.

Oh God, I can't believe I'm here, in America, at an ice-hockey match, with a super-hot guy. I love my life.

The game starts and it's a whirl of fizzing ice and crashing sticks. So much for looking at hot men skating – I can't make out what's going on for more than a second. The boys are enjoying it though. Jake keeps calling out things like, 'Forward! Back!', Bryce keeps yelling, 'You suck!' and other, ruder stuff, and Anthony is just generally whooping.

I go into a bit of a trance listening to all this, letting it wash over me, and I'd even say I was enjoying it, until there's a big skirmish on the ice and suddenly a hockey player jumps over the barrier and lands in my lap. He grunts at me and jumps back onto the ice. No one even comments on it. Now I'm really shaking – I think it's the shock, but also he's left an embarrassing-looking wet patch on Tori's designer jeans and it's making me feel even colder.

Jake stops yelling his instructions for a minute – I hope the players manage to continue without him. He remembers I'm here. Or rather, that my Cleavage Top is here.

'You cold?' he asks my chest.

Freezing! 'A little bit.'

'You want my jacket?'

YOU BET! 'If you don't mind.'

Jake takes off his sporty-boy jacket and puts it around my shoulders. And he doesn't take his arm away, or his eyes off my boobs.

This is more like it. I lean into him slightly.

I get a melty feeling, one I don't remember feeling in the closet.

He whispers in my ear, 'Sorry about them.'

I whisper back, 'That's all right.' Wow. I'd forgive him anything right now.

He whispers, 'I like your shirt.' Then he kisses me.

Hurray for the Cleavage Top, doing its job at last!

We kiss for a few minutes, ignoring the immature slurpy sounds that Bryce and Anthony are making. Like they don't do the same with their girlfriends at every opportunity. Anyway, it feels nice. Much nicer than the night of Tori's party.

Then the whole room explodes into whooping, cheering and jeering and the band strikes up. Wait a second, this can't all be because I'm finally enjoying Jake's kisses, can it?

Jake pulls away.

Bryce thumps him on the back and says, 'You totally missed it.'

Jake cheers as if he hadn't missed it at all.

He doesn't kiss me again during the match, because I think he's scared to miss more action, but he keeps his arm around me.

And when he takes me home, he walks me to the door and kisses me again, deeper. I'm losing myself in his minty taste when Bryce winds down the window and shouts, 'Jeez, Matthews, I'm freezing my ass off here!'

Jake whispers in my ear, 'Next time, baby.' The tickle of his breath makes my knees buckle. Oh yes, this is more like it.

Then he slaps my butt, like he did that first night when we kissed in the closet, and I give my trademark Josie giggle.

On his way back to the car, he calls out, 'See you!'

I watch Jake drive off. I pull his jacket around me. I feel warm all over. Jake kissed me and I didn't think of Sluggy Steven once. Jake left me his jacket. He talked about next time. I'm definitely the envy of the cool girls now. Even if he didn't try to get to second base.

'At last,' says Mum as she pushes open the door and walks across the wooden floor into our messy lounge. 'Now we've stopped showing off our accents to the taxi driver, I'll get the gossip. Was that the boy who was asking about you? Frap's son?'

I nod, trying to look neutral. 'David.'

'Hmm. He seemed nice. A bit forward, carrying on like that under a mother's nose, all that dirty dancing.'

'Mum! No way was it dirty! David's just a friend.' I go into a little dream-world thinking about David. We danced all night. He didn't care who was watching, and he really knew how to have fun.

'Earth to Jo! Come in, Jo! No, we've lost all contact. But we need a cup of tea! There are important decisions to make. Will it be the posher-than-posh Earl Grey I borrowed from work or the funny old Lipton's which seems to be the only tea available in the illustrious supermarkets on these shores? Oh, my kingdom for some Typhoo! I bet your father only brings Tetley's. With issues like these to discuss, we need Jo to land from planet Boy, but she's unreachable, she's currently in orbit—'

'Mum! I'll have the Earl Grey.'

'Houston, we have contact!'

'Mum! Just make me a cup of tea! Please!' I shake my head. No wonder I didn't stand a chance with the in-crowd. I've got geekiness in my genes.

But who cares? If all that stuff hadn't happened with Jake, I might never have met David. I'm glad I stuck to being Jo the Nerd. So-called losers have more fun – isn't that what Mum told me before?

'Kkkkk! Kkkkk! We've lost contact again! Houston! Do you read me? Important issues still to discuss! Which mug does Jo want the aforementioned Earl Grey in? Over and out!'

Still, if Mum wanted to be just a fraction less geeky, I wouldn't complain.

'The blue *Buffy* one,' I say.

She picks up our old-fashioned kettle-with-a-whistle and starts her usual grumbles as she fills it with water and puts it on the hob. 'You come here thinking it's a developed country, but can they develop an electric kettle? No, they bloody can't . . .'

I tune out her voice right after: '. . . technological advances? I'll give them "toaster oven". What's that even good for? Nothing's more essential than a proper kettle . . .' and I go back to my David daydream.

Mum finally switches to humming to herself, with a goofy smile on her face. She's the one who looks like she's in orbit.

Oh, that's right – I haven't teased her about Moustache Man yet!

'Mum?'

'*Baby!*' Mum sings as she picks up a mug and wipes it. 'Yes, Jo-Jo?'

'Were YOU dirty dancing?'

Mum throws the tea towel at me. It lands on my head and I brush it away. I'm glad she wasn't spacey enough to throw the mug. 'What a thing to say to your mother!'

'Well, were you? Who was that man with the moustache? The one you were dancing with all night? I talked to him earlier in the evening about orses and peegs.'

She doesn't pick me up on the 'peeg' thing. Or, should I say, she doesn't 'peeg' me up on it.

'Yes, he's French. He's just a colleague, Jo.'

'Hmm.' I'm not convinced. She's smiling way more than I've seen her smile in a long time. She plops down on the sofa next to me and pulls the tea towel over her face.

I know just how to test her. 'Mum?'

'Mmm?'

'What's his name? This just-a-colleague?'

She answers straight away, 'Rashid.' Her muffled voice comes from under the tea towel. 'Rashid Lacroix.' From under the tea towel, she manages to pick up the remote control and click the Lifetime channel on. They're showing a movie about interracial relationships. I've seen it before. It's dramatic and moving. People who don't watch TV movies are so missing out.

Mum's missing out too, because she doesn't uncover her face. After a while the tea towel lifts rhythmically and there's a faint sound of snoring. Mum's fallen asleep.

Rashid La-What? Mum never remembers anyone's name like that, never ever.

Oh my God. I think Mum's in love with Moustache Man.

I find a blanket to put over her, turn down the longing sighs and stifled sobs on the television, and then I go to bed to dream about David.

On Saturday Tori asks Albie to drive her to the mall and pick me up on the way. I wait at the window for signs of Albie's car. I don't want Tori to meet my mum if I can help it. Mum's being particularly odd this morning. She's cleaning the house and singing eighties tunes at the top of her voice into a feather duster. The main song she's crooning sounds like it's in French – something strange about Joe and a taxi.

I realize I haven't heard her sing since Dad left.

Her voice goes all husky and high-pitched, just as Albie's car pulls up.

'Bye, Mum!' I shout, opening the door.

'Au revoir, ma chère Jo! Le taxi is here!' my mother calls.

Whatever strange disease she caught last night at the party – the one I missed to go on my date with Jake Matthews – I don't want to be exposed to it any longer if I can help it.

I reach the car and open the door.

'Nice jacket.' Tori gives me a knowing smile.

I put my hands in the pockets of Jake's jacket and shrug my shoulders in a kind of hug.

'Thanks.' I jump into the back seat.

Tori cranes her head round to talk to me. 'Didn't you get my message last night? I waited till after midnight. Weren't you even home by midnight?' She raises her eyebrows at me.

I groan. I forgot I said I'd MSN her about the date. That last kiss from Jake made me forget everything.

'Oh, sorry, I didn't check the computer last night,' I tell her. Then I mouth, 'I'll tell you later,' and glance at Albie.

Tori gives me a look that says, *What? Why?*

I don't know what or why, but I just don't feel comfortable talking about Jake in front of Albie. I look at him again. He catches my eye in his rear-view mirror.

'Hi, Josie,' he says.

I look away. 'Hi.'

He taps his fingers on the steering wheel. 'Hey, I bet Josie will agree with me, Tor. Josie, I've just been telling Tori how I'm the best brother in the world, but she won't admit it. For example, I should be rehearsing right now, not driving to the mall. But here I am, sacrificing my future for my little sister's social life. Is that great, or what?'

'It's great. Thanks, Albie.'

Tori groans. 'Yeah, yeah. Whatever.'

'Madison Rat has an important gig coming up, and I have to be prepared and— Oh, listen to this bit.'

He turns his music up and it fills the car with a throbbing, jangling beat. I vaguely recognize Albie's band from the party at Tori's. I'm less distracted now, and I concentrate on the great guitar sound. Albie's voice is amazing and I love the lyrics. *'I'll be Xander to*

107

your Anya, I'll be Spike to you my Dru . . .'

'It's called *Fire and Ice,'* Albie says, and his voice on the CD almost echoes: *'Fire like me and ice like you . . .'*

I find myself humming along a bit.

'Madison Rat's greatest hit,' Albie says. 'Well, lots of people like it. I wrote the lyrics.'

Wow.

'We used to do mostly covers, like Snow Patrol and—'

'Oh, I love them.' I do. Hailey has their latest album on her iPod, and I used to borrow it all the time.

'But we're breaking out on our own, trying different sounds.'

'It's brilliant.' I don't mean to gush, but it really is.

Albie goes quiet. I hope I haven't said the wrong thing. The music fills the car again. I feel it in the tips of my fingers.

A thought pops into my head, and I say, 'Hey, Madison Rat? I think I've heard of that.'

Tori turns round and glares at me, her mouth open with the first syllable of 'Omigod'.

Albie laughs. 'Can't be us. We're into British and Irish indie music, but we've never toured Britain. Yet.'

'As if!' Tori rolls her eyes.

The beautiful voice sings, *'I'll be Tara to your Willow . . .'*

Oh! I get it. I think.

'Hang on,' I say. 'Is that Madison Rat like Amy Madison, the witch who turned herself into a rat in *Buffy?*'

'Yes!' Albie grins. 'That's amazing. Wow! Wait till I tell the guys. You're the first person ever to get that.'

'That's so cool,' I sigh.

'Josie, be SERIOUS.' Tori's eyes roll again. 'My brother and his friends are NOT cool. I mean that in a nice way of course. I love them all, but . . . really? Retro-emo much?'

'You have very little taste, sis, but I love you anyway,' Albie says, stopping at a red light.

Tori ignores him and looks out of the window. 'Look at that house!'

I follow her gaze. There's a row of houses, all large and identically rich-looking. Colonial style, I remember the estate agent – or the REAL estate agent – saying when Mum and I were house-hunting.

'Which house?'

'Josie!' She looks exasperated. 'That one!'

I'm still not sure. 'The pale yellow one?'

'Of course! Wouldn't you just DIE to live there?!'

'Er . . . yes?' I say. As we move off, I see a house that's exactly the same, except it's pale blue. 'And that one too, huh?' I try.

'Uh, not so much . . .' Tori says slowly. I've clearly got it all wrong. I just don't get it.

As soon as Tori waves Albie away at the mall, she

interrogates me about last night.

'Bryce and Anthony went on your date? That's weird.'

I feel my face fall. 'That's what I thought.'

'And he didn't even try to, you know, finish what he started in my closet?'

'Not exactly. He kissed me a little. He slapped my butt.'

'Gross.'

'The kisses were nice.' This time. In fact, I wouldn't mind more of those.

Tori looks thoughtful.

'Is it bad, Tori? It's bad, isn't it? Tell me.' I look at her hopefully, pulling Jake's jacket tight around me.

'Not necessarily,' says Tori slowly. 'He could be backing off because of, you know.'

'No? What?'

'William. He might be following the guy code, the one about not making moves on another guy's girl.'

'Oh,' I say. Oh no. That would mean no more kisses, and no more respect from Chelsea's crowd. That's no good.

'But it's good. Maybe you should stick with William for a while longer. Healthy competition – keep him guessing. Plus Jake must really like you a lot to give you his jacket.'

'Uh-huh.' I'm feeling slightly better.

'Although you have to get him to stop that butt-slapping.'

'I don't mind.'

'For real?'

'Yeah, it's what he does. It's no big deal.'

'Sure, OK.' She frowns and looks me up and down. She picks some chocolate off the sleeve of Jake's jacket. 'Eww, though. You canNOT wear that thing in public any longer. Time for some new clothes!'

Tori drags me to one of those brightly lit tidy shops that used to terrify me, and before I know it I'm trying on a mound of Tori-selected clothes. Mum has finally given me money – enough for one thing in this shiny mall shop or twenty things in a thrift store.

'Josie, those pants are PERFECT for you.'

The trousers are black and, as far as I can see, exactly like the other ten pairs Tori has picked out for me.

'Ugh, but not those!' She discards the identical twins of the ones I'm wearing.

'Why not?'

'Oh, Josie.' Tori shakes her head. 'Trust me. Hey, these are even better.' She picks up another pair. Ah, identical triplets!

If I can't figure this out for myself, Tori is going to have to dress me for the rest of my life. And she'll have to choose my house too.

Several baffling minutes later, we stand in a queue

to pay for the trousers, or a line to pay for the pants. I'm totally getting the hang of speaking American.

The television screen above the counter is showing one of my favourite TV movies. There's a close-up of a girl's face, two fat tears making their way down a track on her left cheek. I'm always impressed by the crying in this film. I point it out to Tori.

'She's admitted to her mother that she's not the girl she pretended to be— What?'

'You watch these movies? You remember them?' Tori's eyes are wide and filled with horror. 'Trash over-load!'

'But it's about trust and deception and . . . it's supposed to be trashy,' I say. 'Lifetime is the best channel in the world! That's what I like.'

Tori shakes her head vigorously. 'Trust me, Josie, you do NOT. You need to develop some taste. OK, forget this garbage' – she waves dismissively at the television screen – 'what REAL movies do you like?'

I think. 'Pretty much anything Joss Whedon's been involved in. Although *Buffy the Movie* was possibly his un-finest hour—'

'Stop! Stop! Jeez, you're worse than my brother. Josie, I'm so glad you met me. I have SO much to teach you.'

Mum's getting ready for a date with Rashid, the French Moustache Man from her work party. She's seen him a lot since that Friday night. I can't believe she has a better social life than me.

At school, it's got so I can't even look at David any more without blushing. I'm not sure if Rachel's noticed. Kendis certainly hasn't. She's totally wrapped up in Trey and we rarely see her any more.

Lucky her. Wish I could get absorbed in David. He's been friendly to me since the party but nothing more. I can't figure him out.

Mum tries on lots of different outfits and swishes around in front of me, her face lit up and eager for approval. It reminds me of when I did this in front of Albie at Tori's house, when I thought I could be a cool girl. The thought makes me cringe. So much for that.

At least the cool gang have pretty much stopped taunting me now. Jake still smiles at me, which is too weird. Rachel never seems to see that. But if Chelsea or Kristy so much as look at me when she's around, she does that stabbing voodoo-doll thing with her hands. Or other, ruder gestures. She really can't stand them.

Mum settles on a dress I've never seen before. It's black and slinky. It looks good but it doesn't look like her. It's not a hundred different colours, for a start.

'Have you been shopping at the mall?' I can't hide my shock.

She looks defensive. 'It's right across from work,' she says. 'This woman at work, Mandy-Mindy something, she took me there one lunch time. This dress was in the sale. Margy said it looked, um – what was that technical word she used? Hot.'

I look at Mum. 'Mum. What's happening to you?'

'It looks good, doesn't it?' She gives me a look that dares me to say 'no'.

'Yes, Mum, you look great.' But it's just not HER.

'Well, thanks, Jo,' she says. She hums some eighties song and I leave her alone.

I fire up the laptop, thinking I'll chat to Hailey online and then spend the rest of the evening on my homework. Even though I don't need any credit from my schoolwork here, I still want to look good in class. I'm so sure David's not into giggly girls who get bad marks to impress boys, girls like the Delicates back home. Trouble is, I'm finding it impossible to concentrate in class with David there.

Hailey's not replying to my instant message. She can't be in bed already – it's only . . . two in the morning in England.

Oh.

I get out my books but I keep fiddling online, Googling random things like 'Dirty Dancing' and 'David Bowie', thinking about dancing with David. I wonder if he likes me at all. I mean, THAT way? We haven't focused on his problems in Personal Relationships yet. I can't wait till we do. I want to hear all about him. I know he's there because of that fight with Bryce, when he stood up for Kendis. Did he fancy Kendis?

I wonder how I can find out. Maybe I could ask Rachel? It's a scary thought. You can never tell how Rachel's going to take things.

I browse Lifetime's movie listings, and then some of my usual *Buffy* forums. There's a huge flame war going on in one of them – a heated discussion about whether Spike can sing. *The trouble with Internet communication,* says one reply, *is that you can't read facial expressions. People think it's OK to say things they wouldn't say face-to-face.*

I rummage among my books. There it is – the Personal Relationships contact sheet. Kooky Karen thinks it's a good idea if we Express Ourselves outside the sessions, so we list our phone numbers and stuff for her to copy and hand out. I added mine but I'd be extremely surprised to get a call from Druggie Daniel. I'd be equally surprised to hear from David, Rachel or Kendis. I might hang around with them every day but they never mention getting together outside school.

Maybe *I* should mention it.

I could ask David out. I survived school after the Jake thing. I can do anything.

But it would be good to get some input first. You know, about whether David would laugh his head off if I asked him out. I may be brave but I'm not stupid.

I look through the list at the email addresses and MSN details. I add them. It tells me they're both online – wow. David's name is BadArseBoy, which makes me grin. Rachel's is RachGrrrl. Should I send Rachel a message? Why wouldn't I? Rachel's my friend, isn't she? I always spent hours on MSN with Hailey before I moved time zones and she started going to sleep so annoyingly GMT-ily early.

Besides, Rachel won't be able to read my facial expression. It's OK to say things I can't say face-to-face.

I type a quick 'Hi' to RachGrrrl.

I don't hear anything for ages and I'm about to turn off the computer when I get a message from her:

```
RachGrrrl: Limey, is that u???
>
JoRosenberg: Yes! It's Jo from school.
Sorry. Should have said.
>
RachGrrrl: Thought ur last name was
Reilly.
>
JoRosenberg. It is. Rosenberg is from
Buffy. Never mind. Hey, what is the
maths homework?
>
RachGrrrl: What is 'maths'? u total
limey. u want help with Werewolf
Wilson's class?
>
JoRosenberg: Not really. ;)
```

```
>
RachGrrrl: OK.
>
JoRosenberg: OK. :)
>
RachGrrrl: OK.
>
JoRosenberg: OK :) :)
```

I wait. I squint at my screen. It doesn't say that RachGrrrl is typing. I'd better send another message.

```
JoRosenberg: Have you finished the
Wilson homework, then?
>
RachGrrrl: Thought u didn't want help?
>
JoRosenberg: What are you doing now?
>
RachGrrrl: Werewolf Wilson homework. u?
>
JoRosenberg: Nothing. Surfing.
```

Another pause. It's not going well. How am I going to get onto the girly things about David and whether he has any girlfriends and whether there's any chance he likes me? This isn't going to work. I'm ready to give up

and type something like 'catch you later' when a
message pops up.

```
RachGrrrl: Been IM-ing David. He said
hi 2 u.
```

This is more like it.

```
JoRosenberg: Is he really a BadArseBoy?
>
RachGrrrl: What do u think?
>
JoRosenberg: LOL.
```

Here goes. I'm going to say something. How hard
can it be?

```
JoRosenberg: So is it all an act to get
girls?
>
RachGrrrl: I could care less.
>
JoRosenberg: What?
>
RachGrrrl: What do u think?
```

Grr. This is just annoying. I don't even understand
what she's on about. I should have known I couldn't

have a girly chat with Rachel. She's not a very girly girl.
She's a grrrly grrl.

```
JoRosenberg: LOL.
>
RachGrrrl: r u hot 4 David? want me 2
say something?
```

No! Yes, yes. No! Why, what did he say about me?
What do you know? No. Nooo! I don't type any of that,
I'm not mad. Rachel's mad for suggesting she'd tell
David I like him.

```
JoRosenberg: Are you mad?!!! ;)
```

Another pause. She'd better not be messaging David
again. She'd better not say anything about me. Is
Rachel so out-there that she doesn't know the rules of
girl friendships? Even if Hailey's biggest filmstar crush
came round for tea, I still wouldn't mention Hailey to
him unless she OK'd it first.

```
RachGrrrl: ur hot 4 David! I knew it!
Why do u think I would b mad?
>
JoRosenberg: What?
>
RachGrrrl: ?? u asked if I was mad at
```

u 4 being hot 4 David???
>
JoRosenberg: No!!!! I don't mean angry.
I mean mad. Crazy. You know. Remember
I'm a Limey.
>
RachGrrrl: u saying I'm crazy????
>
JoRosenberg: No!! Have you done
question 3 yet?
>
RachGrrrl: Working on it. Sorry, gotta
go. Catch u at the Mill.
>
JoRosenberg: Yeah, OK, bye. Thanks for
chatting.
>
RachGrrrl: Yeah, it was fun. IM me
again sometime, OK?

Now I just feel exasperated. I wish I hadn't done
that. I hope Rachel doesn't think I fancy David. I know
I do, but I don't want her to know it. I don't think she's
that sort of friend.

I read Hailey's old emails, full of news about running club and Jonathan, who hasn't kissed her yet. I
write her a long message, mostly about David. I add a
bit about how much I'm looking forward to her visit.

I switch off the computer and switch on Lifetime. I settle into the lovelorn pain of a teenage girl, based on a true story.

 'Josie! Over here!' Chelsea calls, as if I didn't know exactly where she was sitting – the cool table.

I stand at the front of the lunch queue, holding a tray full of gloop. School lunches are the same as in England, give or take a chip or fry or two. (Actually, I'm still speechless for ages anytime I get asked the question, 'You want chips, or fries?' Umm ... but chips ARE fries – what do you want from me? – brain overload – wa-ooh-wa-ooh-waa – meltdown!)

'Nice pants, Josie,' Kristy says as I sit down. I'm still not sure if she's being nice or nasty. Ever. And can she see my pants? I only feel a tiny bit better when I remind myself she means trousers, not knickers. I pull at the black material.

'Thanks, they're new. They cost fifty dollars.'

'Oh-kaaaay.'

I understand THAT tone, though. That means: Too Much Information. Back home, Hailey and I reserve TMI for details of bodily functions, like say I was desperate for the toilet and I said, 'I'm bursting for a wee,' Hailey might say, 'Jo! TMI! Just go!' Boringtown's girly Delicates take it slightly further than us, as they like to pretend their femininity stops at long hair and pushed-up boobs – they don't get cramps or run out of tampons, or if they do, they certainly don't talk about it. So, yeah, I'm used to different levels of TMI. But with Chelsea's crowd, it extends to lots of perfectly innocent things I babble about.

I add the price of clothes to the A-crowd TMI list in my mind. If the list gets any longer, I might have to stop talking altogether.

'Hey, look at Brittany Clarke. Who does she think she is?' Chris shifts the attention away from me. She doesn't do it on purpose, but I'm grateful anyway. 'Who wears skirts that length? What is THAT?'

'She probably thinks she's cool,' says Ana.

'She probably bought it at a thrift store or something. Gross!'

Tori shifts uncomfortably. 'Chris . . .'

'What, Tori? Oh, yeah.' Chris looks at me, then whispers something to Kristy.

I want to tell them that I don't shop at the thrift store any more, but I don't want to draw attention to myself.

'Hey, Josie's from England, her style's a little different,' Tori says. She's so nice to me. But how is it possible that I still look different? Everything I'm wearing is Tori-approved, or Tori's actual clothes.

'Well, there's someone who's a lot different,' says Kristy.

'I know, look at Nicole's hair! Think she's just fallen out of bed?'

'Yeah, with the janitor, I've heard.'

Everyone laughs.

'Omigod, Kristy, here comes that slut Kendis with picture-boots freak boy.' Chris points to the stylish tall girl and the scruffy-looking short guy, the ones who were friends with that arrogant girl, Rachel, who I spoke to my first day of school. For a second I wish I was with them instead of sitting here. The boy is chatting and joking with Kendis, and I bet they're not laughing at people's clothes and hair.

'Josie, that's David McCourt. You probably know him, he's some kind of Brit. He is SUCH a loser. And he thinks he's so tough,' Kristy says.

'Yeah, he tried to fight Bryce last semester,' says Ana.

'Yeah, Bryce just looked at him and the freak crumpled,' says Chris.

'I heard he cried,' says Tori softly.

'I heard he pleaded. *Oh, please, Bryce. I'll do anything, Bryce. I'm down here already . . .*' Kristy laughs.

'That's still no excuse for that weird hairstyle. Or for wearing those boots. I mean, who wears those?' Chris sniffs.

David's boots are battered and only half laced. One of the boots has a cartoon face on it that looks like it's been painted in silver nail varnish. I'm pretty far away, but from what I can make out, it looks like a picture of David.

How cool to have a caricature of yourself on your boot.

Argh, I must remember that he is UNCOOL. I am the one who's cool, in my neat, perfect, mall-bought and Tori-borrowed clothes which carefully match the clothes of all the girls around me.

Their laughter switches to the next person who walks in, a slightly overweight girl whose makeup is 'so last semester and highlights her chins'.

Chelsea isn't joining in. She keeps looking at the door.

Jake Matthews and his friends appear in the distance, all laughing and macho-jumping on each other. Things are going well with me and Jake. We've been kissing a lot – almost every time I see him around school.

I wave at him, but he doesn't see me, and I lower my hand, embarrassed, glancing at the girls. They don't notice – they're still busy mocking Last Semester Chins Girl.

Chelsea stands up, flicks back her hair and says, 'See you guys later.' She disappears in the direction of the boys.

I wonder about her. She's been very quiet for the last couple of days, and not half as mean or bossy.

'Lesbo loser alert!' Kristy calls us to action.

Rachel scans the room and walks over to sit with Kendis and David. She takes a small bottle out of her bag and shakes it. She hunches forward in her chair and paints on her black lace-up boot. It looks kind of like the cartoon on David's boots. It also reminds me of the mean graffiti that Chelsea instructs Chris to wipe off the walls when we stop at the restroom for a makeup session before class.

'Kendis used to be OK,' Ana says as we all survey Rachel's table. 'I don't know why she started hanging with freaks. Oh, wait. Yes I do.'

Everybody laughs.

'Oh, I KNOW. Just look at her. She IS a freak,' says Chris.

OK now, why is Kendis a freak? I'm just not getting this What Not To Wear At The Mill thing. I size up Kendis, trying to join in with all the American Trinnies and Susannahs around me. She's not alternative-looking like Rachel. No battered leather like David. Her clothes look expensive and classic and a lot like what we're wearing, apart from the fake fur coat.

'Why is Kendis a freak?' I say. As soon as the words are out of my mouth, I regret them. Everyone stares at me like I've just landed from Venus. I've been getting this look since I arrived in the USA, and I'm almost used to it. This must be why the US immigration people call me and Mum 'aliens'.

Kristy whispers something to Chris and they both laugh.

I can't keep kidding myself. They're definitely whispering about me.

But I'm one of them! I've got the clothes, I've got the shoes, I've got Jake Matthews – isn't that enough?

'Kristy, Josie doesn't know about Kendis,' Tori says. She chews her lip.

'Is it the coat? What is WITH that coat?' I try, putting on my most scandalized voice. Jo the Nerd would have loved the black and cream fur. It looks cool with her skirt. I add, 'Do you think she's actually TRYING to look like a dog?'

'I know, right?' Ana giggles.

I did it! I said the right thing!

Everyone relaxes.

Tori looks startled. 'I mean, you know, we have to remember Josie doesn't know all the stuff that happened last semester.'

'Oh yeah.' Kristy takes a deep breath and leans towards me, her eyes lighting up with gossip. 'So last Spring Dance, Kendis and Bryce hooked up. She must have paid him or something. He's way out of her league.'

Now I think I really am an alien. What does she mean 'out of her league'? Kendis is striking and stylish, and Bryce is a lot like Jake Matthews – he's perfect-looking and athletic, but sort of bland, really.

Oh wait, Jake's my boyfriend. The hottest boy in

the school, remember. Our lips get deliciously glued together whenever I see him. And I just called him 'bland'. Oops.

'So anyway,' Kristy continues, 'Kendis is getting all slutty with Bryce, and he's a guy, you know, so what can he do but give in? And then she goes crying home to her mom, like, all, *Oh I can't believe it, Mommy, he wanted me to TOUCH him.*'

'In her dreams!' Ana says.

'Yeah, and then all this stuff happened and her mom practically sued Bryce's dad, and it was like, whoa, major stress for Bryce.'

'Yeah, Bryce nearly lost his place on the team – Coach Harrison was all do-the-right-thing and all,' says Chris.

'Poor Bryce.' Ana sighs.

'Yeah, and poor Chelsea. As if Bryce would even look at anyone else when he's with Chelsea. And Kendis was totally stalking him, like she didn't care,' says Chris.

'No respect,' says Ana.

'Well, she's all out of the closet now anyway,' says Chris. 'Look at her with the witch. Oooh, kiss kiss, I love your silver lipstick, Rachel, can I have some?'

'Put it right HERE.' Kristy puckers up and laughs.

'So Rachel's gay?' I ask.

Kristy mimics me. '*So Rachel's GAY?* Get you, you sound so cute and innocent. Yeah, she's a total dyke.

Watch out around her.' She widens her eyes.

'She seems like an interesting person.' Uh-oh. There I go again. Why did I say THAT? I was doing so well. The alien stares are back.

'Josie, what's with you?' Ana says.

'Yeah, should we tell Jake he's dating a dyke? Is your mysterious BOYfriend from home actually a girl?' Kristy says.

'Should I MOVE?' Chris says, shifting dramatically away from me.

'Tori, didn't you say Josie's been at your house a lot? Trying on your clothes?' Kristy whispers to Chris and they laugh again.

I feel desperate. 'You know, because witches could be interesting, in a total loser kind of way. And that guy with her – what a loser. What a bunch of total freaks. Freaks!'

The alien looks stop and there's some laughter.

'I knoooow,' Ana says.

'So is that The Mill's total loser table over there? Or is there worse?' I ask.

'Oh, there's worse,' says Chris. 'Look at that guy.'

'What a freak,' I say, not bothering to look.

Over the next few weeks I relax more at school, apart from my continuing problem with stringing two words together when David's

128

around. It's usually better to keep quiet around Rachel, anyway – she's always storming off in a temper at random things.

I know it's OK to laugh, though, at Rachel's idea of turning up at school for Halloween dressed up as Chelsea. She's thrilled with me when I find her a designer handbag exactly like Chelsea's in my favourite thrift store. On the day, Rachel looks all awkward and wrong in her pastel skirt and top, but it's definitely funny. It makes her hair look blacker than ever. She only lasts about ten minutes – long enough for Chelsea to see her and be 'SO not EVEN at ALL freaked out, LOSERS' – before she changes back into her black Rachel clothes. But she gives me the handbag to keep, saying it suits me. I don't ask what she means by that.

I wanted to dress up as a fluffy-bunny, Anya-from-*Buffy* style, but I don't think David and Rachel would get it, so I don't bother dressing up at all.

After that is the build-up to Thanksgiving, with David moaning about it being a turkey-murdering holiday. I don't tell him how much I relish the opportunity to be pseudo-American for the day.

I persuade Mum to invite Rashid for a roast-peeg dinner, and on the big day I force them to say what they're thankful for, like in my favourite movies. When it's my turn, I say slushy stuff about family. I don't tell the whole truth. I don't say I'm thankful that David smiled at me twenty-six times last week, for example. Neither do I tell them I'm thankful I'm going home after Christmas, which I think Mum half expected me to say. I'm not so sure about that any more. I can't move that far away from David's dimple.

Every day I spend loads of time with David, mostly in maths classes, because I signed up for so many of them back when I was obsessed with hearing people say 'math' in American. They have fifty-eight flavours of maths here – it's better than ice cream. I have to study these obscure things, like the Cartesian Plane in Advanced Geometry, which turns out not to be an aircraft belonging to a low-cost airline. I spend my lessons relating everything I learn to David. I'm the complex person 'Jo', where 'Jo = Rachel's friend + David's friend/maybe more'.

On Fridays, just before lunch, I have Advanced Algebra with Mr Wilson. Mr Wilson is OK, but he's the hairiest man I've seen in my life. He's not just Moustache Man like Mum's French boyfriend – Mr Wilson is Moustache, Beard, Hairy Nostril, Hairy Hands and Probably Hairy Back Man. David and Rachel call him Werewolf, and David has this thing of trying to get the word 'hair' into everything he says in class. Werewolf Wilson doesn't seem to notice, probably because of David's naturally dodgy accent.

Advanced Algebra is one of my favourite lessons because Werewolf Wilson insists on seating us in alphabetical order and I sit right behind David, with Rachel Glassman miles away at the front of the class. I can stare at the back of David's head and dream of running my fingers through his hair. But today I'm having trouble with that. Rachel's turning round a lot and I keep catching her looking at me, as if she's trying to catch me looking at David. I wish I'd never sent her that instant message about David. She's been looking at me suspiciously ever since, and it's been getting worse week by week.

I concentrate on my algebra book instead of the locks of hair tickling the collar of David's black leather jacket, and the class isn't half as much fun as usual.

Mr Wilson asks David a question and David replies, deadpan, 'HAIR, let's see . . . Is it a quarter or a HAIR-th? I'm not HAIRy sure, sorry.'

Mr Wilson says, 'It's not even a fraction, David, but good try.'

Rachel covers her face with her hair and puts her head on the desk, shaking with laughter.

Mr Wilson asks me instead. My lack of David's-collar-gazing pays off and I give Mr Wilson the right answer for a change.

'Oh, listen to HAIR. She's HAIRy good,' David mutters, turning to flash his wonderful dimple at me.

That's the highlight of the lesson for me.

At the end of class, as we're walking out, Mr Wilson

says, 'Miss Reilly, could you stay behind for a moment, please?'

Rachel gives me a shove, 'Uh-oh, Limey's in trouble!'

She doesn't need to look so pleased about it.

David says, 'See you later. HAIRth fun.' He gives me a lovely smile.

'Wait for me a second, will you, guys,' I say, trying to make my voice light. I hate going into the lunchroom alone. It's torture walking past Chelsea's table, even though they pretty much ignore me now. But sometimes Jake Matthews smoulders his eyes at me. I can cope with all of this better when I'm with my David and Rachel bodyguards.

Mr Wilson talks to me for a while about what a promising student I am, although occasionally distracted. I wonder if he's going to invite me to join some nerdy Math Club, like the ones I've seen in films. I wouldn't mind. I'd be in math heaven. Instead he says, 'You're not working to your full potential, Josephine. I want to give you a chance to improve before I give you a failing grade.' He waffles on about extra homework and hands me a list.

I mumble something about having a tough time and I promise to work harder. If Rachel stops me from watching David like she did today, this might even be true.

I shuffle out of the room, thinking I should at least have told Werewolf Wilson I was 'HAIRving' a tough time. David would like that. I shouldn't care that I'm failing Advanced Algebra, since my grades this year don't matter. So why do I feel sick, a bit like I'm not myself any more? I never, ever got into trouble at Boringtown High.

David and Rachel aren't there waiting for me. Maybe they didn't hear me ask.

I walk the long way to the lunchroom, gearing myself up for going in alone. I can do this. But I'd rather not.

Near the gym, strains of music reach my ears. Loud guitars and a strong beat – a sound that's completely out of place in a school, but there's something familiar about it. There's a poster nearby advertising the Winter Dance, featuring The Mill's own Madison Rat. Another sign, on the gym door, says, WINTER DANCE REHEARSAL IN PROGRESS.

I hesitate outside the door.

A low voice is singing the opening lyrics of an old Snow Patrol song. I recognize it instantly – *Set the Fire to the Third Bar*. It's one of Hailey's favourites. I miss her iPod.

I push the door a fraction. There's only one singer – the male voice. I squint at the stage.

It's Albie, Tori's brother. I open the door slightly more, and the music floods over me. It's wonderful. So Madison Rat is Albie's band? The name sounds familiar.

I'm pretty sure they're too intent on their rehearsal to notice me. I creep inside, pushing myself against the climbing wall and trying to blend in. I get lost in the music.

There's a sad crackle of cymbals and a moment of silence. Then the boys nod at each other and the guitars start.

Albie sings, '*I'll be Xander to your Anya, I'll be Spike to you my Dru, I'll be Tara to your Willow . . .*'

This one's definitely not on Hailey's iPod, but it's equally good. It sounds like it's inspired by *Buffy*. I love it.

But after a couple of minutes the guitars screech and the band members yell at each other.

Uh-oh. I hope they don't look over here.

I sneak out quickly, hoping the shouts have covered the thunk of the heavy door. I listen, but they don't start playing again. It's nearly the end of lunch, anyway. It went so fast, surrounded by that excellent music.

I hear David before I see him. 'Look, Rachel, you know I didn't mean it like that—'

'David, why are you so consistently such an asshole?'

Rachel goes quiet when she sees me.

David smiles at me. 'Jo, you're here! We missed you at lunch. What did the Werewolf want? Did he bite? Did you say HAIR-lo from me?'

He missed me. David missed me!

I laugh and fall into step beside David and Rachel.

They don't ask me why I never made it to the lunch-room and I don't ask them why they didn't wait for me.

Jake's friends don't come with us on our next date, or any after that, but it still takes weeks of going out and in-school snogging before I get to second base with Jake. If he minds that it takes so long, he doesn't tell me. He doesn't say much at all, in fact. We don't exactly talk to each other. We do kiss a lot, though.

I've become an expert at being snogged by Jake Matthews. And I'm also pretty good at second-base-avoidance tactics. I hope these will be useful life skills.

For example, around five times a day Jake catches me by the lockers and goes in for the kiss. Easy! I give him a long kiss and then duck away and say, 'Oh, I'm so late for class! See you later, Jake.' And I leave him staring after me, wanting more. He usually slaps my butt as I leave, and I giggle and wiggle. And I'm always late for class anyway, because being in-crowdy takes a lot of makeup-fixing between lessons, so it isn't a lie.

Although, I suppose, it's not like he's going to want to get to second base by the lockers. At least, I hope not.

Avoiding second base is much more difficult on our dates, but I still have methods. I've talked Mum up into some kind of strict parent from hell. 'I must get in right now,' I say, when Jake and I sit in the car outside my house, 'or else I'll be grounded for the rest of the year.'

Of course, there's not much of the year left. It's almost December, and I've already done the big American stuff I've been looking forward to, like dressing up as a slutty bunny for a Halloween party, and sniffing roast-turkey-scented air all the way home from Thanksgiving at Tori's house. (I left Mum to do her own thing with the Frenchman.)

But anyway, unless we're in the car, I manage not to be alone with Jake at all. It's not so difficult when he's the most popular guy in the school. Wherever we go, guys want to talk to him about baseball or football, girls want to giggle near him and touch their hair a lot.

It's not that I don't fancy him. Absolutely everyone thinks he's gorgeous, and his kisses are as nice as ever. But often, when he kisses me, I think more about whether Chelsea has noticed than how it actually feels. I want Chelsea to see how cool I am, how I can snare the boy I'm sure she likes. I think Chelsea would be perfect for Jake, and I can't see her staying with Bryce for much longer – he's so obvious when he struts his stuff around groups of younger, awestruck girls.

But what am I thinking? I need to stay with Jake, and I need Chelsea to stay with Bryce. No matter how many makeovers Tori does for me, I don't think I could ever compete with Chelsea. And Chelsea would have got to second base by now, I'm sure of it. Probably further. It's definitely time.

In the end, after I've decided to go ahead, it's not such a big deal. I'm nothing like that girl who tried to push Jake's hands away in the closet at Tori's party, not any more.

We're at the movies, watching some movie that Jake chose. It's been out for ages and it's about a robbery that goes comically wrong, or something. I mean, I'm not too sure because I only watch these twenty-second chunks when we come up for air. Pretty much the rest of the time we are kissing. The cinema's empty apart from us at the back and an old couple way at the front. We're cosy in the dark. It's perfect for making out.

I only have to taste the wetness of his mouth or smell the mint-covered cigarette smoke on his neck for my pulse to stir, expecting the cold-tipped heat of his kisses. The longer he waits before his octopus hands begin their dance, the more I ache to move them myself. Maybe he's driving me crazy on purpose to pay me back for making him wait.

At last his hands pull at my T-shirt and I say 'Ummh' because my mouth is busy. And that isn't exactly 'no'. I sense the hands – all eight of them – hesitating at my sides.

I've made my decision, so I say, 'Go on,' but very quietly so I don't disturb the old couple. I also say it quietly just in case I don't mean it.

Jake isn't listening, because he whispers, 'Please, Josie,' and his hands inch towards my bra. So then I say 'Mmmh', which sounds halfway between 'yes' and 'no' the way I say it, and a second later it's too late anyway because my bra is undone (how did he DO that so quickly?) and his hands are on my boobs. It feels strange but warm and pretty nice, I suppose. But my boobs are so small and what is he thinking and will he still want to date me now he knows I have practically nothing there? Although I suppose he must have known that before he touched them, because tonight I'm not wearing my Cleavage Top. I wonder if he notices that sometimes I have boobs and sometimes I don't?

Anyway, he can't mind too much because this goes on for another five minutes or so, with a short break when someone on screen accidentally shoots a police officer, which is somehow funny and the old couple laughs. Then Jake laughs, although he can't have seen whatever was supposed to be funny. And then the hands go to the front of my jeans and then I squeak. Yes, I squeak. This is the trouble with being Josie the Cool. I'm sure Jo the Nerd would NOT squeak, she'd do something far more dignified. Like not be groped by a boy she barely knows in the first place.

'Jake!' I squeak.

He tugs playfully at the top of my waistband but then moves his hands away. 'Next time,' he mutters in my ear.

'Ummmhh,' I reply, which means, *Hold on, it's taken me this long to get this far*, but that murmuring in my ear feels nice. Let's do that.

So he goes back to my boobs, what there is of them. And, apart from the time he moves my hand and puts it at the top of his leg and I squeak again and move it back, that's how we pass the rest of the movie. It isn't too bad at all really. Except that when it's time to go, I spend a while fiddling up the back of my T-shirt and then I give up and stand up with my bra still undone. It feels all loose and strange around my top. I hope no one notices. I should have worn my Cleavage Top and then I wouldn't have had this bra trouble. I'll have to remember that for next time.

Oh yeah, 'next time'. So Jake's new target is third base. What did Tori say that was again? More than breasts, less than all the way? But what EXACTLY?

Kooky Karen hands out a worksheet. It has some cartoony stick figures on it with blank faces and empty speech bubbles coming out of their mouths. We're all half asleep, except Druggie Daniel, who's making a paper aeroplane out of his worksheet. But every single one of us jumps when KK says, 'SEXUAL Relationships. That's what we'll discuss today.'

'Will there be a practical demonstration?' asks David sweetly. I join in with the laughter, but my cheeks are burning hot, thinking about David talking about . . . that stuff. Hanging around with David hurts. Sometimes I'm sure he's flirting with me, and my heart goes all fluttery, but then I see him flirting with other girls, and my heart goes all sinky. He kind of flirts with everyone, really. I think it's just the way he is. He's congenitally flirty. Or maybe just friendly, and I'm imagining the rest.

'There will be a discussion' – KK points that last word at David – 'and remember that everything you say in this room is confidential. You can explore your feelings and be as candid as you wish.'

Candid? There's no way I'm being candid in front of this lot. I hope we don't have to go around the room making a list, like in the first meeting. If we do, how will I stop myself from blurting something like, 'My name is Jo and I want to tear David's clothes off,' and then having everyone repeat it?

It might be kind of interesting to hear what other people say though. Like David. Just for an example.

'Now I want you to fill out your worksheets,' says KK. 'The figures on them can be men or women – you decide. They're talking about a sexual encounter, or arranging a sexual encounter.' Arranging a sexual encounter? What planet is KK from? 'Hello, I am call-ing to arrange a sexual encounter.' 'Certainly, madam, let us see what availability we have. How about next Tuesday at eleven?' 'I have a dentist's appointment at eleven. How does twelve-thirty sound?'

KK says, 'Write down what you think the figures are saying to each other.'

Ummm.

I wish I was somewhere else.

I give my first stick figure a nose and some messy hair. It's not necessarily me, we just have similar hair-styles and noses. Cartoon girls should have noses. I write in her speech bubble, *What is second base?*

I move on to the next figure. I draw hair that slightly flops into one little stick-figure eye. I give the figure a dot on its cheek, like a dimple. It's not necessarily David, it just has similar hair and a dimple.

I write in his speech bubble, *I'll show you.*

Then I stop and look around the room to see if I can see what anyone else's stick figures are saying.

Druggie Daniel's page is an elaborate aeroplane now and he aims it at the door, without letting go. Rachel has written loads, and one of her stick people looks a lot like an exaggerated Kooky Karen. I mean A LOT – Rachel's so good at drawing. I bet she could sell her caricatures if she didn't draw them on toilet walls. I love what she's done with her boots and David's boots. Maybe I should look in the thrift shop for some boots and see if she'll draw on them for me? I'm scared to ask her though.

The other figure on her worksheet has straight black hair and an exaggerated Rachel look. I wonder what that's about? She's drawing herself and Kooky Karen?

I can't see David's worksheet from this angle, but I try anyway and as I do, he looks up. I catch his eye and he smiles at me. I feel a jolt. My heart thumps. I smile quickly and look down.

I cross out everything I've written. You can still read it, so I draw boxes around the words and scribble in the boxes until the stick figures have blocks of blue ink in their speech bubbles. Ha! Take that, stupid stick figures! Try having a sexual encounter if all that comes out of your mouth is blocks of blue ink! Then I change the hair and features on the stick figures so that they look nothing like David or me. Then I don't know what else to do, so I sit and chew my pen.

Finally KK collects our worksheets and shuffles them in her hands.

'Let's see . . .' she says, and picks out a worksheet. From the corner I can see, it looks like Rachel's.

Kooky Karen suddenly looks all flustered. There is a red patch on her neck and it shows under her hippyish gathered top, and it's spreading even as I look at it. She takes a deep breath.

'It's good of this person to share these feelings.' She looks very seriously at Rachel, which makes the confidentiality thing kind of pointless. I'm glad I scribbled my figures out.

Kooky Karen twists a strand of her red hair tightly round one finger. Then she has trouble removing the finger and she winces. 'It's very common at your age to develop, ah, affections for teachers and people in authority.'

Rachel has her hands over her face and she's shaking slightly. I'm used to not seeing her eyes, but I can't even see her mouth, so I don't know if she's laughing or crying. Probably laughing though, knowing Rachel. I'm feeling sorry for KK, because I think Rachel is playing some kind of mean joke on her. I'm not sure if KK deserves this. She's annoying, but I sort of like her.

'You might want to get these feelings out in the open. For example, how long have you wondered about being, ah, gay?'

What? Rachel's gay? Really?

Oh, this must be the joke. I imagine what the Rachel and KK stick figures are saying to each other on Rachel's worksheet. Rachel stays silent and shaking. She's definitely laughing.

I feel really sorry for KK now.

'You don't need to talk until you're ready,' she says. 'But remember you're among friends here. Some of us may even have experienced exactly what you're going through. For example, ah—' Kooky Karen stops.

The tension is too much.

KK's got that sincere, serious look on her face and she holds her head high. 'For example, I was your age when I realized I was, ah, gay. And it was very difficult for me.' She softens her voice. 'We could talk about it.'

There's a silence. We're not sure what to say, or if we're supposed to say anything. KK has everybody's attention now. Even Druggie Daniel puts his paper aeroplane down.

'Rachel? If you're ready to talk, we're ready to listen.'

Rachel moves her hands away from her face. She has a wide troublemaker's smile.

She pushes her hair out of her eyes and a mock-sincere expression crosses her face. It's the look she pulls when she does her Kooky Karen impressions. 'I'm ready to talk, Karen,' she says. She glances around the room, looking dramatically at each of us in turn.

KK looks confused.

'The truth is I wrote all that about someone in this room,' Rachel says. 'But not you.'

 I leave the cinema with Jake, warm in my post-second-base glow.

I wish he would hold my hand. We might bump into someone from school. I love that jealous look I see in other girls when I'm with Jake – especially when they're girls like Kristy. Or – even better – Chelsea.

But Jake doesn't hold my hand. Maybe it's just as well. I need to hunch my shoulders up to stop my undone bra slipping around any more. Maybe I should go to the toilets to sort it out. But I don't want to leave Jake's side.

'Want to go get ice cream?' he asks.

I stifle a laugh as I picture an ice-cream van parked outside the cinema to catch the kids on their way out, as if we were about seven years old and at the park. But of course Jake means going to an ice-cream café-type place. Which is still open at this time of night, to catch the kids on their way out of the cinema.

It's a cool-looking place, with wooden tables and funky décor and about fifty-eight flavours of ice cream on offer. It's full of kids from The Mill, but none of Chelsea's crowd. Of course, Jake seems to know them all.

'Matthews! Hey, how's it hanging!'

'Dude!'

Jake goes off to high-five, low-five, in-between five, and say things like 'The game was a bust, man' at top volume. I stand near the counter, trying to see if there's a toilet here. The claspy bit of my bra is itching my side, and there's no point in worrying about leaving Jake now, since he's quite happily left me without a second glance.

'What can I get you?' A rosy-cheeked girl waves her ice-cream scoop at me.

'I. Er.' What should I do? Order, or ask for the toilets? My brain freezes. How do you say 'toilets' in American again? Maybe I'll stick to asking for ice cream. 'I'd like a—' What do people have here? I do a quick survey of the tables, but everyone's hanging out rather than eating. It's like the lunchroom at The Mill, with nicer tables and brighter lighting.

The ice-cream scoop hovers impatiently.

'A banana split,' I say, because it's the only American-style ice-creamy concoction I can think of at such short notice.

Uh-oh, maybe not the right thing to order. I'm getting alien stares from the girl. Unless it was my accent that caused that.

'Banana? Did you say banana?'

I nod. I'm not going to risk speaking again.

'Because it sure didn't sound like banana. You from out of state?'

No, I'm IN a state, I think, and then I giggle. I get another alien stare for that, but her scoop gets to work.

Meanwhile I feel about in my pockets and panic.

Yikes! I don't have any money.

Oh no. I thought Jake would pay for everything. Yes, I know how that sounds. How old-fashioned am I?

Anyway, should I have ordered something for Jake?

And make it twice as much stuff I can't pay for?

I haven't thought this through.

I shoot Jake desperate glances but he's busy mock-pitching now, gorgeous muscles a-rippling.

The girl bashes at her cash register and looks at me expectantly.

'I— Can you hold on?' I beg.

'Let me get this,' says a deep voice behind me.

I turn to see who my saviour is.

'Oh, Albie, it's great to see you!' SO great. I throw my arms around him and give him a bear hug.

Then I remember about the bra. I move away.

Albie pulls some money out of his pocket.

I glance nervously at Jake. He's mock-batting now.

Yeah, as if he'd be jealous if he saw me hugging Albie. Jake knows he's the highest-ranking Mill male, second to none.

This is just great. I threw my semi-bra'd body at my best American friend's brother, who is paying for a banana split I don't want, while my boyfriend has forgotten I exist.

'Thanks, Albie,' I say as he pays.

'No problem. It's really good to see you too. Is my little sis here?' He follows my gaze. 'Uh, of course, you're here with Jake, huh? OK, well see you later, Josie.'

He heads towards the back of the room.

The girl behind the counter nudges an enormous plateful of banana, cream, chocolate and ice cream towards me.

'Thank you,' I say to her.

'You're welcome,' she replies.

'Thanks,' I mutter as I pick it up.

'You're welcome,' she repeats. I see her face working up to a good alien stare.

But it's no good. I can't fight my British urge to thank her for welcoming me.

'Thank you,' I say again.

'You're WELCOME.' There it is: the full-alien.

I bite my lip to stop myself muttering any more thanks. It's so difficult. I've sent assistants in the mall into total 'you're-welcoming' tailspins, just over simple transactions. Tori finds it hilarious.

I pick up the plate and walk towards Jake. His friends are closed in a full circle around him.

Behind Jake's crowd, sitting on his own, Albie is scribbling in a notepad. He has iPod earphones in his ears. He gives me a little wave.

Jake mock-catches a ball and his friends cheer. He doesn't see me. He hasn't even looked for me.

I look at my banana split.

I don't think I've thanked Albie enough.

I walk past Jake and towards Albie. I put the banana split on the table. 'Can I leave this here for a minute?'

He pulls his earphones out and looks at the plate. 'Sure.'

'Just while I use the, ah—' I still can't remember the word. In fact, my mind feels even more blank now.

'Restrooms are out back.' Albie points.

Restrooms! That's it. I smile gratefully, pushing the plate nearer to him. 'You can eat this if you want. I mean, you know you can, since you paid for it and all, but I mean—'

'No problem. I just ate. But thanks.'

'You're welcome,' I say.

In the restroom, I quickly reach back and do up my bra, but it's all twisted and I can't breathe. I have to undo it again and fiddle and wriggle for a full minute before it's OK. I wonder if this is the kind of problem the girly Delicates have to cope with? All the time I thought they were pathetically fainting at the thought of putting condoms on bananas in PSHE, they were cutting off their circulation in some post-second-base bra scenario. I feel a new-found admiration for the Delicates.

When I get back, comfortable at last, Albie is sipping coffee and scribbling away again. He hasn't put his earphones back in.

He gives me a warm smile and says, 'Hey.'

I 'hey' him back.

I wonder if it would be rude to sit with him when I'm out with Jake? But it's only Albie. I slide into the seat opposite him.

'Your banana split,' he says, pushing it towards me.

I can't possibly eat anything banana-related right now, after what I was thinking in the restroom. I stifle my laughter and stare at Albie's notebook. It's covered in blocks of blue ink, like he's crossed something out a million times. It sobers me up.

'Oh, sorry, are you studying? Is it OK if I sit here?'

'Sure.' Albie smiles. 'I was just working on some Madison Rat lyrics. Want to help?'

'Me?'

'Josie!' It's Jake, appearing beside me. 'I wondered where you got to.'

So he didn't forget I existed.

Jake glances at Albie. 'Hey, Windsor. Listen, Jose, you all set? Because I have an early start tomorrow and Coach Harrison says . . .'

I stand up as Jake goes into details.

Albie doesn't say anything to Jake, but then, Jake's still talking.

'Sorry about the banana split. But thanks a lot,' I say.

Jake's hand settles on the back pocket of my jeans. '. . . if I perform as well for the second half of the season . . .'

'You're welcome. Really.'

'Thanks, Albie.'

Jake's voice rattles on: '. . . because of course it's not all about how I play but also . . .'

'Bye, Josie.' Albie scribbles in his notebook.

Jake steers me towards the door. '. . . and if the other team suck, then . . .'

The rosy-cheeked girl behind the counter shoots

me an envious glance as we walk past. I bet she doesn't think I'm a weirdo alien now.

Karen the Counsellor has her face set all hard. It's the longest I've seen her without one of her two trademark expressions on her face: the loony smile and the sympathetic half-frown. She folds her arms. She still has those red patches around her neckline. She says, 'OK, Rachel, you made your dramatic statement, and I guess you think you've embarrassed me, but I'm not ashamed of my sexuality, and you shouldn't be either. Whoever it is you like, male or female.'

Rachel's hair is in her eyes again, so I can't read her face.

'Do you want to talk more?'

Rachel shrugs.

'Well, the object of these worksheets was to raise some issues, so I'm glad you have. But I'm not going to push you. Talk when you're ready, or see me after the session.'

Rachel keeps her head down.

'OK. Does anyone else want to comment?'

I wonder what Rachel is playing at? If this is all a joke, it doesn't seem that funny.

'Let's move on,' Karen says, flicking through the worksheets. She pauses at one with very little writing or drawing on it. No blocks of blue ink, so I know it's

151

not mine. She keeps her gaze on the paper, as if she's trying not to give it away this time.

'This is interesting. This person wants to ask someone out, but is scared. When that happens, what is it we're really scared of? Rejection? Giving up power? A lot of relationships, even teacher–pupil ones' – she looks at Rachel – 'are about power. Let's talk about power play.'

I relax and listen to Karen discussing relationships. Crazy thoughts flit through my head. Could this worksheet be David's? Could it be about me? Maybe he wants to ask me out but he's scared! Oh, wow! I can't help looking over at David, and I catch his eye again. I smile and my heart thuds. I shrink down in my seat and try to concentrate on what Karen is saying. Ironically, fear of rejection can often lead to the very rejection you fear. Blah blah anxiety blah self-esteem blah blah that dimple is so cute. Will he look up? Will he smile at me again? My heart leaps at the thought. Does he like me? Thud-thud-thud. I'm going to be the first person in the world to die of David-smile-induced heart failure.

At last it's the end of class, and we all file out. Rachel and David are beside me as usual. Kendis disappears to find Trey.

I'm quiet. I don't feel like talking to Rachel because I still can't believe she was so mean to Karen. But I don't think I want Rachel to know that.

David's not annoyed with Rachel at all. He says, 'Soooooo. What was all that about, Ray? Ray the Pretend Gay?'

'Did you see her FACE?' Rachel says, and she cackles.

David laughs too. I don't know why that makes me feel so disappointed. It still shows up his gorgeous dimple, it's still the same lovely laugh. But why does he think it's funny?

'So, Rachel, who do you have the hots for? Lenny? Or Druggie Daniel?'

'Hey!' Rachel stops laughing. 'What makes you so sure I'm NOT gay?'

'Oh, I don't know,' says David. 'Maybe the string of boyfriends you've had.'

'That means nothing, Mr Oh-So-Pure.'

I push my annoyance aside, because this is interesting. David – pure? Or not pure? Once again I wish Rachel was the kind of girl I could giggle and gossip with, and find out details like that. I'd have talked about that remark for weeks with Hailey.

'OK, Rachel, who's your crush? Is it Kendis? I wouldn't blame you. She is sex on legs!' David's smile twinkles. Beautifully.

My brain catches up with what David said. David likes Kendis? Of course he does. He got into detention because of her, didn't he? Oh, no. Although she and Trey are so into each other. But still. I'm nothing like Kendis.

'David, what's that quaint British expression you taught me? Shut up, you tosser! Is that the correct usage?' Rachel's face is starting to match her lipstick.

David doesn't look bothered. 'Maybe it's our lovely Jo?' He gives me an exaggerated wink.

He said I was lovely! Wow! He winked at me!

No, wait. He didn't say I was sex on legs. Or even legless sex. He doesn't associate me with sex at all. Just 'lovely'. Bleurgh.

'I said shut up! I'm not telling YOU!' And Rachel storms off.

I'm glad it's David she's mad at and not me. She hasn't even looked at me since the KK session.

Anyway, I have David to myself now. But what's the good of that if I'm some kind of sexless limpet to him?

I think about what Karen was saying, the parts I listened to in between daydreaming about David. Ironically, fear of rejection can lead to the very rejection you fear.

We pass the gym, and a series of posters advertising the Winter Dance, featuring Madison Rat.

I'd just love to go to one of those American dances I've seen in all the films. Plus I'd love to hear Albie's band play again.

And David is an excellent dancer. I wouldn't be in this state now if we hadn't danced all night at Mum's party.

My mouth feels dry. I think I might be sick. Or faint. Help! I'm going to do it. I stop walking.

'You all right, Jo?'

'David,' I say. Thud-thud-THUD. I'm going to die. 'Would you, er, you and Rachel, er, you, like to go to the . . . d— ice skating with me?'

Noooo! Why did I say that? And what's 'dice skating', anyway? I mean, I really do want to go ice skating some time – it's on my list of Bostony things to do. And I would love to go with David. But that's not what I wanted to ask! And why did I ask Rachel too! What is WRONG with me?

'OK, why not?' David replies casually. Well, why wouldn't he be casual? It didn't sound like I was asking him on a date or anything. Argh! Now, what was Karen saying? Self-esteem something-something. Nothing to lose.

'Oh, also,' I say. Do it, do it, do it! Thuddity-thuddity-thud. The last thud was me dropping dead. 'Would you dancer wint with me? I mean, go? I mean to the Winter Dance with me?'

David twinkles his dimple. My knees wobble. I've got that legless thing going on right now.

'Of course, yeah,' he says. Wow-wow-wow. He still sounds casual, but wow-wow-wow anyway. 'Rachel and I were planning on crashing that for a laugh. All three of us should go. Let's go as vampires or something. Rach would like that. You should see

155

the effort that Chelsea's crowd put into their dresses. Last year Rachel spilled orange juice on Kristy's dress on purpose and she nearly . . .'

Oh. That wasn't exactly what I had in mind.

But still. I'm going to the dance with David. Kind of. It's a start.

Of course, he could be scared of rejection too. It might have been his worksheet Karen was commenting on. All this casualness could be a cover-up!

When we get to class, Rachel is already there, drawing in her notebook. She snaps it shut when she sees us and says, 'Hey, you total losers. What's up?' At least she's talking to us.

'Nothing much.' David acts like she hadn't shouted at him and stormed off. I guess he's used to it. 'Jo asked me – us – to the dance.'

I try to smile at her but she won't meet my eye.

That's when this thought jumps into my head. Could it be that she's really gay? Maybe she thought Karen's session was a good way to tell us. I bet Rachel would do that, pretend her feelings are a joke.

And David suggested it before but I was too distracted by him to notice. Could her worksheet have been about . . . me?

Could Rachel be in love with me?

 So I've done Halloween and Thanksgiving, but I haven't done the American high school dance, as seen on TV. It's ages till the prom, of course, but at The Mill everyone's talking non-stop about the Winter Dance, which is only two weeks away. All my friends talk about is what they'll be wearing. Oh, and who's taking who, even though they all have senior boyfriends and it's pretty obvious. But apparently you're supposed to be asked, even if you've been going out with someone since a week after you arrived at the school and they snogged you in a cupboard.

I don't understand why Jake hasn't asked me. We get on really well, in a second-base-only kind of way. We still don't really talk about anything, apart from his team, and, oh yes, there's 'Please, Josie', 'No, Jake', 'You're so hot, baby', and all that stuff. Still, it's not like we've ever had an argument or anything, not like Greg and Tori. Greg's forever hissing angry words at Tori. Tori tells me arguments are a normal part of a healthy relationship, but I'd rather be with Jake than Greg. Jake presses me against my locker and kisses me wordlessly, while Greg slams his fist against Tori's locker and storms away.

It's Saturday and I'm at Tori's house again. She shows me a mall's-worth of dresses and tells me when exactly she wore them. It sounds like she's only worn each dress once. She tells me about all the other dances she's been to and who hooked up with who.

'You want to borrow this dress? I wore it, like, a

157

year ago, I don't think Jake will remember. Don't tell him it's mine. It's a bit retro, but the style might come back in by then.'

By just under two weeks' time? And I'm supposed to worry about Jake thinking I've borrowed a dress? On top of worrying that he hasn't even asked me to the dance?

'So what do you think?' Tori asks, shaking the tiny retro number and handing it to me. 'Won't Jake think you're totally hot in this?'

It's time to confess.

'Jake hasn't asked me,' I tell her. 'Yet.'

'No!' Tori looks even more horrified than I expected her to. Instead of reassuring me, she adds, 'You have to do something about it, Josie.'

'What, like ask him myself?' I've been considering this. After all, this is the twenty-first century, right?

'NO!' The horror on Tori's face deepens. 'That would just be bad for your relationship.'

'Bad?' Worse than never talking to him at all?

'But you can talk around it. You know, talk about my dress, say how hot you'll look in it at the dance. But don't tell him it's my dress, of course.'

Of course. I haven't forgotten that rule already.

'We don't really, you know. Talk,' I say.

Tori laughs and looks at me sideways. 'You're so cute and funny,' she says. Then she sighs. 'I remember when me and Greg were like that. I don't know, it hasn't been the same lately. Greg's so . . . Did you get to third base yet?'

The question takes me by surprise. 'Not yet,' I say. 'I've sort of avoided it.' I'm not sure why. I think I've wanted to, especially when I've been in the middle of kissing sessions, but for some reason I've always pulled away.

Tori nods. 'After the Winter Dance is a good time. I mean, you don't have to. But if you wanted to, it would be a good time. It's practically a school tradition from way back. Like going all the way after the prom.'

Gulp. At least I've got some time before the prom. If there's any chance I'll still be Jake Matthews' girlfriend by prom time.

In the distance I can hear strains of a booming bass – Albie's band are rehearsing. I think I want to stop talking about clothes and Jake.

'Hey, Tori?' I put the dress down. 'Let's go and listen to Madison Rat.'

Tori groans, but then she smiles. 'I guess we could. Then we can break up the rehearsal and ask one of the guys to give us a ride to the mall.'

'OK.' It's a trade-off.

I follow Tori into her basement party venue. Madison Rat are in full flow. The throbbing sound touches the corners of the room. There's a tall boy with red hair bashing the drums, an overweight dreadlocked boy holding a guitar and stooped over a keyboard, and then there's skinny Albie with his electric guitar and his spiky-haired good looks. He's different on stage – he acts like he owns it completely, like it's his kingdom. This is what Jake Matthews is like in the school corridors.

Albie's low voice is crooning a Snow Patrol song into the microphone.

The sound floods my ears and makes me tingle. I can't hide that from my face. Tori shakes her head at me as if I'm a lost cause.

Five seconds into the next song, for no apparent reason, the music twangs to a halt and a squabble breaks out. The band members shout at each other. I catch the following phrases: 'It's in F!', 'It's in effing F, for ef's sake!' and 'You're an effing F, you effer!'

I give Tori a questioning look and she shrugs.

'They always do this,' she loud-whispers. 'Mom says they've been like this since they were in daycare. They fought every morning and made up every afternoon.'

Sure enough, the music starts up again, from almost exactly where they left off.

Tori nudges her head towards the door. I nod – she can go if she likes – and lean against the wall to concentrate on Madison Rat. But Tori tugs my sleeve and shouts, 'Come on!'

I follow Tori, almost walking backwards to prolong

my full Madison Rat exposure. Albie's singing another song I recognize, one that's usually sung by a breathy female vocalist. It sounds fantastic sung by a man. Boy. Whatever. It sounds unbelievably brilliant.

'Josie?'

We're just outside the door. I can still hear the music without straining too much.

Tori waves her hand in front of my eyes. 'Great, you're alive. So it's time to break up the rehearsal.'

'What?'

'The mall.' Tori turns an imaginary steering wheel.

I look at her. She can't interrupt them – she just can't!

Tori rolls her eyes. 'Look, wait here. I guess I'll go get Dad.' She walks away, mumbling, 'I don't know what to do with you.'

I sit on the bottom step and lean one ear against the door, wondering how it would look if I went back in to listen properly. But the music stops again and I hear raised voices.

'You tell me I'm in the wrong key again and I'm leaving the stinking band!' It's a screechy, nasal voice.

'So leave already!' That was a low voice – Albie, I think.

'Yeah, you stink anyway!' Different voice. Maybe the drummer.

'Go get some rhythm, then come to me and say that!'

'You go get some!'

'Yeah, you're just not getting any, that's your problem!'

'You're an a-hole!'

'Who you calling a-hole?!'

'You! A-hole!'

'You can't even curse! You curse like a freshman!'

'You can't even score! You can't even score a freshman!'

I wonder who they're shouting about. Who's not getting any? Who can't score?

The bickering stops and the music starts up again.

I stifle a groan when Tori appears at the top of the stairs.

'Dad's finishing up on his royal family forum. Come on, let's get away from that Rat noise,' she says.

I drag my feet up the stairs. 'I like it.'

'Yeah, I totally know YOU like it, but that's my point exactly, made-for-TV-movie girl.' Tori looks me up and down. 'Anyway, is it the music you like, or my big brother?'

I feel my cheeks burning. I don't like Albie – not that way. I just think he's talented. And misunderstood by his sister. And anyway. 'I've got a boyfriend.'

'Yeah, or two. What's the deal, anyway? My dad just mentioned Prince William and it reminded me. You haven't talked about William in ages and I think

162

Kristy's getting suspicious. She asked me about him.' Tori sits down on a red couch in the hallway, underneath a portrait of Princess Anne. 'It might be time to break up with him, if you know what I mean.'

Why is Kristy asking Tori and not me?

'You think so?' I didn't think anyone cared. Except maybe Jake.

'Well yeah . . .' Tori hesitates. 'And also because . . . Jake's getting so into you. It's not really fair on him, don't you think?'

Tori's so noble. I've never even thought about Jake's feelings. I'm glad she thinks he's into me though.

'OK, I'll break up with William.' I squash up next to Tori. 'How? I'll have to cry, won't I? And how heartbroken should I be? Will I have to miss parties and stuff?'

Tori considers my questions. She is such an expert on all this stuff. I'm so glad she's my friend.

'Maybe bring a small onion to school and chop it in your locker first. Or go for the natural, no onion but sad-faced approach.' She looks thoughtful. 'You can totally go to parties with a broken heart. In fact, it's practically a licence to hook up with boys, and girls can't really call you on it, not right after a break-up. As long as you don't overdo it.'

'You mean, it's like Slut Exemption? A Get Out Of Slutsville Free card?'

'Yeah, pretty much. But you're with Jake already, so

it could be different for you.' She nibbles on the tips of her manicured nails for a while. 'Josie, look, I wasn't going to tell you but . . . I think you should know. Chelsea's saying she'll tell Jake to dump you if you don't break up with William real soon. She says you're playing him.'

Oh no. First Kristy, now Chelsea. When exactly does everyone talk about me and my imaginary boyfriend behind my back? I'm with the in-crowd every chance I get. They must be discussing it in class, passing notes or something. I wish I didn't do all those advanced subjects with nerds. I need to keep a closer watch on my friends.

'But you said Jake was really into me. Why would he dump me?'

'Oh, I don't know if he will, but Jake and Chelsea are close, you know. Also Chelsea usually gets what she wants. And, well . . . she has a thing for him, Josie.'

Yes, I think I guessed that a long time ago. I try to make light of it. 'For William?'

She gives me a stern look. 'You know who I mean.'

'Well, Jake's mine. Chelsea's a bitch.'

Tori examines her fingernails. I expect her to side with me, but she says, 'I don't know, Josie.'

What? Am I losing Tori to Chelsea already, just at the mention of Jake dumping me?

'I feel kind of sorry for Chelsea. I don't know what I'd do if my 'rents freaked on me like hers did in the summer. Well, it was her dad who totally lost it – I mean, had a breakdown, that's what my dad says – but Jake must have told you how hard her mom took it.'

I shake my head, but I don't think Tori notices.

'Chelsea doesn't talk about it, but Albie told me. He works for the Cooks – well, Mrs Cook right now, with Chelsea's dad being in the hospital. At least Chelsea was staying at the Matthewses' house when the worst of it happened. You know?'

I know? No! I had no idea. Chelsea's dad had a breakdown? Chelsea stayed at Jake's house?

Jake never says a word to me. He just kisses me. We never talk about the most glamorous girl in the school, Cookie to him, who is supposed to be my friend, who likes him. Jake never mentions anybody's dad totally losing it. Sometimes he'll tell me when the Red Sox or our school team, the Millers, totally lose a game.

Tori finally registers the expression on my face and slaps her hand over her mouth. 'You didn't know?'

I shake my head.

I've never even been in Jake's house, but I sat outside it in his car once, when he forgot his cell and we went back to get it.

Chelsea has lived there.

And I need to feel sorry for her.

'I can't believe you didn't know. I was sure Jake would have told you.'

'We don't talk, remember, Tori?' I feel dazed.

'Seriously? I thought you meant you're very into each other.'

'No, I mean we don't tell each other anything. We just kiss. And stuff.'

'Oh. Well, it happened a long time ago,' says Tori quickly. She looks at her watch, as if saying that has reminded her about time in general. 'My dad said five minutes. Typical. Probably got chatting to those old British people again.' She frowns. 'You really don't talk? At all?'

'Um. Not really. I can never think of a single thing to say to him.'

'Right.' Tori fiddles with her watch. It's gold and delicate and designery, and I wish I had one like that. Maybe I should ask Kelly to find me a convincing knockoff version.

'Josie, are you sure Jake's the right guy for you?'

I open my mouth to answer, but I don't know what to say.

Of course he's the right guy, or I wouldn't be in the cool gang. He has to be the right guy, or I wouldn't be here now, about to go to the mall with my cool friend. And who says you have to talk to a guy? Isn't that what friends are for? Guys are for kissing, right? Friends are for talking to. Isn't that how it works?

'Ah, the European princess!' Tori's dad's booming voice saves me. 'How are things at the palace?'

166

'Um, OK,' I mumble, feeling my cheeks grow hot. I'm never quite sure what to say to Tori's dad. I feel like I'm letting him down because I can't answer any of his loud questions about the Queen of England. The only vague link I have to royalty is my imaginary boyfriend called William.

And I need to officially dump William very soon, or Jake will dump me.

And then the cool crowd will too.

I don't know what to wear for my date to the ice rink tomorrow. Maybe I could find a fake fur coat in the thrift shop. I could try to look more like Kendis.

As if that will make any difference. I'll still be me, just like I was when I wore Tori's clothes, way back. How can I get David to like me?

It isn't a date anyway, of course. Rachel's coming. And now I'm doubly worried about that. Why does everything feel so complicated?

Hailey will know what to do. I phone her.

'Jo! Hey, listen, can I call you back?'

'I guess.' I twist the phone wire round my fingers – Mum couldn't afford a cordless phone so we bought this wonderful curly-wired antique from the thrift store. 'Why?'

'Ha! "I guess"? You've gone American. Didn't take long. Aaah-some! Get you.'

'Yeah, yeah. It's wicked good,' I say, in my best Boston accent, which is way better than her fake American one now. 'Why do you have to call me back?'

'Oh, sorry, Jo. I'm on my way out to the shops.'

'Isn't it, like, nearly evening there?'

'Yeah, well, LIKE, some shops are open till late even in boring old Britain.'

'I know that.' Why is she being so snippy?

'And Jonathan wanted to go to that sports shop on the trading estate . . .'

'Jonathan?' She's going SHOPPING with Jonathan?

Suddenly I feel really lonely. My best friend's a million miles away, going shopping with a boy.

'He's nice, Jo. I can really talk to him.'

Huh! Talk to him? Hailey and I don't talk to boys. We fancy them from afar. Or a-near, like the way I fancy David. But I certainly can't talk to David, not without getting my words in the wrong order. Since when did Hailey develop the ability to talk to a boy she fancies?

'But Hailey, you don't even like going to the trading estate.'

'No, Jo. YOU don't like going there.'

Oh yeah, that's true.

There's a silence.

'So how's it going with you and that David you like?'

I twist the wire miserably. 'Hailey, you have to go. I'll tell you later.'

'Yeah, OK. I'm sorry.' She sighs. 'He's not my boyfriend, you know. Yet. I'm working on it.'

'Go. Have fun.'

'Thanks.'

'Hailey?'

'Yeah?'

'Tell me all about it another time.'

'I will.'

Mum tiptoes past me as I hang up. She's all dressed up, looking distinctly un-Mum-like, smelling like a perfume counter. I can't ask her either. She has a boyfriend too.

Everyone's changing except me.

Mum's in a pushy, un-Mum-like state. Un-old-Mum, anyway. She's always in a total nark with me these days. It's just as well I hardly ever see her.

'Josephine, you need to ring Hailey.'

'OK, first I'll send Tori a message and—'

'What is happening to you? I know you're busy with your new friends, but you never used to be rude. Hailey left three messages on our voicemail last week, and I know you didn't call back. I bet you haven't been emailing her either.'

She's right, I haven't. Hailey still sends me messages with full accounts of Jonathan and life. She always ends with, *Where are you these days? Call me!*

The messages have been getting shorter though.

It's not that I don't feel guilty about it. I do. I don't want to hurt her by not replying. It's not just about being busy with Tori and Jake, either. Not exactly.

Mum holds the phone out to me, her face all stern.

'Just phone her. Honestly, Jo-Jo, Hailey's just what you need to get your feet back on the ground. You've been so caught up with this Giles boy, we hardly ever see you—'

'It's Jake, Mum.' And who's WE? I only have one parent in this country. In fact, yes, Mum's totally one to talk. She's been out every single night lately, with the Frenchman. But it means I can get away with more, like going to parties on school nights and wearing barely-there skirts without her even knowing.

'Josephine. Call her. Good friends are rare. You'll thank me for this one day.'

Whatever. I pick up the receiver, and Mum leaves the room, shaking her head. Hailey's number trips off my finger onto the phone's touch pad. I used to call this number every day, at least twice a day. Until I moved here.

I feel another pang of guilt.

But what am I going to tell Hailey? The longer I leave it, the harder it is to excuse the fact that I haven't been in touch. And I know exactly why I'm avoiding her. It's because I'm sure she'll get all funny with me about the way my life is now. She'll call me a Delicate. She'll make me doubt what I'm doing, trying to hang onto Jake and keep in with the in-crowd.

I hear the British ring-tone, a solid-sounding *bring-bring*. It sounds more commanding than the flimsy single *bring* I'm used to now.

But there's no answer. She's probably out with that Jonathan.

Now that I'm in phone-Britain mode, I dial Dad's number. He usually calls me every Wednesday evening – a five-minute chat which is almost identical every week. I know I'll shake him up by phoning on a different day, but hey. I'll make him live a little.

Kelly answers in her chirpy telephone voice.

'Oh! Is everything all right?' she asks. 'Your father's out. Golf. He wasn't expecting a call from his daughter today.'

I don't talk to Kelly much, but when I do, she always works the words 'father' and 'daughter' into the conversation a lot, like she needs to remind herself of exactly why she has to talk to a loser like me.

'Is Lolly there?' I miss Lolly's nonsense-talk so much. She's never around for my Wednesday calls from Dad. She gets put to bed at something crazy-early like 6 p.m., so that Kelly can have evenings free to put teabags on her eyes and cucumber slices on her nose.

'Lauren's at the childminder. I've got a facial

booked in an hour. We weren't expecting you to call.'

'I know, you already said,' I say. 'I was being spontaneous.'

'Ah.'

I imagine her sighing inwardly at my use of a big word. She thinks I'm such a geek.

'Well, I'll tell your father his daughter called,' Kelly says. 'Bye.'

But – hey – I'm not a geek any more.

'Wait! Kelly?'

'Yes?' She sounds wary. I don't know if I've ever actually called her 'Kelly' before. I usually avoid using her name, if I talk to her at all.

'Can I ask you something? I mean, just quick. I won't make you late for your . . . face thingy.'

'I . . . suppose so.'

'It's about handbags.'

'Handbags?' Now she sounds suspicious. She's waiting for me to trip her up with some scientific formula for handbag-surface-area-to-diamanté-stud ratio calculation, or something.

But that's something Jo the Nerd would calculate. I'm Josie the Cool now and there are more important things I need to know.

'Yeah, handbags. How can you tell if they're genuine designer or knockoffs?' I ask.

'At a market?' she asks, her voice relaxing.

'No, in a thrift— charity shop,' I say. I don't shop there any more, of course, but that Louis Vuitton handbag, the one like Chelsea's, is still tucked away in a corner of the window. I'd buy it if I could be sure it wasn't a fake.

I hug my knees to my chest. I'm a genius for thinking of asking Kelly this. A spontaneous genius.

'Oh. Those places smell,' Kelly says. I imagine her wrinkling her beautiful nose, itching to spray air freshener. So what if she's a snob though? She could really help me for once.

'It's Vuitton. It looked real to me.' I've been studying Chelsea's bag, for comparison. 'And it's ten dollars.'

'Ten dollars!' She sounds impressed. 'Is the snap monogrammed?'

'The snap?' I shut my eyes, picturing the bag that will either cause increased in-crowd respect, or more alien stares. 'I don't know.'

'What about the stitching on the handles? Is it yellow?' She's excited now. 'Do the sides of the handles look red?'

'I don't know. Maybe.'

'Oh God. It's a bargain. Buy one for me! I can't wait to visit. I always knew America would be shopping heaven.'

'There's only one. In the charity shop,' I say, in case Kelly has forgotten that she doesn't approve of my shopping habits. Or rather, Jo the Nerd's shopping habits. I think she'd quite like going with me, Josie the Cool, to the shiny mall.

'Buy it! Oh God, buy it! But, oh, check the lining first.'

'What should I check for?'

We continue having what is probably the longest conversation we've ever had since the day Dad first introduced her to me and I gave her the killer look I'd been practising in front of the mirror especially for her.

By the time I get off the phone, it's time to go to the mall with Tori like I arranged. And by the time Albie drives me back from Tori's, and we chat wonderfully about music all the way back, it's too late in England to call Hailey.

Anyway, I have to get ready for my date with Jake tonight.

When I see Mum later, she doesn't ask me about Hailey, or tell me to call again. She doesn't even comment that I'm wearing Tori's brand-new Extra-Ultra Cleavage Top or ask if I'm going to wear a jacket tonight, when the first light snow of the season has been forecast. She just gives me a look and gets herself ready to go out on her own date.

I'm in the back seat of a car with David. Unfortunately Rachel and her mum are in the front.

We're on our way to the skating rink, though we probably could have found a frozen puddle to skate in, it's gone that cold outside. For the last week or so the ground has been covered in a thin film of icing-sugar snow, but last night was the first big, proper snowfall. It's gorgeous. It also hasn't stopped anyone driving anywhere, and even my mum's plans for a big day out with Rashid in some countryside sculpture park didn't get cancelled.

Rachel's mum is driving confidently, ignoring the ledges of white that narrow the road. She's surprisingly normal, except that she's playing wailing New Age music and talking about something called Holistic Barmy yoga – or at least, that's what it sounds like from back here.

'The relaxing effects are amazing.' She taps her polished nails on the steering wheel. 'Jo – is that your name?'

'Uh-hunh-ha,' I say, even though I did try to form a real word. I concentrate on the amazing white world outside.

'Jo, maybe you can persuade Rachel to go. You girls should go together. You need more relaxation. The stresses of modern teenage life are extraordinary.'

Rachel blows air out of her nostrils.

'I'm serious, Rachel.'

'You're always serious, Mom. Don't worry, we get plenty of relaxation. It's called high school.'

I wonder if Rachel's mum said that because I'm giving off hyper-nervous vibes. I'm totally on edge. I'm gripping the seat because I keep having this crazy thought about reaching over and touching David's hand, which is so close to mine. Also, I can't speak in words of more than one syllable today. And calling them 'words' is pretty generous. I just keep thinking, This is it! I'm on an almost-date with David! And Rachel, but still. David!

'Have you ever tried yoga, Jo?'

'Nunh-huh,' I say.

'Jo's into more strenuous exercise,' David says.

Ooh.

I grip the seat harder.

'She's a runner, aren't you, Jo?'

He remembered the conversation we had months ago at Mum's party! He *must* like me!

'Yunh – uh – nunh. My fruhn-huh.' I take a deep breath. 'Friend from England. Not me. I ran. With her.'

There's a long silence.

I can't go on like this. I have to regain the power of speech, and fast.

Luckily we arrive before anyone can expect me to speak again. Rachel's mum spends ages negotiating whether or not she can give us a lift home, based on the length of her post-yoga-class herbal-tea session with her friends. She pronounces the tea as 'erbal', which amazingly sounds posh rather than Cockney.

Rachel ends the negotiations by saying, 'Forget it, Mom, we'll take the commuter rail,' and striding away while her mum's still talking. David says a smooth goodbye, thanking Rachel's mum for the ride, and I say, 'Guh, thanh.'

David and I walk to the rink. Together.

The skating rink is far more basic than the only one I've ever been to in England. It's also really cheap to get in, unlike the one in England, which was so expensive that it had to be a birthday treat for Hailey's twelfth birthday. Hailey's mum took us on a train and two tubes from Boringtown to London. We were crap at skating and we hung onto the rail, giggling and wobbling the whole time. Then we went to the café and ate the most disgusting hot dogs in the world and ignored the loud, rough boys who were laughing at us and making comments about the way we ate. It was a great day out and we always said we should do it again, but we never did.

I've always watched the ice dancing at the Olympics, though, and I've seen re-runs of *Tonya and Nancy: The Inside Story* and *Michelle Kwan: Princess on Ice* about ten times. I like to think I'm just one step away from an ice-dancing career myself. I only need to learn how to skate. It should be easy enough, living here, with cheap rinks and my five-dollar skates from the Walnut Street thrift store.

In the changing rooms – or rather, a series of benches

where Rachel and David expertly twiddle laces on their boots and I fumble nervously with my grey skates, which don't quite fit – I daydream about winning my first skating medal against all the odds, in a true-life rags-to-riches story.

Rachel looks at me expectantly. David concentrates on his laces.

'So is that cool with you?'

'What?' I ask. Yay! That sounded like a word! I'm back. Except that I need to start listening too.

'I said, Limey, I'll need you as a lookout again. I have to increase my graffiti campaign for the Winter Dance.'

Great. That's all I need – more time standing outside the toilets dying of embarrassment, avoiding Tori's brother Albie, who always tries to talk to me if he sees me, and Jake Matthews, who might smoulder his eyes at me, and Chelsea's gang, who generally intimidate me just by walking past. And all so that Rachel can draw something that gets wiped off in minutes. It's pretty stupid, really.

'I don't know, Rachel . . .' Why can't I just say no to her? Especially now that I've got this idea that she fancies me – shouldn't she hang onto my every word, full of wonder, the way I am with David? But I'm more awkward around her than before. I'm always looking for signs. Not that I'd know what signs I'm looking for, or what to do if I found them.

'Rachel, I don't think Jo wants to do it,' David says.
He noticed! He cares about me!

'I think Jo can speak for herself, David. Anyway, shut up, you're male. You're part of the problem. Guys have a thing about school dances, like it's some kind of tradition to be assholes,' Rachel says. 'There's a whole heap of Bryces around. I have a duty to the women at The Mill.'

'I don't have a thing about dances,' David says. 'I don't even particularly want to go, but people keep asking me. Anyway, what's your duty? To piss off Chelsea? Isn't she a woman too? Shouldn't you be on her side?'

'Think what you want,' Rachel snaps. She stands confidently on her skates and tucks her boots under the bench. She makes a show of turning away from David.

'Listen, Limey, we'll go buy some boots next weekend and I'll decorate them for you like mine and David's.'

Wow, I'd love that.

But is that a sign?

Is she asking me out?

David does an impressed whistly thing. 'That's a big deal for Rachel,' he teases. 'She doesn't just draw on anyone's boots, you know.'

Oh really? I fiddle awkwardly with my laces.

'I thought I said shut up, wise guy,' Rachel says.

David shrugs. 'You didn't actually say that.'

'Yes, I act-YOU-ally did, freaky talker.' She glares at David.

'I can't make it,' I say. 'The British are coming.' It's true. My dad, Kelly, Lolly and Hailey are arriving the day after the dance. But if David had suggested meeting up, I bet I would have found a way round it.

A toddler in a red bobble hat jumps towards us, reminding me of Lolly. I can't wait to see my family. And Hailey, though I hope she doesn't talk non-stop about Jonathan.

I've changed my mind about going home with Dad after their visit, though. I'm going to find a way of telling Mum and Dad soon. Someone needs to keep an eye on Mum – she's turning into a total teenager with that Rashid.

Mind you, if I went home, I could get away from this Rachel problem without ever having to confront her. Maybe I can take David with me.

'No problem, we'll go some other time,' Rachel says. 'Your number's on Karen's list, right?'

Another sign? She's asking for my number?

'Uh,' I say.

A group of tweenage girls giggle past us. Rachel rolls her eyes. 'Jesus, Limey, I can't believe I agreed to come skating. Whose lame idea was this? So yeah, Jo, you owe me. You're my lookout next week.'

I finish lacing my boots, trying to copy the circling

knots that Rachel and David have done on theirs. I'm sure I'm doing it all wrong.

David says, 'Look, Rachel, leave Jo out of it.'

I stifle a cheer. He's risking the wrath of Rachel – for me! Rachel glares at him.

David digs the base of his skate into the ground. 'Half the school, anyone who doesn't use the girls' loo, doesn't even get to see your work. You're brilliant – you should publish your comics. Reach a bigger audience.'

'Rachel writes comics?' I mutter.

She turns her glare at me. 'ComiX! With an X. Not kids' stuff. Graphic novels. The feminist ones – not that macho superhero BS.'

'Oh, you mean like *Buffy* season eight,' I say, but no one seems to hear me.

'I can help. I—' David says.

'I don't need help from you!' Rachel strides away as if she wasn't balancing on two tiny blades.

I stagger to my feet and teeter towards the ice.

'Don't worry, Jo, I'll talk to her,' David says, walking confidently beside me. He flashes the dimple at me. Wow.

I'm sure I should stand up to her, but I'm so happy he's offered to do it for me.

David's skates attack the ice. Rachel's already in the middle of the rink doing a pirouette. Her black coat fans round her like one of those little skating skirts.

Rachel in a skating skirt – yesterday I'd have said that was impossible to imagine.

I wobble onto the ice. My first step towards Olympic gold, and my first date with David. Almost.

I grab my Louis Vuitton bag and my Advanced Algebra book and slam the locker door. I chew my lip. I'm not looking forward to Advanced Algebra because Mr Wilson, this super-hairy teacher, is failing me. It makes me uncomfortable – I never used to be the failing type – but I'm not going to show I care. It's not important, anyway. This year is Not For Credit, it's for my Personal Development. Ha. So far I've developed pushed-up boobs and an expertise in second base with the hottest guy in the school. I suppose that's more personal than any equation.

I've chewed most of my lipstick off, but none of Chelsea's gang or any of the hot boys are in my class, so I figure I'll get away with having pale lips for an hour or so. I'll reapply my makeup before lunch – I can't go to the lunchroom naked-faced.

'Hey, Josie, wait up!'

It's Chelsea. Oh no! She's going to see my ghostly lips. I bite my bottom lip hard to bring out some colour. And what if she asks me anything about William? I haven't had a chance to do anything about that yet.

'How's it going, Josie?'

'Um, OK.' I suck on my top lip so that it will match.

'So you're going to be at the party, right, the one after the Winter Dance?'

Ah. The dance. The one Jake still hasn't asked me to.

But Chelsea's asking about the after-dance party, and I don't have to worry about that. It's at Tori's, so I'm invited. I hope I'm allowed to go if I don't go to the dance.

Wait, of course I'm going. All my friends are going with their senior boyfriends, and I'm going with my boyfriend Jake. He'll ask me soon. He has to.

'Um, yeah, I'll be there.' I'm at all the cool parties. Chelsea knows that. I chew on my lip a bit more. Why is she talking to me?

'Why are you making that crazy face?' Chelsea asks. I instantly stop sucking my lips and pout.

'What do you mean?'

'Never mind.' She gives me a strange look. 'Anyway, so you ARE going to the dance, right? With Jake?'

Sneaky. I wasn't ready for that. I nod, and she gives me a look that sweeps from my head to my toes, sizing me up.

'OK. Well, good.'

She's making me nervous. But still, I know she's been having a tough time. Maybe it's not her fault

183

she's always so sharp with everyone. She has a lot to deal with.

'Listen, Chelsea, I heard about, you know, and I wanted to say I'm sorry.'

She narrows her eyes. 'For what?'

'You know.' I shift around a lot. 'About your . . . your dad and all. It must be hard for you and your mum. I heard that Albie was—'

Her face is hard. 'What has Albert Windsor been saying about us?'

I'm shocked at the hateful way she says Albie's name, but I manage to mumble, 'Albie didn't say anything.'

'So what has Jake told you?'

'Also nothing,' I say.

'Yeah, that I believe,' she says. She tosses her hair. 'Look, you and Tori's wholesome brother can just keep your noses out of our business.'

'I didn't mean—' Chelsea is usually drop-dead gorgeous with all her delicate features and perfect figure, but right now she looks ugly. And nasty. And then I feel nasty myself, for thinking that. I probably shouldn't have mentioned the family stuff – I should have known she'd be sensitive about it.

'I've got to go,' I say. 'To Advanced Algebra,' I add, and then I wish I could keep my mouth shut. Less is so definitely more when you talk to Chelsea or Kristy or any of them except Tori.

'Yeah. Don't keep them waiting in Advanced Algebra.'

Chelsea walks away with a flick of her blonde hair, but then she seems to reconsider.

She walks back over. 'There's something different about your face.' Her icy blue eyes examine me. I hold perfectly still, willing my lips to go redder. She says, 'Have you had a nose job?'

I laugh, but she looks serious.

'No,' I mutter, and I manage not to add any detail, even though I'm itching to explain that I'd never do anything like that. I like my nose – it's a Reilly family nose, my dad's nose, although I couldn't really imagine it as an 'after' picture at the Noses R Us Clinic. I suppose it's not the smallest nose in the world. Dad's never complained, though, and it never stopped him getting girlfriends. Even when he was with Mum, it still didn't stop him.

Chelsea sweeps over me with her eyes again. Oh no, now she's bound to spot that I'm not wearing lipstick, and she'll report me to the Cool Girl Lipstick Brigade and ban me from sitting with her at lunch.

'You're right, you haven't,' she says. 'But you should really think about it.' She smiles sweetly. 'I'm telling you as a friend, Josie. Friends should be honest with friends, don't you agree?' She makes the word 'honest' go on for about a minute.

'Um, yes,' I mumble. I'm gobsmacked, really. I don't know what to say. I know full well that it's in the cool girl job description to be mean. But this is so randomly mean, and out of nowhere, that I'm not even sure if she really is being mean. Maybe she really means it. Or maybe she meanly means it.

In any case, what can I say back? Have you ever thought of looking slightly less perfect? I know a place that could give you a tattoo of a boil on your chin, which would give your face a much more interesting look – all that clear skin is just boring?

I do an impression of a small, pale-lipped goldfish for a while. Chelsea keeps looking at my nose.

'OK. Well, bye.' And she smiles sweetly, does another trademark hair-flick, and walks away.

I walk slowly after her, late for Advanced Algebra, rattling the lipsticks in my bargain designer bag and wondering if I can buy industrial-strength nose concealer to put in there with them.

'Jo, are you all right? Can you move?'

I'm in a heap on the ice. It's embarrassing enough without Rachel calling out from the other side of the rink and lots of people staring at me, including that Lolly-like toddler with the red bobble hat who has just skated past me backwards in a figure of eight. I refuse to feel bad about that – I once read that babies are born knowing how to swim, so it's probably the same with skating. I must try this on Lolly when she visits.

David and Rachel skate expertly over, and David does one of those professional stops that spray ice all over you with a big 'fizz' noise. Not that it matters as I'm already soaking wet. And sore. It's about the twenty-fifth time I've fallen over. But who's counting? Rachel and David aren't – they're skating off enjoying themselves, although they have this ironic 'this is so not fun that it's fun' thing going on, especially Rachel, who complains every time she skates past me that this is a lame thing to do. It's really bugging me. She didn't have to come with us. And it's obviously a lame thing she's done a lot in her life.

I'm starting to think that I won't get that gold medal at the Olympics after all. Unless they have an event where you have to stand for a full minute without falling over. With a few years of training, I could qualify for that.

'Jo? Hello?' Rachel is saying. 'Come on. Get up. Hold my hand.'

Oh.

Uh-huh.

I really would prefer to hold David's hand. Except that I might pull him over when I fall. Though that mightn't be so bad.

I must look great, all wet and icy and red in the face.

I still haven't taken the hand Rachel's holding out to me.

I know I'm being stupid. There is no way Rachel is in love with me. I am as bad as those boys who think that if a boy is gay he probably fancies them. Those sporty boys are always going on like that, as if it's bad, and catching or something. Yesterday I saw a group of those boys jumping all over each other in the hallway, and Bryce shouted something to Jake Matthews like 'Keep away from me, fag!' There was lots of laughter and wolf-whistling. As if Bryce thinks Jake is even remotely gay – he just stole Bryce's girlfriend, for a start. I can't believe I once thought those people were my friends. I can't believe I sat with them at lunch and I even went to a party with them. I can't believe Jake still catches my eye and smiles at me at least once a week.

Am I as bad as Bryce? At this rate, Rachel will be drawing damning pictures of me in her jock-bashing graphic novels, or whatever they're called.

This is stupid. I'm not like Bryce.

I take Rachel's hand and she yanks me to my feet. She pulls me along the ice and for one exhilarating minute I feel like I'm actually skating. Then I lift a leg, which is quite difficult, as my jeans are soaked and heavy. I keel forwards, then wobble and fall in a heap. Rachel laughs, but it's not her usual sarcastic laugh. She is in such a good mood right now. She seems thoroughly in her element on the ice.

Or with me?

'David, get over here,' she calls. 'We need reinforcements.'

This is it. David's going to hold my hand. My heart does a triple lutz. (See, I know the terminology.)

I barely have time to wipe my wet gloves on my equally wet jeans before David holds out a dry hand and smiles sympathetically at me. He's not wearing gloves – I can't imagine him wearing anything as ordinary as gloves. There's that dimple again. It's so lovely. I wish I could feel David's hand more instead of just soggy wool next to my skin.

Suddenly I hear someone say 'Whoaaaaaaa!' and I realize it's me. I'm being pulled along by Rachel and David. It's fabulous. 'Try a walking action, Jo,' says David, and I make small steps with my grey scruffy skates. Left leg up, left leg down. Right leg up, right leg down. And I don't fall over! This is the best feeling ever!

'Out of our way, losers!' Rachel calls to some pre-teen jocks who are hogging the centre of the ice, fooling about and shouting abuse at each other. They shout something about the size of Rachel's butt, but they move out of the way before we barrel into them.

'I'll show them what my butt can do!' shouts Rachel. She drops my hand and I wobble dangerously. She skates off towards them, but I only see this out of the corner of my eye as I fall backwards onto the ice, pulling David on top of me.

'Oof!' I say.

'Argf!' He says. His face is right by mine and his body is pinning me to the ice.

Suddenly I don't care about the freezing, wet feeling seeping through my heavy jeans and how cold the back of my head is against the hard pillow of melting ice. All I can think about is David, inches from my face and covering my body.

'We look elegant,' he says. He moves his arms in an upside-down snow-angel kind of way. But he doesn't get up. Instead he looks at me and laughs.

I can see right into his twinkling grey-green eyes.

'Oof,' I say, almost in a whisper this time. I can't think of anything more intelligent to say, and anyway, I can hardly get any words out.

'Are you OK? Can you breathe?' says David.

How do I answer that? I can breathe, but not in the usual way. I can breathe him. He smells like crushed ice and something clean and slightly exotic. Coconut soap or something. He's only wearing a T-shirt and I wonder if he's cold, but he feels so warm, so close so . . . male. I can feel his chest heaving through the layers of my thick winter coat. I remember I'm supposed to answer him.

'Unh,' I say. Monosyllabic Jo is back.

'Hang on,' he says. He does the snow-angel thing again. 'Such grace,' he says, chuckling. 'Hey, let's dance.' He wiggles his arms. He finally shuffles his way off me and stands up, tugging me up with him. I wobble backwards and forwards on my skates. The rink is spinning.

'Thanks,' I mumble. We're standing very close and he's holding me and he's looking at me. I'm a mess – my hair is everywhere and my cheeks feel icy wet. If you replaced my nose with a carrot, I think I'd look like a snowman. But I can't seem to move enough to do anything about it. I don't think any of my bones are broken or else I wouldn't be standing here. I think they've just all gone soft and if I'm not careful I'll be back on the ice again. Except that David's holding me up. He pulls one hand out from under my arm and reaches over to my face. I hold my breath. He takes a lock of my wet hair and pulls it away from where it was sticking to my left eye. He tucks it behind my ear carefully, looking down while he does it. His eyelashes glisten. At least I'm not the only melting icicle here. I breathe out and breathe in again, that coconut David smell.

'There,' he says.

I hear the sudden slice of skates behind me, and that fizzing 'stop' sound. Rachel. Except she doesn't stop in time. I hear her shout, 'Sorry!' as she tears into the small space between us. I go flying, landing squarely on my bum, with another one of those 'oof' sounds. David wobbles but manages to stay upright. He skates a little circle around me to get his balance back.

'Hey,' he says. 'We only just got up!'

'Yeah, I said sorry,' repeats Rachel. She doesn't sound sorry. Her eyes blaze.

'And it was your fault we fell over in the first place. So did you make those boys quake in their skating boots?'

'Yeah, whatever, smartass,' Rachel says. 'Keep talking out of your butt, you're keeping us all warm.'

David shrugs and skates a casual figure of eight around Rachel with his arms behind his back. She glares at his feet the whole time.

At the end of the second loop, David says, 'They're just kids, Rachel.'

'I said whatever. Anyway. You got it right, it's kids' stuff. This is a dumb-ass little-kid thing to do. Whose sucky idea was it to come here?' Rachel turns her glare on me. 'This sucks. I'm leaving.'

She skates away, the tail of her black coat circling like a kite behind her.

'Rachel! Wait!' David speed-skates after her, not giving me a second glance.

I sit on the ice.

What happened to Rachel? I mean, she's normally got a temper, but she's been blowing hot and cold all day. Did she really get so upset about those freshman boys? Or was it because me and David looked like . . . well, we nearly kissed? Is she jealous? Because she likes me? DID me and David nearly kiss? Or is it

192

all my imagination? I don't know what to think.

And how am I going to get up without their help?

I roll myself over so that I'm on my knees on the ice. Two little puddles form quickly, one under each knee. I pull one leg up and try to stand but I quickly slip back down again. A buzzer sounds and people flock off the ice. Everything's quiet for a few seconds and I wonder about staying here all day, but then I hear the distant rumble of the Zamboni. (See, and I even remember what the ice-cleaning machine is called! That's gold-medal worthy, surely?)

There's no sign of David or Rachel. I feel the panic rise in my throat. They've left me here! I try the other leg – maybe it's stronger. Wobble wobble, slip, skid. Help, help, help.

The Zamboni trundles onto the ice, leaving a slug trail of smoothness behind it. How much time do I have before I get run over? Hit by a Zamboni – what an end to my career as the official Ice Queen of Milltown.

I must pick myself up. I scrabble to my feet but it's even worse than before. I do a great comic banana-skin slipping action with my feet, take a few steps forward, and land on my bum again.

The Zamboni makes watery tracks straight towards me. I sniff. 'Hey,' I say, but it comes out very quietly. 'Mind out.' Sniff sniff.

And then a miracle happens. The Zamboni stops, and a boy climbs out. My knight in shining armour, or puffy jacket and woolly hat. My snowy mountain rescue. Swoon. Hmm, my knight's face looks familiar.

'You all right? Oh, hey, Josie, it's you!'

It's Tori's brother Albie.

Another Saturday, another trip to the giant shed that is Milltown mall. Tori says it's our last chance for a full day of pure shopping before Friday's dance. There's a big snowfall forecast for tomorrow and Tori doesn't want to go out in it because she doesn't 'have this year's snow clothes picked out yet'. I don't ask her what she's going to wear to school on Monday if it's still snowing – I'm sure there's some subtle cool-girl dress code issue I'm missing.

Albie's so busy with rehearsals and work right now that Tori doesn't even consider asking him to drive us, so I'm treated to another Mr Windsor experience. This time he talks non-stop about an Australian he met online who's called Bruce Windser ('with an "e" but he could still be related'). Bruce sounds as deluded as Tori's dad, but hearing about his Aussie obsession with Princess Anne makes the journey go quickly.

When we arrive, Tori's dad does his usual checks. 'All set? Do you have your cell, Tori? Is it charged?'

'Yes, Dad, I'll call you when we need a ride.'

'You make sure you do. Have a good time, princesses!'

Tori cringes.

We enter the World of Shiny Shops. The piped cheesy music instantly puts my ears to sleep. I wish they'd pump some good music in – some Madison Rat. Maybe I should write that on one of the suggestion slips at the information booth.

But I'm not scared of malls any more. I've been coming here every week and now I understand what they're really for. They're full of people from school who need to notice the latest makeover that Tori has given me. It's better than school – here, no boring teachers or classes get in the way of seeing and being seen.

The first thing Tori does is drag me to an accessories shop. She presents me with an array of belts, handbags and jewellery.

'Everyone can afford designer accessories,' she tells me for the five-hundredth time. 'I mean, brand-new ones. Not that your Louis Vuitton purse doesn't totally rock. It's so great how your stepmother worked out it was genuine. I can't wait to meet her. Maybe she can teach me a few things.'

'Maybe you could teach HER a few things – like how to be fashionable without being a total snob. And she's not my stepmother!'

Tori lifts her eyebrows at me.

'OK, technically she is, but call her Kelly. Please. Don't use the M-word about her.'

'Josie, you have issues! You're as bad as Albie. You should go see The Mill's counsellor – I've heard she's cool.'

'I don't need to – I'm sorted.' At least, I think I am. 'Why does Albie see a counsellor?'

'He doesn't, but he should. Ask him some time. Anyway, I'm a retail therapist. Let's find a new purse to go with that dress you're wearing to the dance.'

'Later.' I don't want to think about the dance. Tori knows that Jake still hasn't asked me. I haven't found a good time to announce a split from William either, and there's an unused onion sitting in my locker. Maybe I do have issues after all. 'Let's go to the first floor and see who's here,' I suggest.

Tori looks at me strangely. 'But we're ON the first floor. Ohhh . . . I remember.'

We take the escalator and arrange ourselves casually by the railing overlooking the ground – er – first floor. We scan for faces we know. Tori spots one straight away.

'Omigod, Josie! It's Jake! Perfect. You can get him to ask you to the dance right now.' She beams with excitement.

I feel sick. I'm not ready! But Tori's not going to let me get out of it. I've been her project more than usual lately, now that she doesn't see Greg much.

Jake is leaning by the fountain talking to a blonde

girl. I worry immediately – who's that girl? And anyway . . .

'Jake said he had practice today.'

Tori shrugs. 'Must have been cancelled. Greg didn't tell me, but then . . . Aren't you going to say hi?' She gives me a little shove. 'Don't be scared. He's your boyfriend, remember?'

Oh, yeah. That's right. I lean over and call, 'Hey, Ja— Oh.'

I stop in my tracks because the girl next to him turns round and looks right at me. And it's Chelsea.

'You all right, Josie?' Albie asks.

'Jo,' I mumble.

He hits his forehead with the base of his hand. 'That's right, sorry. Tori still calls you Josie.'

I'm surprised Tori still calls me anything. Oh no! I hope they don't laugh about me together, with the cool crowd. I bet Chelsea and Jake will love hearing about this. I know Albie's not exactly one of their group, but he's definitely friends with them. I still overhear them talking about parties in his basement.

Albie holds out his hand. 'Guess you're not used to the ice, huh?'

I have no choice – I take Albie's hand and let him yank me to my feet. He steadies me the way David did just minutes ago. My cheeks are burning but the rest of me is shivering.

'Been down there a while? Here, get in and help me resurface the ice.'

I'm still embarrassed, but I can't help smiling. Woo-hoo, I'm going to ride in a Zamboni!

He hoists me up and I land awkwardly with my feet turned out, but more or less in a sitting position. Just call me Jo the Graceful. Albie jumps up in one masterful leap and squashes in beside me, taking the wheel. There's only one seat.

'I've always wanted to go on a Zamboni.' The words are out of my mouth before I can help myself. That's right, I don't sound even more like a dork NOW. Needing to be rescued by the fit brother of an ex-friend isn't enough for me.

'Ssh!' Albie says.

I look at him in surprise.

'It's called an ice-resurfacing machine,' Albie mock-whispers. 'Don't let the lawyers from Frank J. Zamboni and Co. Inc. hear you. Zamboni's a trademark. This here ice-resurfacer is a lesser model.'

I laugh and rub my wet gloves together. Albie starts the engine and we glide across the ice. Albie is talking a lot and I can't hear him very well over the roar of the engine, but he doesn't seem to expect me to answer, so I relax and enjoy the ride, watching the snow pile up in front of us.

'. . . approximately one and a half thousand pounds of snow . . .' Albie is saying. '. . . operation of an average of twelve minutes . . .'

I remember Tori complaining about her brother being a nerd, but he looks pretty cool to me. I've heard him at the lockers talking sports with Jake Matthews and the cool juniors, and I've heard him in the lunch queue talking equations with the Mathletics Club, or whatever they're called. Maybe Albie's some strange hybrid cool nerd type. He's friends with everyone, transcending nerd/cool boundaries.

I catch a few more words: '. . . machine covers around two thousand miles each year . . .' He sounds so enthusiastic.

Probably about twelve minutes of operation later, Albie steers the Zamboni off the gleaming ice, turns off the engine and says, 'Feel better now?'

I nod and beam a smile at him. 'That was brilliant.'

Albie looks at me. 'I love the way you talk. Dad's right. It's so classy.'

Classy? Me? I fall out of the Zamboni with as much grace as an elephant on stilts and narrowly avoid falling over by grabbing the barrier. Albie climbs down on his side and says, 'I kinda love my job even if it takes me away from the band. But I want to help my boss out, and we need the money for band stuff, and I know you're thinking my parents are rich but I like to stand on my own two feet, and you know . . .' Albie kicks some clumps of snow off the front of the machine. 'So yeah. I like driving the Zamboni.'

'Ice-resurfacer,' I say.

'Ice-resurfacer.' He grins. 'Sorry. Hey, want to grab a coffee? There's a Starbucks near here. I'm on lunch now and you still need to warm up.'

'I've got to find my friends,' I mumble. I check his face for signs that he's making fun of me, but I can't find any. Then I scan the rink and what I can see of the changing rooms for David and Rachel, but I can't see them anywhere. Why didn't they wait for me?

I sneak another glance at Albie. He's gorgeous, with his spiky hair and that skinny rock-star thing going on. As rock star as a guy can look in winter clothes that have clearly been selected by his sister the style guru. What would Rachel say if she saw me here with him? Maybe nothing, despite Albie's cool-boy clothing. Probably even Rachel, who has a gold medal in snark, couldn't have a bad word to say about Albie.

It must be great to be Albie, and never have to worry about how people see you.

I wish I had a mobile, or cell, as they call them here. Mum wanted to get one, but then she said they all had two-year contracts and stuff and I told her it wasn't worth the trouble. Rachel and David have cells. Albie probably has one. Should I ask to borrow it? But I don't know Rachel or David's numbers. Argh!

If David saw me with Albie, would he be jealous? Maybe it's just what I need to get David to ask me out properly.

I open my mouth to tell Albie that I'd like a coffee, but I've left it way too late, because he says, 'Um, OK, some other time then. I'll tell Tori you said hi.'

'No, don't!' Oh, great, Jo. First I insult him by not even replying to his invitation for coffee, then I insult his sister. 'I mean—'

'Don't sweat it,' says Albie. I can't tell if he's annoyed. He's kicking the snow on the Zamboni again.

I really want to explain, but Albie mutters something else that I don't catch, and then he walks away, pushes a door marked STAFF ONLY BEYOND THIS POINT and disappears.

I hope I haven't offended him. I seem to be upsetting everyone today.

I hold onto the barrier for another second, watching the staff-only door swing, and then I stagger away, leaving wet skate marks on the ground as I go. The changing area is deserted except for two mums putting shoes on their struggling toddlers.

I go to where Rachel, David and I left our things earlier today, but there are no funky Rachel-illustrated boots there, just my boring old shoes.

I spend about an hour undoing my skates, or at least that's how it feels. By the time I'm in my shoes again, moonwalking towards the door because my feet feel so weird without the skates on, even the mums and toddlers have gone. I leave the skating rink, trying not to panic and thinking, What now? How am I going to get home?

It's not like I've never taken a bus before, of course. In Boringtown I used to travel on public transport by myself all the time – everyone did. We took the bus to school, and the train to the shops at the weekend. It was nothing special. But I've never done it here. So Hailey was right about the car culture after all. What a time to find out.

I know that the public transport system in Boston is called the T, so I cheer up when I see a snow-topped sign marked 'T' on the pavement – clearly a bus stop. But there is no reassuring bus number or map or timetable posted. Should I wait here? I remember Rachel suggesting to her mum that we'd catch the commuter rail home. I decide to look for a train station instead.

I walk towards a railway line I can see in the distance, and there I find the station, which is just a sign and a track running right through the street. There's a timetable displayed behind some badly scratched glass. I squint at it for ages but the section for Sunday only seems to list three times: 9:30, 10:30 and 11:30. I don't know what the time is, but we got to the rink at around 10, and I'm pretty sure it's later than 11:30 judging by how hungry I feel. I wonder if Rachel and David got on the 11:30 train. Why didn't they come back for me?

If I've missed the last train, how am I going to get home? I can't see any taxis around, and anyway, I only have ten dollars and some change in my pocket. I wasn't expecting to need more than that. And Mum's out with Rashid the Moustache Man again. She has no time for me any more. Where did that thought come from? My teeth chatter.

OK, so I'll call Rashid. There's a pay phone on the platform. But how do I find the number? I'm racking my brains for his last name – it was something French. Suddenly I don't like Rashid at all. He's a mum-stealer. A mum-stealing peeg. I don't even know the number for directory enquiries. Even if I did, how could I call them and ask for the number of someone whose name I only vaguely remember? Rashid Le-Croissant? Trust me to develop my mum's bad name memory just when it matters.

Help.

I'm stranded.

Some white stuff lands on my nose. I bat at it with my wet glove, and then more arrives. The sky fills with flurries of white dots.

It's beautiful.

It's cold.

I'm stranded and alone. And it's snowing heavily.

I love my life.

Chelsea waves to me casually, as if she wasn't standing with my boyfriend at the mall. My boyfriend who told me he had practice. I know they're friends and all, but right now I feel like if I hear him call her Cookie once more I'm going to make her crumble.

If only I could.

Tori looks surprised but she recovers quickly. 'Hi, Chelsea!' she calls.

'Hey, Tori.' Chelsea doesn't say hi to me.

Jake doesn't exactly look happy to see me. But he doesn't ever show much emotion, one way or another. I don't know if he actually has feelings that aren't sports-related or third-base-related.

He nods up in my direction.

'I didn't expect to see you guys here today!' Tori calls. 'Are the others here too? Is Bryce with you? Have you seen Greg?'

Jake points to his ear and shakes his head.

'Hold on, we'll be right down!'

I follow Tori in a daze. On the escalator, she says to me in a low voice, 'Don't worry, Josie. They're old friends, remember?'

I try not to worry.

'Hey,' I say to Jake when we arrive on the lower floor.

'Hey,' he says back. On hearing the word 'hey' from him, my lips enter kiss mode – it's what they're used to, after all. But the kiss doesn't happen. I fiddle with my hair.

'So did practice get cancelled?' Tori asks.

'No, I cut.'

'Oh,' I say. Jake lives for practice. Why would he skive off to spend time with Chelsea? I blink a lot.

'Josie and I are out shopping for the dance,' Tori says.

I look at her in alarm. *Not now*, I try to make my eyes say. *This is the WRONG time for Jake Winter Dance hints.*

But my eyes aren't communicating well, because Tori goes on talking – dance this and dance that.

I shift awkwardly from leg to leg, sneaking glances at Jake. After a while he looks up and smiles lazily. His amazingly differently coloured eyes do their smouldering thing at me. I smile back, relieved. Maybe Chelsea had something urgent to confide about her family. Why wouldn't he cut practice to see her, you know, as a caring friend?

'And Bryce says he can get hold of a keg,' Chelsea is saying.

I'm relieved she's talking about Bryce and his abilities to supply top-up booze for Tori's party. What was I worried about anyway? Chelsea's obviously going to the dance with Bryce.

'You'll be there, right?' Tori asks Jake directly.

I stare at the ground and cringe.

Jake says, 'Yeah, I guess.' There's a short silence.

'Well, good.' Tori claps her hands together and nods. 'Chelsea, I saw this . . . thing that would be perfect at the party – it's just to die for, you have to see it . . .' She walks away, still talking.

Chelsea hesitates but then she says, 'See you guys in a second,' and follows Tori.

'Tori's pretty obvious, huh?' I say to Jake. Yeah, and so am I.

'Huh?' says Jake. He's staring at Chelsea in the distance and I feel like slapping him to snap him out of it. He's MY boyfriend. Chelsea's with Bryce. His friend.

'I mean, about the dance . . .'

'Oh yeah, the dance,' says Jake. He runs a hand through his hair. 'So am I taking you?'

I don't know, I want to say. *Are you?*

'Er,' I say. 'Yes? Why not?'

'Chelsea said your dad and one of your friends was visiting. So I guess . . . William could take you to the dance?' He drags William's name out for three long syllables.

I don't believe it. Where did Jake get this idea?

I wish I'd never invented William. He causes trouble wherever he doesn't go.

'It's, um, Hailey who's coming,' I explain. 'My girl friend. And the day after the dance, anyway. But not William.'

'A girlfriend? You never talk about her.'

I never talk about a lot of things.

I have to get rid of William. There's no time for onions. 'Jake, you know, it's over, anyway. With William, I mean. I guess it was all over long ago, I was just waiting for the right time to tell you, uh, him. He was having a rough time, with the, um, exams. No, parents.' I should have thought about this in advance. 'With his parents' exams. Um.'

'Oh.' Jake's smile is not the warmest I've ever seen, but it encourages me.

'Yes, I don't want to be with William. I want to be with you,' I say. I take his hand.

He pulls me close and kisses me. He pushes his body into mine. Now I really do feel relieved. The coolest guy in the school is still my boyfriend and Chelsea's just his friend. William's gone and everything's going to be OK.

'No more William,' Jake says, coming up for air. He seems so pleased. He must really like me.

I nod.

'Does that mean we can go all the way now?' He doesn't wait for an answer. He starts kissing me again, deeper. 'You're so hot, Josie.'

Oh, THAT'S why he's pleased.

I wait until his lips move to my neck. 'I thought you played baseball, not soccer.' I try to make my voice light.

Jake stops nuzzling. 'Huh?'

'You know. All those bases you told me about ages ago. Aren't we supposed to get to third base first?' I sound so breezy.

'Oh.' His arms hold me tight. 'Yeah, right. Whatever.'

He licks hungrily at my ear. It's making it difficult to think. His arms move over my back. My legs turn to rubber. I sigh.

'So we'll do it then?' he murmurs.

Help! What? I thought we'd agreed on third base? 'What?' I say. It comes out very high-pitched.

'Go to the dance? The party afterwards would be the perfect place to, you know. Reach those bases.'

This isn't at all how I imagined being asked to my first ever American dance. This never happened in any of the films I've seen. And what is Jake doing, arranging this, er, what we're going to DO, how far we're going to get, in advance? Shouldn't that kind of thing just happen, unplanned? Or at least sort of naturally?

'Hey, guys!' Tori waves. A fed-up-looking Chelsea trails behind her. Tori walks up to us, beaming, looking at me with her face all did-he-ask-you-yet?

'I'd love to go to the dance with you, Jake,' I say, extra-loudly. It's childish, but Chelsea glares at me and it gives me a thrill.

'Great,' says Jake, more quietly than me, but that isn't difficult.

'Josie, didn't you say your British friend was visiting?' Chelsea asks me, her voice sweet but her eyes like stones.

'Yeah. Hailey.' What is with everyone today, asking me that? 'And my dad and Kelly and baby sister Lolly. They're coming the day after the dance.'

'And William?'

Oh, I get it. So it was Chelsea who told Jake I'd be going to the dance with William? Well, so what – I've already taken care of this.

'No,' I say sadly. 'We broke up.'

Ha! If Chelsea had any ideas about stealing my boyfriend, she can forget them now.

'Oh really?' Chelsea piles more sugar into her voice. It makes me feel slightly sick. 'Is that what you told Jake?'

'It's true,' I retort.

'Oh, it's TRUE?' Chelsea drawls, looking at Jake.

I feel very hot all of a sudden. There's a pounding sound in my ears. What does she know?

'Chelsea . . .' Tori says. She is looking from me to Jake to Chelsea and back again. There's worry written all over her face.

OMG. Has she TOLD them? Has Tori told Chelsea that I made William up?

Surely she wouldn't do that to me? Tori's my friend. And, if it slipped out by accident, wouldn't she warn me?

Whoosh-whoosh-whoosh go my ears.

'So you told Jake the TRUTH about William?' Chelsea says, as sweetly as before but with her eyes narrower.

In the silence, the plinky mall music works at my nerves.

'Chill, Cookie. It's cool,' Jake says.

'It's not cool, Jake. Josie lied to you. She lied to you for, like, months. Don't you care?'

'Tori, did you tell them?' My voice is squeaky with panic. 'Did you tell them there's no William? Did you tell them I made him up?'

Chelsea looks at Jake triumphantly. 'See!'

Jake frowns. There's another silence.

Chelsea says, 'I TOLD you, J. But you're all, like, I gotta get me some of that cute accent.' She puts on a silly voice that sounds nothing like Jake's deep throaty twang. '*Josie's a nice chick.*' She tosses her hair. 'Huh! She's a nice liar!'

I can't argue with Chelsea.

Jake says, 'Josie, did you make William up? All this time?' His frown deepens.

Oh God. He's going to break up with me, and for a good reason. Not for some shallow, I-wear-the-wrong-clothes type of non-reason.

Instead of dealing with this, I turn on Tori. She's shaking her head. My voice gets louder. 'Why? Why did you tell her? I never told anyone your secret about Carl!'

Tori goes pale.

I don't care. She told my secret! She's ruined everything!

'About Carl? Carl Earlwood, Kristy's Carl?' Chelsea asks. She looks at Tori.

Tori shakes her head more. Her eyes are wide.

'Yeah, about how Tori slept with Carl.'

Oh God. What have I said?

'It was a real long time ago. Before he hooked up with Kristy. It was nothing,' Tori says quickly. She looks like she's going to cry now. She's glancing around frantically as if she needs an escape route.

'Interesting,' says Chelsea, smiling at me. For one ridiculous second I feel happy that she's on my side now. 'And does Kristy know?'

Tori's face crumples. 'It was nothing,' she repeats, each syllable on the same dull note.

Jake leans against the wall. He breathes in loudly, blows out. It's like he's smoking without a cigarette. 'Cookie,' he says, 'leave it. Carl Earlwood's a total pussy. Kristy's a fake. Leave them to it, it's not important.' He puffs out a series of invisible smoke rings.

'It could be important,' Chelsea says. 'I'll decide.'

'I have to – I have to go,' says Tori. She doesn't look at me. She runs into the mall crowd.

I fight the urge to run after her. Like she'd want to speak to me now.

'So, Jake? You really still taking Josie to the dance after THAT?'

'Sure. It's no biggie. Josie and me will work it out.' He looks at me with a gleam in his two-tone eyes.

'You are unreal, Jake Matthews. UnREAL.' Chelsea flounces off in disgust, flicking her hair as she walks.

Jake gives me a slow smile, slightly apologetic. 'Don't worry about her. She always gets steamed up over nothing.'

My stomach's still churning. 'It's not nothing.'

He shrugs. 'Listen, Josie, I don't know what craziness made you lie to me all this time, but, you know, I think I'm sort of glad there was never a William.'

His amazing eyes flare at me.

He kisses my ear and says, 'Now there's nothing standing in our way, Josie. There never was, huh? You were just scared. You shoulda said. But you'll like it, I promise.' He sucks on my earlobe. It's lovely but . . . I can't concentrate.

'I've got to go,' I mumble.

The truth is, I don't feel like hanging around with Jake. I came here to go shopping with my best female friend.

And whose fault is it that she's run off?

Oh.

Instead of kissing Jake goodbye like I probably should, I do this lame little wave.

As I turn, Jake smacks my bum like he did that time in the closet, millions of kisses ago.

I don't giggle like I did that day, and almost every time since. I don't say anything. I put my head down and walk away.

If I sit here any longer, I'll turn into a snow-girl. I'm already doing a pretty good impression of one. I've pulled on the big fluffy hat that I bought at the thrift store. I didn't feel like wearing it before, around Rachel and David, because Rachel once told me it looks like I'm wearing a cat on my head. I admit it was more a style buy than a practical one. Who knew I'd REALLY need a hat? In Boringtown it snows for about a day or two a year, a layer of wet whiteness that quickly becomes grey slime. We all complain about it and everyone has trouble getting to school, and the news talks about the cost of the snow to businesses. Our feet and our mums' cars get stuck in sludge. We shiver and put on scarves and gloves and impractical hats like Moggy the Kitten, the one that's on my head right now.

But it's different here. This is properly cold, and this is proper snow. And the cars don't even pretend to be stuck. All the wipers are going and everyone's moving along. I've never seen anything like this. It's hard to see much though, because of the beautiful flurry of full white fluffy flakes. They're gathering on the brim of

Moggy and on my shoulders and on the tops of my legs. They're swirling around me, and the flakes are getting bigger. I stick out my tongue and catch one. It's wet and tasteless and almost magical. If I didn't feel so cold, and if the snow wasn't settling so completely all over me, I could stay like this for ever.

As it is, I need to find some shelter. I don't remember passing Starbucks on the way to this odd station, but it must have been there. I wonder if Albie will be there even though I said I wasn't going. Was he was planning on going anyway?

I stand up and trudge in the direction I came from, marvelling at the gentle crunchiness of the snow beneath my feet. I leave tracks behind me with my plain black unillustrated shoes. I see the bus stop again, but still no sign of any buses. Then I pass the skating rink, and I glance inside, just in case. I see a group of boys with hockey sticks and matching beige and brown sweatshirts, and a man in black who's barking orders at them. No David, no Rachel.

Beyond the skating rink there's a branch of Milltown Citizens' Bank with its large foyer and cash machine. It's all carpeted and almost inviting. Just as I wonder about breaking in and sheltering there, I spot Starbucks.

I push the door and walk in, shaking the snow off myself like a little dog who's been swimming in a puddle. In fact, a little dog could come here and have a swim, as I've left a huge puddle on the floor myself, with all the snow I've shaken off Moggy. I take a second to adjust to the dim lighting – all that white stuff has made it very bright out there. At first it doesn't seem like anyone's here apart from a bored girl with a ponytail who's slowly wiping the coffee machine. She nods at me.

Then I see him in the corner. Albie, huddled over a magazine, studying it intently and sipping from a large cup. Turning into a snowgirl has made me brave, and I stride over and say, 'Hiya.'

He jumps, spluttering coffee over his magazine. He dabs at it with a napkin.

'Sorry, I didn't mean to scare—'

'No, I'm sorry, I'm not usually such a klutz. Oh, it's all over my hair!'

'No, I'm sorry, I really— What?' How did the coffee get into his HAIR?

'Here. Look. I have a beauty spot on my temple and I look like I'm wearing a toupee.' He points to the magazine. It's a photo of him, posing with a guitar, his face splashed brown. 'I'm such a dork, spilling my coffee. I was going to save that article for Mom— Uh, I mean, the guys.' He pushes his hair back with the hand that's holding his coffee, and now he has a coffee spot in the same place as the Albie in the photo. It makes me smile.

'It's not every day I get my picture in the *Improper Bostonian*.'

'Is that a big deal then?'

'Kind of. Lots of college kids read it, and maybe we'll get a gig, or— Wait, you're shivering again. Can I get you a coffee?'

I've got so used to shivering, I didn't even notice I was doing it any more. 'Yes, please,' I say gratefully, sinking into the seat opposite Albie.

'So how do you like it?'

This throws me for a second. People are always asking me what I think of living in the USA, but I wasn't expecting this question from him right now.

'It's OK,' I say. 'But I'm probably going home after Christmas.'

Albie gives me a confused look. 'Huh?'

Maybe the cold has gone to my head, or there's something about Albie that makes me feel super-comfortable, but for some reason I blurt out, 'You know, don't you? You were there. You know what happened with Jake Matthews and all that. I got off to a bad start at The Mill. I just wanted to leave, you know. But then I started hanging round with these other guys, only now they've abandoned me too. It must be me.' I sniff and a big drop of water plops onto Albie's magazine. It has to be a snowflake from Moggy – surely I'm not crying? Wait. Maybe I am. Another tear falls down and lands on Albie's photo, spreading across his nose.

Oh no. This boy rescues me and I repay his kindness by ruining his day and his magazine photo.

'I'm sorry! Have I made the photo worse?' I sniff and another big tear falls, but I manage to catch that one in my wet glove.

'No, it's good. If it spreads far enough, it will dilute the brown up there. Hey. Here.' Albie stands up, hands me the coffee-stained napkin and glances nervously at the coffee counter, as if he's trying to make up his mind whether to say something or not. Maybe he's plotting his escape from the mad British girl.

'I sorta meant, um, before, how do you like your coffee?' Albie asks, and as I groan and put my head in my hands, he adds quickly, 'But it's OK, I wanted to hear the other stuff too. Let me get you that coffee first, though. I think you could use it.'

'Um, just regular coffee,' I mumble through my hands, and I'm relieved that Albie walks towards the counter without asking any more questions. I can't do any of that non-fat-mocha-hold-the-sprinkles thing I've heard other people specify in this country.

I pull Albie's magazine towards me and read the article. It calls Albie a *hot new talent from suburban high-school band Madison Rat, with lyrics influenced by 90s TV show Buffy the Vampire Slayer*. I realize why the band name sounds familiar.

Albie comes back with my coffee and a muffin. 'Here,' he says.

Wow, how did he know I was starving? I thank him loads. Then I point to the article. 'Madison Rat, huh? As in that witch in *Buffy*, Amy Madison?'

Albie gives me a delighted smile. 'Wow! How did you know? No one ever gets that!'

I smile back. 'Gingerbread, season three, episode eleven.' I take a huge bite of muffin.

'You rock!' Albie says. 'I mean. Uh. Cool. So . . . What's your favourite season?'

I hug my coffee with both hands.

'I like winter,' I say without thinking.

Albie looks at me strangely again. 'Yeah, I like winter too,' he says. 'But I kind of meant, which is your favourite season of *Buffy*? Oh wait! This is your British humour, right?'

'Um, not exactly.' It's like I can't stop until I've humiliated myself as completely as possible.

I take a deep breath and try again. 'Season six.'

'Six? Really? That's interesting. I've never heard anyone say six before.'

'It's the way Buffy has to kind of reinvent herself, you know, after the huge changes in her life. I've always liked the way she does that. It's like she doesn't know who she is any more – no one knows who she is. So she's got the freedom to be anyone.'

'I never thought of it that way. I just thought the monsters weren't as good. I'm more of a season two guy myself.'

'Dark melodrama? The true pain of love?'

Albie grins. 'Plus it's the season where Willow's the cutest.'

I laugh and take a huge gulp of coffee. I've thawed out now.

'Although six has that musical episode. That was awesome,' Albie says.

'Wouldn't it be fun if we went round singing instead of talking?'

'Yeah, that would work for me. I'd love that. I sing way better than I speak.'

We keep chatting for a while, about school and life and everything. I talk about Hailey and he talks about his friends in the band. Then he asks me the question I've been dreading. 'Why did you stop hanging with Tori? She misses you coming round.'

I don't know how to answer. Surely he knows?

'I'm sorry, it's none of my ... I remember what happened, but ...'

I take in Albie's deep eyes and dark hair. He's nothing like the blond Windsor family. He has a serious expression and softly red cheeks against his olive skin.

Wow, he looks gorgeous right now.

I shake the thought away. I've gone boy-crazy since coming to the US.

'You look nothing like your sister,' I say, to explain why I've been staring at him.

'That's because I'm adopted,' Albie states.

I laugh, but Albie doesn't join in.

'No, I really am. I'm surprised Tori never told you. I've known all my life, it's no big deal. Mum and Dad were desperate for royal baby Windsor, but it just wasn't happening for them. It took years to do the paperwork to get me, and in all the stress Mom didn't even realize she was pregnant with Tori until after I arrived.' He smirks. 'But I'm the wanted one, she's the accident.'

This time we both laugh. Albie is so laid-back about everything.

'I know I look nothing like them. I'm the dark-haired sheep of the family. But I'm still part of the royal family. Albert and Victoria Windsor.' He laughs.

'Oh God! Is your name Albert? And of course, Tori's—'

'Really, call us Albie and Tori.' Albie grins. 'I guess sometimes I'm not as cool with it as I think. The adopted thing, I mean. I want to earn my own money, even though Dad gives me a generous allowance.'

'Oh.'

'Tori and me are real close though, you know. And I know she misses you.'

'I really don't think she does.'

'No, she does. She was so happy when you arrived. I know she's not cool with those other friends of hers. That Kristy Melbourne laughs at her. And Chelsea, even though her mom . . . Well, the others just agree with whatever Chelsea says, and sometimes I want to tell them . . .' The aggressive grimace looks out of place on Albie's face, but then he shrugs and relaxes back into his usual easy smile. 'But I'm her dorky big brother, so what do I know? I guess they're Tori's friends. She can take care of herself. She even used to take care of me sometimes, back in elementary school.' He laughs and plays with his coffee cup.

'I don't believe you,' I say.

'Swear. She was a force when she was six years old. A seven-year-old boy didn't stand a chance against her. You ask her.'

I turn my coffee cup in my hands. 'I really can't talk to her after, um.' I don't look at him. How did we get onto this again? 'That party. You know.' I keep my eyes focused on swirls of coffee.

'I know there are two sides to every story,' Albie says.

I look up and meet his eyes.

'Did you know I ran after you that night? I was worried about you.'

I'm shocked. 'YOU were my stalker? You freaked me out. I mean, just for a second.'

'Sorry. I was calling your name. But you totally outran me. Are you a pro runner?'

'I used to run with Hailey back in England. But it's her thing, not mine.'

I swirl my coffee around a bit more. Neither of us speaks for a while.

'Albie? Have you ever said or done something and wished you hadn't?' I ask, not looking at him. 'Do you ever wonder what life would have been like if you hadn't said or done it? I don't know what got into me that night. I'm sure I'd be happier if . . . I just think everything would be OK. But I couldn't . . . you know.' What am I thinking of, having this conversation with Albie? A guy! I can't believe it. I'm talking to him like he's Hailey. I'm usually scared to even talk to guys. I can't talk to David at all.

'Hey, don't worry about it. You should be yourself. What else can you do?' Albie says.

'Who's myself, though?' I glance at him from under my eyelashes, in case he's looking at me as if I'm crazy. But he isn't. He's fixing me intently. I decide to continue. 'I mean, I'm myself with my mum, and I'm a different person with Hailey, but it's still me. A different me. You know? And I'm myself with my friends here too.' At least, I think I am. Except that I'm scared of Rachel, and David makes me nervous. So maybe I'm not myself. In fact, I'm more myself with Albie, but I don't mention that. 'So there's more than one me. Which one am I supposed to be?'

'I think I know what you mean.'

I smile. He smiles back. We sit smiling for a while.

Albie breaks the smile-silence. 'Wouldn't it be great

222

if we could all just be ourselves and say what we want to the people we want to say it to?'

'Maybe it would be boring.'

'I don't think so.' Albie looks like he's about to add something, but his cell phone rings. I watch him fumble in his pocket.

So this is how it feels to be friends with a guy you're not crushing on. I've never really experienced it.

This makes me think of David again, and that near-kiss moment we had today on the ice rink. Should I just have kissed him, instead of hesitating? Would that have been true to myself? I think so. I feel my face growing hot at the thought. I hope David is looking for me right now.

'Is Chelsea with you?' Albie says into his phone. He turns away from me slightly. His voice lowers. 'With Kristy? I understand. It's OK, don't worry. I'll come over.' He presses a button and looks at me apologetically. 'I have to go. I'm sorry.'

'That's OK.' What a weird conversation.

'Want a ride home? I'm going to the Cooks' house. That's near you, right?'

'Chelsea Cook? You're going to Chelsea's house?'

Albie looks slightly uncomfortable. 'Yeah,' he says. He stands up. 'Are you coming?'

I've been lying awake all night wondering how I could have done that to Tori, even if she did tell my secret about William.

223

It's been snowing heavily. Outside my window, the street looks white and magical. Inside, I feel dark and terrible. I need to talk to Tori about it. But I don't think she'll ever want to speak to me again.

I wander into Mum's room, thinking I can maybe spill it all out to her, get some advice. But she's fussing around with clothes and makeup, acting like me before a night out with Jake.

'Oh, I'm glad you're up! I'm having a day out with Rashid today. We're going to this gorgeous sculpture park and then for lunch and— What do you think, Jo-Jo, is this OK? Is it a bit over the top for daytime? Should I wear lipstick or not? And mascara? You know about this stuff, don't you? Hey, should all three of us get together? But your father's visiting soon and maybe it's not appropriate . . . Look, don't think . . . Are you OK with this . . . ? With—'

'You look just great, Mum. Really.' I want to tell her not to change herself. She doesn't need to.

Mum comes over and gives me a hug. She smells like airport gift shops. She doesn't smell like Mum.

'Look, I'm glad you're happy here, Jo-Jo.'

I want to cry. She's so excited about her day out, I can't tell her that I lay in bed last night thinking of going home with Dad after Christmas. I could run away from Tori and Chelsea and Jake. I could be laughing about all this to Hailey in Boringtown McDonald's within the month.

But I need to sort things out with Tori before I escape. I think I owe it to her.

Mum leaves in a flurry of sophisticated perfume. I put Lifetime on and half watch two whole movies, waiting as long as I can, worrying the whole time. I pick up the phone and start dialling Tori's number a couple of times, but I can't do it. Maybe it would be easier face-to-face? I grab my coat.

The snow's floating down again and, as it's only Sunday lunch time, not many paths have been cleared yet. I run, jump and skate over the snow and ice to get to Tori's as quickly as possible, before I change my mind. But when I get to her front door, I freeze.

What am I going to say? There's no good explanation for what I did. I've got to beg for forgiveness then.

I take a few deep breaths, then I knock at the door.

Albie opens it. He's wearing full snow gear. It suits him. He looks like a mountain rescuer. I want to throw myself into his arms like I did that day at the ice-cream parlour.

Oh no. Would Tori have told him? Does he hate me too?

'Josie! Great to see you. How's it going?'

So he doesn't know.

'OK.'

'I haven't seen Tori yet, I've been at work. She

might still be sleeping – she's kind of a Sunday sloth. But go on up.'

My heart sinks. 'No, I'll, um, let her sleep,' I say. I don't want to wake her up, not when I'm the last person she wants to see.

'Well, would you like a drink? I'm having a coffee before I head back.'

'Coffee would be great.' Why did I say that? I should go.

'And I could make you a banana split.' He smiles.

'No, thanks. But thanks.'

'You're welcome.'

I follow Albie into the kitchen, feeling like a fraud. As soon as he hears about what happened, he'll want to throw the coffee right at me.

He rattles a whole cupboard's worth of equipment onto the worktop. Watching him is fascinating. He shakes coffee beans into an old-fashioned grinder, chatting as he turns the lever.

'I've been at the rink this morning, and I have to go back later. Sucks really, because the band could use the extra practice, but this is something I have to do.'

'You have to work Sundays?' He's putting me at my ease, as usual.

'Yeah, for the Cooks. Chelsea's mom and dad own half the town, including the ice rink. They've had a rough time recently—'

'I heard about that.'

'Yeah. So I help Mrs Cook out more than I used to.' He tips the ground coffee into a machine. 'Plus I guess the money's good too.'

'The money?' I look around at the shiny kitchen with every imaginable gadget on display. I think about Mum's tiny kitchen and our throwaway plastic sporks that she keeps washing and re-using. Why would Albie need money?

'Yeah. I, um . . .' He pauses. 'I don't like to spend my parents' money. Tori says I have issues.' He shrugs. 'Maybe I do, I don't know.'

I frown.

'Oh, did Tori never tell you that I'm adopted?'

'No.' I have wondered why he's so dark when the rest of the family is so blond. But his eyes are large like theirs. I always thought he was a bit like his dad, actually. Only without the tweed jackets and the royal family obsession. 'What's that like? I mean—' Maybe it's rude to ask questions like this.

The coffee maker sputters and Albie pours a cup for each of us. 'It's OK. I don't mind. It's not a big thing, I've known all my life. I used to tease Tori about it. You know, about how I was really wanted and she was an accident.' He laughs.

I totally can't imagine him ever being mean to his sister.

'Anyway. Sorry. I'm talking too much as usual. How do you like your coffee?'

'Just like that is fine.'

He hands me the cup. 'So how are things with you? You still liking it here?'

'It's OK.' And then, for some reason, I add, 'Except that I want to go back home now. Something I did . . . I've just blown it big-time.' My voice trembles. I don't know why I'm telling him this.

He gives me a kind look. 'I'm sure it will turn out OK.'

'I hope so.' I want to tell him not to think less of me when he finds out. Except how do I say that? Anyway, it should be what Tori thinks that's important.

Important. I think of Chelsea saying that she'll decide whether what I told her about Tori and Carl is important. Meaning she'll decide whether or not to tell everyone, or how to tell them. How to make the maximum deal of it to lose Tori all her friends. I've seen how everyone is with Kendis, after they threw her out of their gang. Or rather, I've seen how everyone ISN'T with Kendis. She might as well not exist for them any more, except to be laughed at.

I don't know if it would be the same for Tori, seeing as she has such a good party house here. I think Chelsea wouldn't want to lose that, but she could still do plenty to make Tori miserable.

And Kristy is the cattiest girl I've ever met.

Poor Tori, being used by Chelsea and the gang, and now by me. I am the worst friend in the world.

'Hey, Albie . . .' I say.

'Yeah?'

I wish I could ask him for help. I take a huge gulp of coffee which burns my throat.

'What, Jo?' He's looking at me seriously. Jo? It's the first time anyone's called me that since I met the cool girls. A million Jake kisses ago. A lifetime. I was a different person then.

'Nothing.'

Albie's cell phone rings. 'That's my boss now,' he says apologetically.

'I'd better go.' I head for the door, calling, 'Thanks for the coffee! Bye!'

I struggle down the snowy street, crunching uncleared snow, leaving soft tracks. There's only one thing for it.

I've got to go and see Chelsea. I've got to persuade her that it's not important.

Albie drives me home, happily chatting about the bands that influenced him and how great the British pop music scene is. The whole journey to Main and Lexington goes far too fast. I wish I could spend more time with him.

'Bye, Jo, it was really great talking with you.' Albie grins.

'Bye, Albie.' What should I say? Thanks? Likewise?

I love the way you talk? 'Yeah,' I say, quick and smart as ever.

'Yeah,' he echoes.

I get out of the car and watch it disappear up the road, towards the big houses of Winter Street.

Yeah? What a lame thing to say. But then Albie said it too.

Why am I worrying about what I said to Albie, anyway? He's just a friend. It's not like with David, where I worry about every glance, every smile.

I can't believe I'm the same girl who partied at Albie's house. It feels like a million years ago. But then, even this morning with Rachel and David feels pretty long ago.

Mum should still be out with Rashid, but as I get near the door, I can hear a strange sound inside. It sounds like crying. How weird. Maybe the television's still on?

I turn my key in the lock and push open the door.

The sound gets louder and I realize with a chill that it's not the television. It's Mum. She's sitting on the sofa, sobbing.

'Mum, what's wrong?' I rush over and crouch down close to her. She looks at me and tries to say something, but it all comes out as sobs. I've never seen her like this. Not even when Dad left.

'Is it Rashid? What happened?' I feel ready to kill

him for hurting my mum. I want to rush straight out again and find him and—

'No!' Mum sobs. 'No, no! It's me! It's me.'

'Mum, what?' I reach for her hand and hold it, waiting for her to calm down. These awful thoughts go round in my head about what might have happened.

'Thank you, Jo,' Mum says finally. She sniffs, but she doesn't sob again, thank goodness. 'Don't worry, honestly. I'm being stupid. It's nothing. What are you doing home? Weren't you going skating with Frap Junior?'

'David. Yes, I went. What's the matter, Mum? What happened?'

'I – I broke up with Rashid.' There's a trail of mascara running down her cheek. Mum never usually wears mascara. 'I just couldn't do it, Jo-Jo. The whole new boyfriend thing, I mean. It wasn't fair on him, so I broke up with him.' She sniffs again. 'Can you believe it? Three years on and I'm like this. And your dad's coming next week. Why aren't I as strong as him? He's got his new family and everything. He's moved on, and I— Anyway, how was your day? How was the skating?'

'Mum,' I say. 'Never mind me. And never mind Dad. He moved on before he left us.' It seems like a mean thing to say, but it's true, isn't it? Mum can't go comparing herself to him. She's nothing like him.

And what was it she said to me about Hailey, about

it being hard for the one left behind? Well, Dad went off and lived his life and kept moving, and Mum was left behind, coping. She coped with the empty space he left in our house, she coped with me, and her job, all the time acting as if nothing had happened, putting dinner on the table, mopping up my tears and tantrums. And then she had the guts to move to the USA and start all over again and take me with her, and buy sporks. And I've whinged and moaned and said I wanted to go home. But she still coped. I think she's stronger than Dad could ever be.

'Dad moved on before he even left us,' I repeat, because Mum doesn't show any signs of having heard me. 'I'm sorry, but he did.' I move to the sofa next to her, and hold her other hand. Something occurs to me. 'You never cried before, did you?'

'I know, I'm sorry, I didn't mean to. I didn't think you'd be home till later.' She gives me a small, sad smile.

'There's nothing wrong with it, Mum. Honestly.' What would Kooky Karen say now? Mum should express her feelings. I think she's been hiding them too long. 'You SHOULD cry. Dad was awful to you. To us.' I feel like crying myself now.

'Jo!'

'Well, he was. How could he treat you like that?'

'I wasn't entirely blameless, Jo,' Mum sighs. 'We'd been going downhill for a while. It was complicated.'

She hasn't let out one of those horrible sniffles for ages.

'Oh, not that again. Next you'll say I'll understand when I'm older.' Although maybe I'm starting to understand now. Already, things don't feel very simple for me. I thought I would like someone, he'd like me back and that would be it. But I like David, I think he likes me back, and it all feels impossibly difficult. 'So did you like this Rashid?'

She nods sadly. 'He's fun. I mean, he WAS fun. IT was fun.'

'More fun than Dad?' Dad likes his fun to come in a box marked FUN. He likes to pre-order it a few weeks ahead and then collect it, pop it in the microwave for three minutes and consume it quickly before moving on to more important matters, like tax returns. 'Though it wouldn't be hard to be more fun that Dad.'

'Jo.' Mum gives me a Look. 'Your father loves you.'

'Doesn't mean he isn't boring.' I shrug. 'So what happened then? With fun Rashid? I thought things were going well. You were singing French eighties songs and everything.'

'Things WERE going well. I'm just not ready. You know. You've seen Lifetime movies. I can't COMMIT.' She smiles sadly.

I want to tickle Mum, or do something crazy to make her laugh. It's making me ache.

'And I don't like changing myself like this, you

know.' She touches her eyes and wiggles black mascara-stained fingers at me. 'But how else . . . men want women to make an effort. Your father was always trying to get me to wear different clothes, change my hair, look more like—'

'Kelly?' As soon as I say that, I wish I hadn't. 'I mean—'

'No, it's true. That's it. She's the kind of woman men like. It's—'

The phone rings. Mum gets up, wiping her hands on her new mall-bought clothes.

'Let's leave it,' I say, but it's too late.

'It's for you, Jo,' she says. She mouths, 'A boy.'

A what? I take the phone.

'Jo? It's David.'

David.

Mum wanders into the kitchen.

David phoned me.

Wow.

His voice is warm and low and full of concern. Concern for me. 'We couldn't find your number. I'm so sorry we left you on your own at the rink. Are you OK?'

'Where were you? I waited for ever—'

'I know – oh, Jo, things got crazy, you know how Rachel is—'

'I looked for a bus stop and then I went to the station but there were no trains and then it started to snow—'

'Jo, I wanted to say . . . something. It's . . .' He sighs. 'Can I come over and talk to you?'

He wants to come over and talk to me!

I glance over at Mum in the kitchen, overfilling the weird kettle. The water's flowing out of the top and she's just standing there.

David sounds worried. 'Or would you like to come here?'

I've never been to David's house. We're not that sort of friends. Yet.

'Yeah, that would be better.' That would be great!

'OK.' He still sounds worried. 'Because I want to explain . . .'

'Don't worry about it.'

I feel vaguely bad about leaving Mum right now, but I think she'd understand. I can't wait to see David. I can't believe this is finally happening.

Mrs Cook, Chelsea's mom, answers the door. Her nose is the same shade of pink as her silky nightgown and she's shivering. She looks at me blankly. I feel like making some excuse and running away. This whole situation is nerve-racking. What I have to say to Chelsea, meeting Chelsea's mom like this, being here at all, at Chelsea's house. I've been here for parties and all, but I'm not exactly Chelsea's closest friend.

'Can I help you?' Mrs Cook says distractedly.

'I'm Josie, Chelsea's friend from school!' I try to sound cheerleadery like her daughter. I figure she'd like that. I stop just short of calling her 'ma'am', like people do around here when they're being polite.

'Oh. Chelsea's upstairs with Kristy. Hold on. CHELSEA!'

Oh no! I'm too late. Even if Chelsea hasn't already spread the gossip, how am I going to talk about this with Kristy here?

Chelsea's annoyance drifts down the stairs. 'What NOW, Mom?'

I shoot Mrs Cook a sympathetic smile but she doesn't notice. Her eyes are dull and she looks tired. 'Your friend . . .' She glances at me.

'Josie,' I say.

'Josie . . . is here.'

A pause. 'Who?'

Mrs Cook looks at me again. I nod, and fight the urge to run away.

'Josie,' she repeats.

Another pause, and then I hear some footsteps. Chelsea appears at the top of the stairs.

'We were just talking about you. Come on up.' She disappears.

I try to act normal but each step I take is a thud of dread. I can do this. I can do it for Tori.

'In here, Josie!'

Chelsea's room is enormous and filled with pink

fluffy things – slippers, shawls, even photo frames. There's a white floaty canopy over her bed. I've only ever seen rooms like this in catalogues, and I didn't know they existed in real life. Everything looks like it's been placed precisely to look as perfectly feminine as possible. There's even a lacy hammock full of cuddly toys. If that was in my room, I'd apologize for it, but in Chelsea's room it just adds to the effect of teen girl perched prettily on the cusp of adulthood. There's a row of lipsticks lined up on her dressing table. Her closet is open and displays a large collection of clothing covered in protective bags. I bet it's all designer stuff. It's like Tori's closet to the power of ten.

Kristy appears from inside the closet, holding a tiny red cocktail dress.

'Hey, Josie,' Kristy says, acting as if it's normal for me to spend Sunday morning with her in Chelsea's perfect bedroom.

Chelsea sits on her bed, leans back and crosses her legs daintily at the ankle.

'Sit,' she commands. She pats the bed. I perch on the edge, pushing the filmy white canopy out of the way when it brushes against my nose.

'We were just talking about you,' Kristy says, shaking the dress so it sparkles at me.

'Oh,' I say.

'Chelsea said you told her something interesting

yesterday,' says Kristy. 'She's being all mysterious. Maybe I can get it out of you instead.'

No one says anything. Kristy holds the dress against herself. Chelsea fixes me with her icy blue eyes.

'Oh, it's just . . .' I say. 'Look, it's really nothing.'

Chelsea lets out a sweet, tinkly laugh. 'I didn't think it was nothing,' she says. 'And I think Kristy deserves to know.'

'You guys! Tell me,' Kristy says.

I look at Chelsea, willing her to shut up. Tori was right to be worried – I know that Kristy will take this the wrong way. Chelsea will make sure of that.

'Let me tell her, Chelsea.' I don't know what I'm going to say, but it has to be better for Tori than anything that comes out of Chelsea's mouth.

'No, let me,' says Chelsea. 'Kristy, guess what I found out? One of our closest friends has been holding out on us.'

Kristy waves her hands impatiently. 'What? What?'

I hold my breath.

'So it turns out . . . Josie made William up. There is no William. Isn't that priceless! You were right all along.'

Kristy gasps. 'I knew it! I knew it! I said that, didn't I?'

Chelsea says, 'Poor Josie. She wanted to be part of our elite so bad, didn't you, Josie?'

I grit my teeth. I try to feel relieved.

'And I was asking Tori about William just the other day, after what you said, Kristy,' Chelsea says. 'I swear she knew – she acted like some little kid with a secret – but she didn't say anything. Isn't it touching how loyal SOME friends can be?'

My stomach plummets a few more depths.

So Tori didn't tell them?

No, I realize. She didn't.

I did.

I told them.

And I told them Tori's secret too.

I am the worst friend in the world.

'But you have to feel sorry for Josie. She hasn't had the chances we've had in life. She probably has to tell a few lies, spread some GOSSIP.' Chelsea looks at me sideways. 'You know, just to make people notice her.'

I can't speak.

'I'll bet she doesn't even know that's a Nordstrom dress.' Chelsea points to the dress Kristy's holding. 'Am I right, Josie?'

I nod. I hate this, but what else can I do?

I've got to talk to Chelsea alone. I've got to do it soon, for Tori's sake. These are Tori's friends, and I know they mean a lot to her.

Maybe I meant a lot to her too. Before.

'Poor little Josie.' Kristy's laugh rattles.

'Kristy, didn't you want to try on that dress?'

asks Chelsea. 'Be my guest. Take your time.'

'Why, thank you, Chelsea.' They sound like they're play-acting. Although I don't know if I've ever heard Kristy say anything that sounded sincere.

Kristy closes the closet door primly behind her. So this is my chance. Now or never.

'Look, Chelsea . . .' I whisper.

Chelsea looks at me with her eyes narrowed. 'What? You didn't mind me telling Kristy what a loser you are, did you? I think she already knew.'

'Chelsea, you won't tell Kristy about Tori and Carl, will you?'

She gives me a wide, crocodile smile.

'I mean, please don't. Tori thinks a lot of you.'

'Yeah, and Tori's just adorable. Wouldn't it be a shame if she had no friends except losers like you?' She clasps a hand over her mouth. 'Oh wait, didn't you stab her in the back? How sad – she doesn't even have you! And I'll bet Greg will dump her once he hears this.'

I don't know how Chelsea can say things like this and still smile.

'But it was years ago. It was nothing.'

'Sure, yeah. That's not what Kristy will think. It depends on you, of course.'

Is she threatening me? 'Do you want something from me?' I squeak the 'me'. What could I possibly give her?

Chelsea's smile disappears. She gets up, moves to her dressing table and picks up a thick makeup brush. She looks at my reflection in her mirror. 'YOU are SO not right for Jake.' She looks down, concentrates on dipping the brush in a tub of powder. 'But, you know, if you LOSE him' – she looks at the ceiling, her brush poised – 'everything should turn out just fine.'

I can't believe it. 'You mean if I break up with Jake, you'll—'

'I mean' – Chelsea dabs powder on her nose, blotting out her perfect 'barely there' features – 'I won't say anything to Kristy – or Greg – if I don't, you know, HAVE to.'

I stare at her reflection, stunned.

'Of course, without Jake you won't be one of us any more, will you? And maybe Tori won't want to know you anyway. But, you know. You never really belonged, did you? This was going to happen sooner or later.' She smiles at herself in the mirror. 'You should think about it.'

The closet door opens and a sparkly red Kristy appears. 'Think about what? Don't I look fantastic?' She twirls around. 'Not that I'd wear it out of your house, Chelsea. Only losers wear their friend's cast-offs, right?'

'Listen, I've got to do a . . . thing. I'll see you guys at school,' I say. I run out of the room, not looking at either of them. My cool American so-called friends.

I stumble down the stairs, my head reeling. I nearly don't notice that there's a couple hugging, just outside the open front door. It must be Mr and Mrs Cook. I walk past quickly.

Then I glance back. I recognize that snow jacket. The mountain rescue gear. I saw it this morning.

It's Albie.

Albie with Mrs Cook.

Just when things couldn't get any weirder.

I stop and stare, even though I know I shouldn't. They don't notice me.

I hear Albie say, 'It'll be OK, Mrs C. He'll be back soon. Everything will work out fine, you'll see.'

Mrs Cook moves away. 'I'm so sorry, Albie. I didn't mean to have another meltdown. Thanks for coming over.' Her nose is redder than it was earlier. She looks like she's been crying.

'No, it's OK. Do you need me to help out with anything else?'

'Just the afternoon session at the rink – if you could run the Zamboni again and clear up a little.'

'Sure, no problem, Mrs C. I'll take care of it.'

I walk on quickly, before either of them see me. Of course it's not what I – for a minute there, with my warped, third-base-obsessed mind – thought it looked like. It's just typical Albie, going out of his way to be nice, to make Mrs Cook feel better. He's got the kind of arms that make everything all right.

I hurry towards home.

I'm beginning to understand what Mum meant years ago when I asked her why Dad was leaving us and she said, 'It's complicated. Relationships are complicated.'

I fall over about fifty times on my way home, but even walking through snow and ice is easier than sorting out my life.

I make my way to David's house, walking out of my run-down area and into in-crowds-ville. Milltown's like a sandwich, with two posh areas on the outside and a scruffy bit in the middle, where me and Mum live. Tori lives at one classy end of town, and she once told me that Chelsea and Chris and Ana live at the other side – the area I'm going to now. Who'd have thought David would live near Chelsea?

The walk takes me ages because people have left walls of snow at the boundaries of their properties. It's not like in my street, where we all live so close together that, once we clear our paths, the whole pavement has a clear track running through it. Here, the houses are so far apart that the only way I can get anywhere is like this: walk-walk-walk CLIMB UP SNOW MOUNTAIN stagger-stagger-stagger CLIMB DOWN SNOW MOUNTAIN walk-walk-walk. Rest, repeat. It's taking ages, and once I sink into soft snow at the top of a badly constructed snow wall. I stay there for a minute, with snow almost up to my chin.

It's the second time today I'm turning into a snow-girl, but this time I don't care. This time I'm on my way to see David.

I kick at my snow prison. I get out, even if I don't look very dignified doing so.

During one of my relaxing walk-walk-walk phases, I see a mailbox that says COOK. I love looking at mail-boxes – they're so American. COOK? It must be Chelsea's house, where Albie was headed when he dropped me off. I turn my head. I want to take a good look at where someone like Chelsea would live. But I see the strangest thing, up by the main door to the house. It has to be Albie. He's wearing the same practical Zamboni-operating clothes that he was wear-ing earlier.

That's not so strange, of course. He did tell me he was coming here. What's strange is that he's in the arms of a woman in a nightgown. A nightgown, in this weather. I shiver just thinking about it. But also, I think she might be Chelsea's mom. And Albie and the woman who's probably Chelsea's mom woman are hugging.

Wow.

Is Albie WITH Chelsea's mom? Is that why he wishes he could discuss his feelings? Is he scared about people knowing?

I understand the world even less than I thought I did. I put my head down and hurry past, slipping slightly on some ice. If it's what it looks like, I wouldn't want to embarrass them. For some reason I feel a bit strange about what I've just seen, although I don't know why. Women date younger men sometimes, don't they?

No, I can't shake the thought. I don't know what bugs me so much about it. It feels like when David was talking about Kendis. It feels like . . . jealousy.

The whole world seems to revolve around couples – getting together, being couply. And everyone's doing it except me. I've never even got to second base.

I concentrate on getting to David's house as quickly as possible. I can't go on like this, being this person who's scared to take a step out of line. Why didn't I go further with Jake in the closet that day? What was my problem? Why haven't I told David how I feel about him? Why haven't I SHOWN him?

David's house is a lot like Chelsea's, only pale blue instead of pale yellow. I might have known he'd live somewhere like this, despite his bad-boy attitude and the black clothes and the boots and all his talk of the in-crowd having it all. I think he has just as much – he just uses it differently. He's the right kind of different.

By the time David opens his door, I'm determined to do something about my feelings for him. It's time.

He's standing there, looking so hot in his black

leather jacket, with those grey-green eyes fixing on me, his hair flopping into his eyes, his smile directed at me. Me!

'Jo,' he says.

I don't trust myself to say anything. I follow him into the house, wondering whether I'll have to make small talk with his parents. I met his dad once at Mum's party, but I've never met Mrs McCourt. 'Are they here?' I wonder, and then I realize I said it out loud. I feel myself blush.

But David answers as if I haven't said anything stupid. 'Mom and Dad are out with my brother. And Rachel just left. She said she couldn't face you, uh, and she'd apologize to you on Monday. She's sorry. We're both sorry. Really, Jo.'

I almost forgot that Rachel was the reason that David rushed out. He ran after her. Or maybe I was the reason, if it was me that made Rachel so angry. I can't believe Rachel would be so sorry that she couldn't face me, though. That has to be David being nice. Being David. I can't imagine Rachel being too scared to face anything. Although maybe, if she has those feelings for me . . . It all comes back to that again. Feelings. Attraction. It causes all the trouble.

I follow David into a large room with white leather sofas and a huge plasma television screen. Wow, I'd love to watch Lifetime movies there some time. I wonder if David would mind? Maybe we could snuggle up on the sofa and—

I suddenly realize it's my turn to say something. At least I didn't think out loud that time.

'Hey, it's all right,' I say.

'No, it's not. We shouldn't have left you there like that,' says David. He looks serious. I've never seen him look like this. I want to throw my arms around him and tell him it's all OK.

He looks at the ground. 'Jo . . . there's something I need to say to you and it's really awkward. I don't know how to say this.'

My heart's pounding. Just say it, I think. Don't be scared.

I feel the same way.

He looks even more gorgeous when he's so serious. His eyes are churning like the ocean. 'Sorry to bring you round here. But I can't tell you at school, it's too . . . It's just . . . About—'

'Stop, David. Really. You don't need to say anything. It was pretty shitty leaving me at the rink like that, but I understand. It's difficult with Rachel—'

'Yes—'

'Ssh,' I say. I don't want to talk any more. I lean towards him. It's only a short distance. I look at him. 'David,' I murmur, and then I think, *Do it*. I breathe in.

And I kiss him.

I kiss him on the lips. Just like that. At last. I've done

it. I've kissed David. And it felt fantastic. Every bit as good as the kiss I've been dreaming about all this time. I can't believe this is happening at last.

'Oh God, Jo,' David says. My heart pounds even harder at the sound of his voice.

'Ssh,' I say again. I don't care any more. I'm not even here any more. The whole world revolves around – this. I understand now. I lean towards him again, and this time I put my arms around his neck. I pull him towards me and I press my lips against his. And I lose myself. I'm spinning, I'm melting. There's nothing left of the snowgirl now, not even a hat.

At first David's hesitating. Well, maybe he wasn't expecting it. I've taken him by surprise. I've taken myself by surprise, so it's not surprising. I keep kissing him.

'No, Jo. No,' David says. He moves away, but only slightly. 'I—'

'Yes,' I say. 'Yes.' I kiss him again. He stops resisting, if that's what he was doing, and then he's kissing me back. We fall backwards onto the white leather. He's moaning something that sounds like, 'No,' but that's not what his body's saying. His mouth on my mouth, his tongue against my tongue. Fire. I move his hands to my breasts. I want this so much. This hasn't blossomed quickly, this longing. This has been building since the day David first looked at me. I can't believe we're finally here, now. Second base. I don't know what I was afraid of.

David groans and pulls away. 'Jo – Josie—'

It's strange to hear him call me that name. I ignore him. I lean forward and kiss him again. He gives in again. For a second. Then he pulls away and kills me.

'Jo. We shouldn't be doing this. I'm not – it's not—This didn't happen . . . I'm sorry. I—'

Oh God. Oh no. I feel sick. I spring to my feet.

'Jo? I need to explain—'

I don't want to hear this. I feel a different fire burning my face. Not passion. Shame. I get up and run to the door. Could I really have read this situation so wrong? It takes me three attempts to open door, but I don't look back. I can't look at David.

I finally get the door open and call out, 'You're right! It didn't happen. It doesn't matter!' and then I run down the street, jumping over a snow wall to get away, skidding on the plain, jumping up again and away, as far and as fast as I can go.

Home, finally. I'm expecting the house to be empty – Mum's with Rashid – so I get a shock as I climb the stairs and I hear the television blaring from our flat. It's cheesy TV-movie music. Did I leave it on when I went out? I don't think so. I creep up the last two stairs and put my head round the door slowly.

Mum is sitting on the sofa. She looks tired, defeated. Her face is blotchy. I don't think I've ever seen her like this, even straight after Dad left. I was the one who did all the crying then. Mum was the one who made popcorn and gave hugs.

I've never really thought about it before. Mum made herself busy looking after me. I don't think anybody looked after her.

'Mum?'

'Oh, Jo-Jo!' Mum wipes at her eyes. I wonder how long she's been crying. 'You're home. Were you at Tori's house?'

'Yes – no . . . Never mind. What's the matter, Mum? What happened?' I feel my heart sink. I've been so full of my life, I've been completely neglecting Mum. We used to be so close, and now I hardly ever see her. I'm off with my new friends, she's off with her boyfriend. I've never even met him. I should at least have gone to that party at Mum's work, instead of that stupid first date with Jake, with Bryce and Anthony in tow. I've been so selfish.

'It's nothing, Jo-Jo.' She sniffs. 'Well, OK, we broke up. Me and Rashid broke up.' Her voice wobbles. 'It wasn't meant to be though. I'm not ready, you know. It's too much. I can't be what he wants. I can't be what any man wants.'

'Mum! What are you talking about?' I sit down next to her.

'You said yourself when I first started seeing him that I needed to make more of an effort. Well, I've been trying, Jo-Jo, but I can't keep it up. It's just not me.'

'I didn't say that!' But maybe I did. It sounds like a Josie thing to say. 'Or I didn't mean it that way.'

'I can't do it, Jo-Jo. I couldn't change for your dad and I can't change for him.'

I put my arm around Mum and she hugs me.

'Mum, come on, tell me all about it.'

She lets out a long sigh. 'There's nothing to tell. I've ruined it now anyway. I told him to leave me alone. I told him never to ring me again. I made it pretty clear.'

The phone rings and our old-fashioned answering machine kicks in. A familiar voice says, 'It's only me again. Hailey. Never mind. Bye.'

'I'll ring her back later.' I put my arm around Mum.

'No, Jo-Jo, do it now. Please, for me. I'd like to . . . sit for a while. I'd like you to ring Hailey.'

'OK.' I give Mum a massive hug. 'If you're sure.'

Hailey answers straight away. 'At last, American girl,' she says. She doesn't exactly sound happy to hear my voice. In fact, she doesn't sound happy at all.

'Yo,' I say tentatively.

'Yo.' Her voice is flat.

I feel a lump in my throat. I've neglected Mum AND Hailey. I've just been an all-round terrible person since I got to the USA. It's not like I can blame Chelsea or Jake or anyone. It was my own fault I got so drawn in by the cool crowd.

'Hailey, listen. I'm . . . I'm sorry.'

'What for?' she asks softly. 'For ignoring your boring English friend or for the mess my life has become? Which of course is all your fault because you totally haven't been there for me. And even if you had, it would be your fault for leaving me in the first place.'

That's it. I sob. 'I'm so so so sorry.'

'Oh shut up.' She sobs back. 'I've missed you, you total sap. Anyway, less of your sorry. I didn't call you either. Much. I've had a life too. HAD being the right word.'

'What happened?' I ask. I wipe some tears away. I want to hear this.

'Oh, it's a long story,' she huffs.

Won't anyone talk to me any more? 'I've got time.'

'Hmm. Let's just say that people – OK, boys – send out mixed signals. There should be better signals. There should be standard, well-known ones. Like road signs.'

'You mean like DANGER? And GIVE WAY?' My sniff sounds more like a laugh now.

'No, maybe more like those car-park signs that tell you where to find available spaces. People should put those signs on their heads, listing who they do and don't fancy.'

It's such a relief to talk to Hailey again. She's mad. I've missed her so much.

'Anyway, what about you, Yankee doodle girl? You shagged any fit jocks yet?'

'Hailey! No! No, I've just messed up everything with everyone who matters.'

'Ah, that's my girl! So tell Auntie Hailey all about it.'

'No, tell me more about you first.'

I listen to Hailey's problems until her mum calls her away.

Then I find Mum and sit with her until she can't resist talking to me about the Frenchman. She does that for the rest of the evening, telling me all about the way they both loved their naff eighties music (well, I said 'naff' and she said 'classic'), and he let her borrow his iPod, and all kinds of romantic stuff like that. Eww. And also awww. They sound perfect for each other.

But when I suggest to Mum that she should try again with him, she goes all firm and bolshy. 'No, it's over – it really is, Jo-Jo. And I shouldn't be talking to you about it anyway! Make me a cup of tea, would you?'

As I wrestle with the weird American not-exactly-a-kettle, I think about how I owe it to Mum to get her back with Rashid. It's time I did something nice for her. Tori would know how to help – she's the relation-ships expert.

I wish I hadn't wrecked everything.

All I can think about when I get to school on Monday is David. Will he act as if nothing happened between us? Or will he fall at my feet and say he was wrong to break away from me, and how could he deny the passion between us?

How could he though – deny it? That's what I don't understand. I didn't imagine it. I've thought about nothing else all night.

Well, apart from how I can cheer Mum up. And Hailey too. I rang Hailey last night and she told me all about her Jonathan disaster. Apparently he doesn't like her after all, not like that. I told her about David. We agreed to give up all that love stuff for ever. We both laughed for about five minutes about how useless we were with boys. It felt brilliant.

I don't feel like laughing now. I'm throbbing with embarrassment at the thought of seeing him, and aching to see him at the same time.

There's no sign of David, but Rachel walks up to me, swinging her rucksack until it hits me.

'Hey,' she says.

'Hey.'

'Rrrrgh!' Rachel screws up her face. 'I'm going to say this quickly, OK? Just listen. Yesterday. You made me lose it. But I know it was not a cool thing to do, leaving you there like that. Completely. Not. Cool. So . . .' She squeezes her eyes shut. She mumbles, 'Sorry.'

'That's OK,' I say.

'OK! Good.' She opens her eyes. 'I'm glad that's over with. You coming to class?'

'Yeah.'

David appears from somewhere and walks casually beside us. We all get busy pretending the weekend never happened. Rachel and David have a conversation about something normal – an episode of some reality TV show and Rachel's mom's yoga obsession. None of it sounds quite right though – we sound like we're acting the parts of ourselves in a play.

This weird play keeps going for most of the week. David doesn't talk to me at all, not properly. I feel so bad about everything. If I think about that afternoon at his house, my cheeks burn. It's agony to look at him. I look at him as much as possible, like I'm prodding a bruise to make sure it still hurts.

As we leave school on Friday, the day of the dance, he says, 'So, see you later.' Rachel is with us too. He says it to both of us, really.

Rachel perks up. Maybe she's been wondering what's up with David too. She must have noticed that something isn't right. She says, 'Great, we're still going? Hey, let's crash the I'm-so-cool-I'm-practically-frozen party afterwards. Jo was Tori's best friend a couple of months back anyway, so she probably knows the secret code for getting in.'

I look at her sharply. But she's smiling. I still can't make her out.

David says, 'I don't know, Rachel. Aren't you sick of that crowd? I see too much of them already. Every time we share the air they breathe, a million of our brain cells die. That's what they want, you know. That's how they take over the world.'

Rachel says, 'Yeah, but what if it works in reverse? I'm sure I can find a reversing spell in one of my books. Think of their faces when they see us at their party. They might explode. Or implode. Now that WOULD be cool.'

I mutter, 'I don't think I'll go. Maybe not to the dance either.' Until just now I'd been hoping we could all still go to the dance, like nothing had happened. But now it all seems too much. I can't act natural around David anyway. Mum will be happy to have me at home. We can watch movies and eat popcorn. I think I need to spend more time with her. She's taking the Rashid thing worse than she ever took Dad leaving us.

'You have to come, Jo,' Rachel says, touching my arm.

I remember all those crazy thoughts I had about her. I'm pretty sure now I was wrong about that, the way I'm wrong about everything to do with attraction, or passion.

'Yeah, you should come, Jo,' David echoes. He doesn't touch my arm.

I'd been looking forward to it so much. My first American dance. 'OK,' I say.

We make plans – or rather, Rachel makes plans, and David and I listen.

I wish he'd look at me. I wish he'd talk to me. And I know I'm not supposed to think this, especially after what I agreed with Hailey, but I think it anyway.

I wish he'd kiss me. I wish we could kiss again.

'Tori, wait up!'

It's Monday at school, and I have to speak to Tori. I have to explain.

Not that there's any explanation for what I said.

Tori doesn't look at me, or smile, or speak, but she stops.

'Listen, about Saturday at the mall—'

'It's cool,' Tori says. She stares intently at her books.

'It is NOT cool!' I practically shout. A few people stop and stare at us. 'It's not cool,' I say more quietly. 'I've been the worst friend in the world. Not just to you, but especially to you. And I'm really really sorry.'

Tori looks up, her face serious. 'I didn't say anything, you know. About you and William, I mean. They were asking me but I didn't say. I thought once you broke up with him they'd forget all about it.'

'Yeah, me too.' I sigh. 'I should have known you wouldn't say anything. In any case, it still wouldn't excuse what I did. I'm so sorry!'

'Mmm,' Tori says, studying the book covers again.

'Look, Tori, I don't know if it helps, but . . . I asked Chelsea not to repeat it. And she kind of said she wouldn't.' On condition that I break up with Jake and get banished from her crowd. But I don't say that. Maybe I don't deserve to be friends with her anyway.

'I guess that kind of helps.' Tori finally gives me a small smile.

I know it's not over. But it's a start. We walk towards class. I'm not used to the lack of Tori chatter. I hate this silence.

'She wouldn't say anything anyway,' Tori says after a while. 'Not yet. She wouldn't want to risk the after-dance party. She loves my house as a party place. But would Kristy come to my party if she heard about me and Carl? And Ana and Chris would follow Kristy, you know. They're pretty scared of her. It would ruin the whole party, and it's far too late to find somewhere else.'

I can't believe people say Tori's stupid. She understands people so well. She knows all about friendship and loyalty, and other people's power play.

I'm so relieved she's talking to me again. And she has a point. So maybe I don't need to dump Jake until the Winter Dance. The night I've promised to get to third base with him.

'Josie, it's not your fault you said stuff, anyway.'

'It's not?' And Tori's generous – maybe to a fault.

'Not really. Chelsea kind of tricked you into it. She does that.' Tori nibbles a nail. 'Listen, would you do me a favour? An easy one, I swear?'

'I'd do anything.' I absolutely mean it.

'Just promise me you'll go to the dance with Jake. And have fun – in front of Chelsea. Make her suffer a little.' Tori laughs. 'See, told you it was easy.'

'OK,' I mutter.

'We'll show her.' Tori links her arm in mine. I'm so glad she's still my friend.

So I'm going to the dance with Jake, like I promised Tori. And getting to third base with him, like I promised Jake.

And then breaking up with him, like I promised Chelsea.

THIRD BASE

 I'm ready for the dance. Tonight I'm not dressed as Josie. I decided to wear one of Mum's dresses instead of Tori's, and I added some beads I found at Walnut Street thrift store yesterday. I went with Mum. We had a girls' afternoon out. I've started putting a plan in motion with her, going on about how women don't have to change themselves to please other people.

I wish I believed it myself. I've sneaked these beads on because I wanted to, but now I'm scared the cool gang will notice and say something.

Or maybe I hope they will. I don't know. The more I said all that stuff to Mum, the more I started to think it might be true.

When Jake picks me up, he doesn't say anything. As usual. He doesn't say, 'You look wonderful,' but he doesn't say, 'What the hell are you wearing?' either. I wonder if he thinks I look any different? He drives me to the dance in silence.

Maybe I could still be any girl.

But when we walk into The Mill together, I know that no matter what I look like, I'm the envy of every girl. Because I'm with Jake, and there's no one here who wouldn't want to be me.

I relax and bask in Jake's hot, cool glow.

And I try not to think about what I've promised to do later.

'OK, think post-ironic, people,' Rachel says as we approach The Mill on the night of the dance.

David flashes his dimple at her. 'What does that even mean, Rachel?'

'Just be your freaky self, David.'

The three of us are starting to believe the act, that nothing is strange between us. Rachel talks excitedly about the looks on people's faces when they see us there. I think they might be too busy enjoying themselves to care about us, but she's sure we'll cause a stir, and I don't want to upset her. She's dyed her hair from black to flaming red just for tonight. She's also made a rare venture into colour, and her dress matches her hair. It suits her. She looks great. Her lipstick's black, and her boots are black, with those wonderful illustrations that I want her to do for me but am scared to ask her about again because I don't want to encourage her if she's in love with me.

Yeah, I realize how stupid that sounds.

Maybe I'll ask her later.

David's all in black and looking like the usual wild-boy David. He's still not meeting my eye though. I wish I knew how to fix whatever I broke between me and him. I don't want to think about it. If I turn red again, I'll clash with my purple dress. I borrowed one of Mum's old dresses tonight, the ones she stopped wearing when she started changing herself for Rashid, the ones I'm trying to persuade her to wear again. I also bought some beads from the thrift store.

On the outside, I look like normal Jo, but on the inside I just don't understand anything any more.

Albie's hypnotizing vocals fill the room. Madison Rat sound even more fantastic than usual, doing a glorious cover of a Snow Patrol song. I make a thumbs-up sign at Albie when I think the cool gang are too busy getting drinks to notice me, but he's infusing his lyrics with passion and his eyes are shut. Tori sees my thumbs on their way down and she shakes her head at me slightly, with a smile. Her brother's a musical genius and she can't seem to see it.

The dance isn't what I expected. I thought there would be more dancing, for a start. Instead, there's lots of standing around commenting on what every-one's wearing. Everyone's smart outfits reduce my friends nearly to tears of laughter. Everyone except members of our crowd, of course. I've had some funny looks, but no one has commented on Mum's purple dress, except Tori, who said kindly that it looked better on me than her dress.

I stand slightly to one side, watching the guys as they elbow each other. They look so hot and man-like in their tuxes, but the way they're behaving isn't any different to what I'm used to seeing in the hallways every day. They jostle and mock each other.

My friends giggle at them.

'Omigod!' Kristy yelps suddenly. 'The witchy morons are here!'

'No! David and Rachel came to the dance? Oh God, does that mean Satan's here?' Chris asks in high-pitched alarm, waving her arms dramatically. I think she might be serious.

'The witch is wearing red tonight! And her hair! OmiGOD!'

I look at where Kristy's pointing. David and Rachel are standing together under a banner, looking around, almost daring the room to laugh at them.

Chris laughs extra-loudly. Ana and Kristy join in, and they say, 'I KNOW, right,' to each other a few times.

Something in me snaps. I'm really not myself tonight. I walk over to the banner and hover for a second. Then I move closer to David and Rachel.

'Hey. Rachel, isn't it? I like your hair. It looks really great that colour.'

David and Rachel both eye me suspiciously. I glance back at my friends. Kristy is staring at me with her mouth open. Chris is shaking her head furiously. I'm glad Chelsea isn't here yet – she's the only one I'm still scared of right now.

'Josie, what the—? Get over here!' Kristy says. 'Christ. We need to babysit her.' She looks at her friends, and they all reassure her with 'I knoooow's. All except Tori. Tori has a broad smile on her face.

'Yeah, bite me, Limey,' Rachel says, and makes a rude gesture with her middle finger. But she grins.

'Rachel, you gotta use two fingers.' David demonstrates. 'It's British.' He turns to me. 'I know you. You sit behind me in Werewolf Wilson's class. My dad works with your mom.'

'Really? So hey, does he know a French guy?' I talk to David for a while about Mum's work. He has an amazing smile and he's really fit. I must have been so out of it in class not to have noticed him before. I push those thoughts out of my mind, and not just because I'm with Jake. It's completely obvious I wouldn't stand a chance with David anyway.

'OK, freak show's over, guys!' Rachel yells, and she pulls David away, laughing, onto the dance floor.

I wish I was as carefree as them.

When I join my friends again, Tori whisp[ers]
was THAT about?'

'I don't know, Tor. I guess I'm sick of bein[g told who]
my friends are.'

'Oh, God, you're so right,' she says. She goes really
quiet for ages.

Post-ironic or not, I can't stand the way everyone's been staring at us all night. Rachel seems to be loving it though.

'Let them look,' she says, dancing wildly and incorporating various finger gestures into her dance.

I wish I could care as little as her. I feel so self-conscious I can barely move.

The only good thing about tonight is Albie's band. They are excellent. Albie's a fantastic singer. At one point he turns in my direction and I swear he's looking at me. But he can't be. I feel awkward about knowing his secret. I wonder if anyone else knows about his thing with Chelsea's mum? Life's so weird. It seems to have got progressively weirder recently.

'Nice DRESS. Very RETRO,' a voice attacks me sarcastically. I look up, trying to mask the hurt I feel. Kristy walks by, snickering. She never liked me, anyway.

Rachel shrugs at me. 'Suck it up, Limey.'

I don't want to.

I pull at my purple velvet dress. I wish I looked more like Kristy, or Chelsea, or any of that lot. I thought

I was so special, sticking to my Jo principles, refusing to change, but it didn't get me anywhere. I ran away that night at Tori's house, and I think I've done nothing but run since. And I've still been desperately trying to fit in, only it's been with a different crowd, in a different way. I'm always worrying about what Rachel and David think of me. I've never felt comfortable with them.

I look over to where Kristy's heading, looking for Tori, wondering if I should try to speak to her. She was always so much kinder than the others, and Albie said she missed me. She's with Chris and Ana. Of course. Where else would she be?

Still, what do I have to lose? They've already rubbished my dress. They already hate me. It's time to take some action. I walk over before I can change my mind. The cool crowd are in a huddle, laughing meanly about something. Tori's standing at the edge, not really joining in.

'Hey, Tori,' I say.

Kristy, Chris and Ana stop talking and stare at me.

'What—?' Kristy says.

'Hey,' Tori says. She looks at Kristy nervously, but then she smiles at me. 'What's up? Nice dress.' She sounds like she means it.

Kristy snorts.

'Thanks, but I feel like kind of a nerd, to be honest. I

like your dress. I wish I was still getting those makeovers at yours.'

Tori's voice is quiet over the music, but I'm pretty sure I'm not mishearing her. 'You always looked cool anyway,' she says. 'I never listen to Albie, but he's always right.' She moves away from the others more. 'Look . . . I'm sorry I tried to make you look like me.'

'I wanted to look like you. I'm sorry I never spoke to you again after—'

'Then we're both sorry. We're even.' Tori grins. I remember how much I like her.

Kristy snorts again. 'Tori, are you for real?'

'Come to my party later,' Tori says loudly, ignoring Kristy's open mouth. 'Please?'

'Tori, are you insane?!' Chris touches Tori's arm but Tori pulls it away.

'Bring your friends. They're a cute couple.'

I almost want to laugh. Rachel won't be happy about the invitation. She's been looking forward to gatecrashing this party for ages.

Chris is practically jumping up and down. 'She's crazy. Kristy, she's crazy. What's in this punch? What's WITH you, Tori?'

'Tori, tell me I did NOT just hear that. You did NOT just invite those losers.'

I move away, leaving the cool girls bickering. So Albie was right about Tori. I should feel bad for lumping her in with the others after the Jake thing, and not seeing what a good friend she'd been. I should, but I don't. Because I'm only thinking about one thing.

They're a cute couple.

Cute COUPLE.

I've been blind, but I'm not any more. Because I'm looking at Rachel and David on the dance floor. Rachel's pushing David's beautiful hair out of his gorgeous eyes. David has his hand on Rachel's waist. They're not kissing or anything, but they may as well be, it's so obvious.

Why did I not see this? How self-absorbed have I been?

Rachel and David are a cute . . . couple.

Jake's body presses me against the cold wall of the gym. One of his hands is in my hair and the other is rummaging at the back of my dress. The lights are low, but everyone can see us. We don't care. Everyone's seen us do this every day, anyway, if they can be bothered to look. Against the lockers, outside the lunchroom, under the bleachers.

So when Jake says, 'Let's find somewhere . . . quieter,' I know it can only mean one thing.

This is it. Third base.

'I thought we had to wait for the party. I thought it was a tradition,' I joke.

Jake runs his hands over me hungrily. It makes me tingle.

'Screw tradition,' he says with a knot in his voice. He pulls me out of the gym. The door swings shut behind us. The corridor is echoey and empty.

I hang back as Jake tries the handle of a door marked SUPPLY CLOSET. It opens.

'Josie? In here,' he whispers, underlining his invitation with those sexy eyes.

I go to follow him but a loud voice behind us booms, 'Mr Matthews, where do you think you're going?'

Coach Harrison.

I study my shoes.

Coach strides over and jangles a huge ring of keys. He locks the supply closet door.

'It's a school dance.' He points to the gym. 'Go dance.'

Jake pulls me over and puts his arm around me tightly. He whispers, 'We'll dance later.' It makes my heart pound.

We walk back into the gym. Chelsea must have arrived while we were gone. She shoots me a look that plainly says, *Who do you think you are?*

I think she has a point. Who do I think I am?

No wonder David didn't want to kiss me. No wonder Rachel was weird with me – I was making it pretty obvious I wanted David.

I'm so embarrassed.

Rachel and David have been wrapped up in each other for the last hour and I don't know what to do with myself. There's not much post-irony going on where I'm standing. I think I should just go home. I'm glad Tori was nice to me, and I'm glad I've listened to Albie's wonderful band, but I don't belong here. Tori has Greg and Albie has . . . well, his band, but I guess he has Chelsea's mom too.

'Hey, you.' David appears behind me.

I scan the room for Rachel.

'Rachel's gone to the restroom,' David says, as if he can read my mind. He'd better not. I'm thinking, *How could you? I thought you were mine.*

I say, 'So Rachel's your girlfriend?'

David looks at the floor. 'Yeah.'

'Yeah,' I echo.

'Jo, look, I'm so sorry about the other day. I shouldn't have kissed you—'

'I kissed YOU,' I say quietly, and I cringe.

'Yeah, and I kissed you back. Look, I haven't told Rachel—' Ah, that explains a lot. 'We only just got together. Well, it's been in the background almost as long as I've known her, I guess, but we never admitted it to ourselves, or to each other. Do you know what I mean?'

No.

David's just confirming what a huge fool I've been. I wish he'd stop.

'I think we're only starting to understand it now. I wanted to tell you because I knew you had, ah, feelings – I wanted to tell you before, but you—'

'David, stop.'

'No, I need to tell you. Blame mad-faced Karen – I have a need to share my feelings. Listen.'

I shut my eyes. I feel like I'm in the dentist's chair waiting for an injection.

'I like you, Jo. A lot. But Rachel . . . remember when she admitted she was, ah, in love with someone? In Personal Relationships? Well, she masked it all as a big joke, but that's typical Rachel.' He gives me a love-struck grin. Ouch. 'Well, she meant . . . me. I know it now.'

And I thought she meant me. I laugh out loud.

'What?'

'Nothing.'

'OK. It's just, you know . . . Look, sorry, but remember I'm half American, half British. I half express my feelings and half don't.'

I can't help smiling at that. As if I hid any feelings for him at his house the other day.

'Jo, are we cool? Because I'd hate to lose you as a friend. I really like you. And I'll just have to, you know, ignore the other feelings.'

He gives me an earnest look. I can see Rachel approaching us, dancing her way across the room. She's full of confidence tonight.

She's in love.

'Yeah, we're cool,' I say quickly before she joins us.

'Hey, Limeys, whatcha gossiping about?' Rachel calls. 'Don't make me get jealous – you wouldn't like me when I'm jealous. Yeah, I turn GREEN! Limey-GREEN! And I can do this voodoo stuff . . .' She reaches us and nudges me hard. She smiles at me. I think this might be her way of saying sorry properly for the day at the ice rink, or maybe even sorry for hooking up with David. Rachel's OK. Congenitally rude, but OK.

David gives me one of his cutest dimply smiles.

I quickly practise ignoring my other feelings.

 That's it. My first ever American dance is over. We pile into some limos owned by Chelsea's dad.

We arrive at Tori's house, two by two. Tori and Greg, Chelsea and Bryce, Kristy and Carl, me and Jake.

The boys head straight for the drink. Chelsea and Kristy fade into a corner, whispering. I stand with Tori as the room slowly fills with partygoers.

'Where's Albie?'

'He'll probably be late – the band have to clear up, and I think he has to stop by the Cooks to deliver something.'

'Oh.'

'Hey, things are going well with you and Jake, huh? You're really showing Chelsea!'

I nod, but say, 'Sssh,' because Jake's on his way over.

'Hey.' Jake sits on the arm of our sofa and hands me a drink. He runs his fingers along my arm.

Tori gets up. 'I'll go find Greg. Bye, you guys.'

I notice Chelsea stare at Tori, then at me.

Jake puts his arms around me. My skin buzzes. Is it because I know I have to dump him later that his every touch feels extra hot tonight?

Chelsea catches my eye and mouths, 'Loser.'

Or maybe it's 'Lose him.'

Rachel and David are plotting about crashing the after-dance party. I don't have the heart to tell them they were invited anyway. I tell them I don't feel well and I'm going home.

Mum has a large bowl of popcorn on her lap and Lifetime on television. This used to look cosy but tonight it looks sad. I've got used to her going out and having fun instead.

I don't say much about my evening. We start watching a movie called *Painful Secrets*. We sit in silence, taking it all in. Misery, depression, despair. We munch our popcorn.

After a while Mum says, 'Jo-Jo, didn't you say there was a party after the dance?'

I shrug. I don't want to explain it to Mum. It all feels so stupid, and anyway, we're depressing ourselves enough as it is.

Mum switches off the television and puts down the popcorn.

'Come on, let's do something else. This can't be good for you. For either of us.'

She's right, of course.

'Let's get things sorted for when Hailey comes tomorrow,' she says.

We go to my room and Mum pulls the spare comforter out of my closet. She shakes it out.

I reach in and push some clothes aside to make room for Hailey's clothes. A top and some trousers fall down. They're Tori's, from way back. From the night of the kiss in the closet with Jake. I never had the courage to face Tori again to give them back.

'I washed those for you ages ago,' Mum says. 'I haven't seen you wear them again. They're not your usual style.'

'That's because they're not mine,' I say. 'They belong to someone who's not my friend any more.' But that's not true. 'Or maybe she is.'

I think about the way Tori talked to me tonight. The way she risked her reputation with the cool crowd to invite me to her party.

'Mum, is it OK if I go out after all?'

'Sure,' says Mum, looking happier than she has done in ages.

We're entwined on the sofa, Jake's hands reaching around me, touching, stroking, pulling at me. Each kiss feels like a little spark, and they're adding up, lighting me up.

I'm getting lost in this feeling until Chelsea walks past, spilling some of her drink on my leg.

'I'm so SORRY,' she says, her voice sugary. 'Hey, I'll go speak to Tori, see if she can help you clean up. I have something I need to say to Greg anyway. And Kristy too.'

I instantly go cold all over. 'No, don't!' I say. 'I mean, there's no need. Really.'

'OK, as long as things are UNDER CONTROL.' Her fake smile chills me as she walks away.

I look over at Tori. Greg is turned away from her and his face looks grey. I think they're having another argument. Poor Tori. All she needs is Chelsea stirring things up.

I need to stop this. I need to dump Jake – now. I've kept my promise to Tori.

'Jake . . . ? Mmm. Jake.'

Jake doesn't answer because he's kissing my neck, and because it didn't sound like I was asking him anything anyway.

I've got to tear myself away. Maybe I'll go and speak to Tori first – check she's OK. 'Jake, I've just got to go . . .'

I get up, but he pulls me back down and whispers

in my ear, 'OK. Meet me in the closet.'

He strokes my back as I get up again. It fills me with heat. My heart thumps. My whole body wants to meet him in the closet.

I swallow a huge, nervous lump in my throat and open the side door to Tori's basement. I haven't been here for so long. The last time I was here, I was a different person.

The room is full of couples at various stages of making out. There's no music playing tonight, just the manic buzz of conversation and laughter.

A low voice beside me says, 'Jo! You're here!'

It's David. I can't see Rachel.

'Are you OK?' he asks. 'Felt like coming out after all?'

I nod.

'Rachel's getting drinks. No one seems to care that we're here. She's really disappointed.'

I clutch Tori's clothes, my excuse to be here. Though I have another excuse. I also thought of something I want to ask David, about Mum. So I launch into that explanation, and it covers my awkwardness until Rachel appears. She smiles at me and hands a plastic cup to David. She strokes the back of his head. It's so weird to see her all loved up like this. She's not the Rachel I'm used to.

'You want a drink, Limey?' she asks. Even the way

she says 'Limey' sounds sweeter than anything I've heard come out of her mouth before.

'It's OK, I've got to . . . go.' I don't feel like sticking around the Couple of the Century any longer than I have to.

I find Tori with Greg. They're sitting at opposite ends of a sofa. Greg's arms are folded and he's pouting. He looks like Lolly when Kelly tells her she can't have an ice cream.

'Tori?' I hope I'm not interrupting an argument.

'Oh, hi! You made it!' Tori beams, standing up.

'Here,' I say, handing her the clothes.

She looks confused for a moment. Then she says, 'Omigod, Josie, you can totally keep those.'

'It's OK.'

'Well, OK, but come over and borrow something else sometime. I mean, if you want to. Not that you need to. But come over anyway. I mean it.'

Greg grunts.

Kristy appears beside me, glaring at me with her mouth open. Carl is pouting at her side.

'Listen, Josie, Jo, whatever your name is. Tori has clearly lost her mind. You are not welcome here.' Kristy points at me, and with venom that makes her voice carry, she spits, 'Loser.'

The room goes quiet. Everyone stares at me.

I should never have come here.

'Kristy, let it go!' Carl pulls at her arm.

'I will NOT! She can't respect my friends, and Jake will not stop talking about her—'

'Kristy, leave it,' Carl whines. 'What do you care about Jake? I'M your boyfriend.'

Chelsea steps towards me, followed by Chris and Ana and their boyfriends. The cool crowd are all coming out of the woodwork now.

'Kristy's right.' Chelsea's voice rings out in the silence of the basement. 'We don't want losers at our party, Tori. Tell her to leave.'

'No,' Tori mumbles.

'Yes,' Chelsea states.

'No.' Tori's voice is bolder. 'She's my . . . my friend.'

Kristy narrows her eyes. 'Tori, are you insane? WE are your friends. She is NOT.'

Chelsea's voice is soft. 'Tori, I think it would be great if you apologized to Kristy now. And to me. You can judge a person by the company they keep. If you're friendly with' – Chelsea twists her face in disgust – 'nerds, you can't hang with us any more. And that includes Greg. You can't be with Greg any more.'

Greg grunts.

Tori doesn't even look fazed. 'That's OK. Greg and I just broke up. You know, I've been thinking for a while now, about friendship. Maybe since I met Josie – Jo.' She takes a deep breath. 'And you know what, Chelsea? I'd like you to leave my house right now.'

Kristy spits out more angry words, ending in: '... turning on your friends?'

'I'd like you to leave too, Kristy. Because, right now, I've realized you're a total fake ... and I'm not.'

Kristy goes white. Her voice turns into a Carl-like whine. 'Omigod, Tori. Chelsea—'

'And anyone else here who can't respect my guests,' Tori says. 'Please leave.'

It's so quiet that I think I can hear snowflakes falling outside.

The silence doesn't last long.

The room starts to crackle. Kristy shouts at Carl. Ana pushes Jonny away. Greg swears loudly and hits the wall. All those perfect couples I noticed before seem to be imploding.

Only Rachel and David are still kissing, like they haven't even noticed the commotion.

Most of the cool crowd storm out, cursing. Tori watches them, arms folded, insults flying over her head. Greg is the last of them to leave. 'I hope you're happy,' he calls to Tori. He slams the door.

Tori waves to the remaining, stunned people. 'Guys, it's a party. Go party.'

The noise level creeps up slowly.

'Tori, you're amazing,' I tell her. I can't imagine the courage it took to stand up to Chelsea. Well, I suppose I tried it too, ages ago. But Tori was way more successful.

She shrugs. 'It's been building up a while. I couldn't stand the way they talked about you. And everyone, really. They're the losers.' She looks at her watch and pulls out a cell phone. 'Jo, I gotta go check where my brother is. I know he had a delivery to make to Chelsea's mom. I should warn him I've kicked his boss's daughter out of our house.'

'Mrs Cook is Albie's boss?' I blurt. 'Nothing more?' Oops, I didn't mean to say that part out loud.

Tori looks at me strangely. 'Yeah, he works for the Cooks. What do you mean?'

'Nothing.'

'Chelsea's dad's . . . away, and Chelsea's mom's taken it hard, and you know Albie – he goes out of his way to help.'

Of course. It's just another example of how my couple radar is utterly malfunctioning, or non-existent.

She frowns and heads for the internal door, pushing buttons on her phone. 'I'll be right back, OK.'

I look around. I feel lost. Rachel and David are in a corner, and I move my eyes away quickly. All these kids I barely know stare at me and whisper. This isn't much better than the last time I was at a party at Tori's. I don't want to stay. I'll explain it to Tori another day.

I shut the door to Tori's basement, lean against it and take a deep breath. It's snowing, but not too heavily. I'm not scared of a few snowflakes any more.

'So, Josie, right?'

I jump. Jake Matthews is propping up the wall beside me.

When I get closer to Tori, I can hear her say calmly, 'It's over, Greg. If you can't handle a thing like that, then what's the point of us?'

Greg is spitting names at her.

'I think it's been over for a long time. We need to face up to it.'

Greg makes a fist and looks at the wall as if it's his worst enemy. Then he storms to the bar, calling out more nasty stuff. He grabs a can and yanks it open.

Tori stands in the middle of the room. People are talking, making out, partying. But not for long.

'Listen up!' Tori shouts so loudly that the whole room freezes for a second. 'All of you. There's someone here trying to spread rumours about me. Well, they're kind of true, but that's not the point. If you don't like me, if you can't handle it, then you shouldn't be here.'

Nobody moves. I hear Albie give a cheer from the side of the room. He's standing with his Madison Rat friends. I wonder when he arrived.

'Tori, chill,' says Chelsea, stepping out from a dark corner. Bryce is next to her, his face stony.

'You chill, Chelsea,' says Tori. 'You know exactly what I'm talking about.'

Some girls gasp. Nobody talks to Chelsea like that.

'Tori, we're your friends.' Chelsea rolls her eyes at Kristy as if to say, *What a nut.*

'Then treat me like one. And treat Josie like one too. I'm sick of it.'

Chelsea gives that tinkly laugh.

No one else laughs. Everyone stares at Chelsea.

'It's taken me a long time,' Tori says, 'but I've finally realized who my friends are. And they're not you.'

There's a long silence.

'Are you saying you want me to leave? Because just say it and I will. I'm warning you, though, your life will be hell.'

'Oh, Chelsea, I'm totally so not scared.' Tori looks at me. I've never seen her like this. 'I have real friends now.'

'Riiiight – loser girl who invents boyfriends and tells everyone you slept with Carl?'

Now there are murmurs going round the room. People are mostly saying, 'Kristy's Carl?' although I hear one voice say, 'She invented Jake Matthews?'

Chelsea turns to Greg triumphantly, but Greg chugs his drink and doesn't look at her.

'I already told him,' says Tori. 'And we were going to break up anyway.'

The murmurs start up again. I hear 'Break up', 'Way to go, Carl!' and, that voice again, 'I thought Jake Matthews was real!'

'So you can say what you like, Chelsea. After you've left.'

Chelsea walks to the door, full of dignity. 'I cannot believe you! You'll be so sorry.'

'I'll be so NOT!' Tori calls.

Bryce follows Chelsea like a sheep.

Chris scuttles out with Anthony. Kristy gets up too, pushing at Carl. I'm not sure if they're following Chelsea or going out to have an argument in private.

Everyone's still staring at Tori, so she waves her arms and says, 'Guys! Go party.'

The room rumbles into separate conversations again. I hear girls going over the whole argument, word for word. No one seems to be on Chelsea's side.

'I did it for you,' says Tori, smiling. 'Well, and for me too. But now you don't have to break up with Jake.'

'What?' I'm amazed. 'How did you know about that?'

'It's just so Chelsea.' She shrugs. 'And I saw what she mouthed at you before. I might be not be an honour student nerd like you, but I understand girls like Chelsea.'

'Tori, you are the best friend in the world.' I throw my arms around her.

She beams. 'You're pretty OK yourself, even with that stuff last week. You know, I'm sick of being scared of Chelsea. I've been like that since third grade. I'm glad you came along.'

'Thank you.'

'You're welcome. Now go get your man.' She gives me a gentle push and scans the room. 'Where is Jake?'

I don't answer. I know where he is. He's in the closet, waiting for me to get to third base with him.

The lights from Tori's basement make the snowflakes on Jake's broad shoulders gleam.

There he is, the hottest guy in school, the one who started all my problems and self-doubts.

In the distance I hear car doors slam, and shouts of 'Let's blow this party!' and 'Sucked anyway!'

'Shouldn't you be with them?' I ask. I don't mean to be rude, but . . . Actually, I don't care if I'm rude or not right now. If Tori can face up to them, so can I.

So why is my heart pounding like this?

Jake shrugs. 'Didn't feel like it.'

Wow, you have a mind of your own, I think, but I don't say it. Partly because Jake's looking at me with THOSE eyes. The way he kept looking at me in the corridor, even after I made a fool of myself with him. It makes my knees feel wobbly.

Jake takes some cigarettes and a lighter out of his pocket. 'Hey, did you ever see those drawings some crazy witch kid did of Bryce, in the girls' restrooms?'

'Yeah, I did.' I try to keep my tone aloof. I won't give in to those eyes.

'It totally bugged Chelsea. It bugged me that it bugged her. You know, because she's with me, not Bryce.'

I'm surprised Jake's talking to me like this. He's acting like I'm his friend, or something.

'You wanna know what? I think she still has something going on with Bryce.'

'Oh.' I don't know what else to say. I think I preferred it when he talked to me about baseball.

He takes out a cigarette. 'She thinks I still have something going on with you.'

I nearly fall over in shock. 'With ME?'

He taps the cigarette against his leg, not looking at me. 'Yeah. You know, no one's ever done that before. What you did.'

'You mean the . . . slap?' I say, and cringe.

He smiles. 'I meant the way you said no to me. But yeah, that too.' He touches his cheek. 'I did think you were pretty crazy.'

'Sorry,' I mumble. And I think I am. Because that slap was the beginning of everything that's wrong with my life now. I'm sorry, but not for Jake. For me. If I hadn't slapped Jake, I could have been friends with Tori all along. She might not have needed an upsetting showdown with her friends. Most of all, I might never have been friends with David and Rachel, and felt so betrayed and let down. My life would have been different.

It would have been better.

Jake offers me a cigarette.

I shake my head. 'I don't smoke.'

He shrugs. 'Neither do I, any more.' He puts the cigarette back in the pack. 'Coach Harrison says it's bad for my game. But I, you know' – he flicks the lighter on and off – 'pretend sometimes.' He pushes the pack back into his pocket.

I pretend sometimes too, I think. Like, lately I've been pretending I'm a girl who's totally in control, who knows who her friends are, who can deal with any situation. Who slaps boys who are out of order, who understands relationships. It's a lie. I'm as weak as any Josie the Cool. I wasn't brave in front of the cool crowd, like Tori just now. I couldn't stand up to Rachel. I went to pieces over David. I can't even cope with seeing them together, when it was under my nose the whole time anyway. I shiver. It's time to make some changes around here. It's time to stop being Jo the Nerd.

A flake of snow drifts down and melts on my cheek. 'I'm cold,' I say.

'You' – Jake pulls a hand through his blond hair and turns those eyes on me – 'are totally hot.'

His voice makes me shiver. His eyes scorch me.

I made the wrong choice before. Is it too late to . . . go back?

'Want to get back to the party?' he says in the throaty voice he had way back when. When I nearly died of happiness because he chose ME for the kissing game.

My voice is feeble. 'OK.' Why not?

He makes me feel hot all over with the look he gives me.

I follow him as he steps back into Tori's basement. I think I'd follow him anywhere, to have him look at me like that again.

He touches my arm. 'I'm really glad I ran into you,' he says.

My arm burns. 'Uh-huh,' I say.

'I guess I never said sorry, you know. About before.' Jake leans closer and picks up my necklace. He runs the beads through his fingers.

'Uh-huh.' It doesn't matter now. I watch the snowflakes on his shoulders begin to melt.

He brushes his fingers along my neckline.

I shiver.

Jake moves his fingers. He strokes my cheek.

I shut my eyes for a second. When I open them, his intense eyes are fixed on my lips. I remember why I wanted to go into the closet with him in the first place, all that time ago. I'd forgotten that, in all the anger I felt afterwards. I'd forgotten that I wanted to go there with him, that I wanted to kiss him, desperately. And now I can have another chance. A chance to see what could happen, how it could feel . . . if I didn't say no to him.

I swallow hard.

He kisses my neck.

I shut my eyes again to the sensation. I breathe his minty man smell.

I hope David sees me.

Jake and me.

I wish Chelsea or Kristy could see me now. I hope the gossip gets to them soon.

He murmurs in my ear. 'Come on, Josie. Let's go somewhere quieter.'

'OK.'

We walk in silence to the closet. The same closet we were in all those weeks ago. He shuts the door behind us.

'I'll take it slow, I promise.'

'It's OK,' I say. I mean it. 'I wasn't ready last time.'

'But you're ready now.'

It's not a question. He sits down and pulls me towards him. His kisses are immediately hard and deep. His tongue makes delicious circles in my mouth. He murmurs, 'Josie.'

That's not my name.

What am I doing?

I don't know who I am any more.

And I don't think I care.

I relax into the kisses and let his hands wander. Wherever they want. Wherever I want them to.

'Josie, at last. I was going to come and look for you. I'm getting bored of counting coats in here.' Jake gives me a lazy smile.

He doesn't know anything about what's happened outside the closet just now. That's so typical of him. He's always missing the important scenes – at the movies, at the ice hockey, in life.

I don't feel like talking to him. I never do. I kiss him and we drop softly to the closet floor.

He reaches up for my bare skin with his hands. He also reaches down, making me forget everything with his dancing hands.

My mind empties. All I'm aware of is Jake. Jake's hot kiss, Jake's smooth touch, Jake's hard body.

Jake, Jake, Jake.

A few more minutes of delicious kissing and Jake's warm hands all over me, and I hear a metallic clink. A belt buckle.

I freeze.

He stops.

'Don't you want to?' Jake murmurs in my ear. He keeps stroking my back and putting fluttery kisses on my neck.

The honest truth is, I don't know. Partly, I do. His kisses are totally melting me. Why wouldn't I want more?

I'm creeping out of my trance though.

Why am I doing this? Do I really like Jake? What am I trying to prove? Am I doing this to show David that I'm attractive to someone else? Am I doing it to get back at Chelsea?

But David isn't right for me anyway. He's right for Rachel.

Jake isn't right for me. He's Chelsea's guy, all the way.

I look up. I can make out the outline of Albie's puffy jacket. The stripes on the arms glow in the dark. It's the jacket he was wearing the day he rescued me on the ice. The day we talked for hours about everything. The day he told me, without actually telling me, how much he cared about me, right from the start.

Doing this with Jake doesn't feel right.

'You want to. I can feel it,' Jake says, caressing me. 'You know you want to, baby.'

My shivers turn to shudders.

I know what I want. What I've always wanted. All this . . . all the rest of this. It's a mistake. A distraction from the truth. Why couldn't I see it?

'Jake, you know . . . I'm really sorry.'

Jake's hands stop cold. He looks at me, kind of fed up, but not angry.

'Here we go again. I guess we're not meant to be, huh, baby?'

'I guess we're not,' I sigh. 'And my name's Jo.'

Jake sighs, stands up and pushes his hands into his

pockets. 'You know, I couldn't get you out of my head, but . . . Josie?'

'Jo.'

'This is it, know what I mean? I won't be giving you another chance.'

'That's OK,' I say. 'Listen, I'm sorry, you know, to you and Chelsea. I shouldn't have come in here with you. It's not right.'

'It felt right to me. It felt right to you.' His eyes smoulder again, but they leave me cold.

'No.' Finally I feel like I really know what I believe, and I'm not afraid to say it. It's been a long time since I felt that.

Ever since the first time I was in this closet with Jake.

Jake walks out.

He's so not the guy for me.

Albie's mountain rescue jacket sways above me as the door slams shut.

I think about how different I feel from the first time I was here.

The first time, OK, I stood up for myself, but at the first taunt from the crowd, I crumbled. I ran away and tried to change myself for another crowd. I lost control. I lost sight of myself anyway. I may as well have been Josie the Cool. Jo the Nerd was equally weak. Half a person, a shadow of my complete self.

This time I sit and think about my mountain rescue guy. Albie.

But I don't need to be rescued any more.
I've rescued myself.

 Jake, Jake, Jake. His lips, his hands, his hot breath. It's all I can think about.

It's all I can think about until I open my eyes and glance up. And I see Albie's mountain rescue coat, the stripes on the sleeves glowing in the dark.

And then all I can think about is Albie.

I shouldn't be here with Jake. I don't want Jake.

Jake stops. 'What's the matter, Josie?' he asks.

He doesn't sound annoyed. Just mildly irritated, like he's swatting a fly. He doesn't seem as arrogant as the Jake I got to first base with. Maybe the William thing really did bug him, like Tori said.

Anyway, I think I've changed too. I'm not doing half as much Josie giggling. I've even stopped caring what the cool girls think, at least on some level. Tori's my friend, the others are really not. And so what if they don't approve of me or my choices? Tori doesn't approve either, but she's still my friend.

I touch my beads. I think it might be time to go back to dressing as the real me all the time.

I might keep the straight hair though. Every now and then.

'Hey? Are you OK? Why'd you stop?'

'It's . . . It doesn't feel right.'

'OK.' Jake's quiet. After a while he says, 'Is it because of me and Chelsea?'

'What?' My voice comes out high and sharp.

'You know, right? You saw me with Chelsea at the mall. We kind of . . . hook up sometimes. Chelsea said you wouldn't care, because British girls date more casually, but I wasn't sure.'

'What?'

Does no one stick to one person at a time? Do boys always have to line up another girlfriend in case they change their minds about the first one, like my dad did with Kelly?

Mind you, girls do it too. Chelsea, for one.

'Does Bryce know?'

'Not exactly. Chelsea's going to break up with him real soon. He's been kind of a jerk to her, you know, seeing other girls and stuff.'

There's no sign that Jake sees any irony there.

'Cookie said I should dump you anyway, because of all the lies and all. But I didn't want to because, you know . . .'

'No. Why?' Maybe he really loves me, and he's been too shy to show it. Maybe the sports-talk was all a cover-up for nerves. Maybe I should feel sorry for him. After all, I don't love him.

'Because, well . . . no one says no to Jake Matthews. And all the guys expect me to hook up with you. You know, fully. I can't really . . . not. There's a lot of pressure on me.'

It figures. I try to stir up some anger, but instead I feel sort of sad and let down. Anyway, Chelsea's right. I did lie to Jake. And I was using him to stay in with her. It's just all wrong, and it has been from the start.

'It's not true,' I tell him, 'what Chelsea said about British girls. We're like any girls, anywhere. You're only supposed to have one girlfriend at a time.'

'But for ages I thought you were with that British guy! Listen, I was going to tell you about Chelsea. It caused a few problems, with both of you wanting a date to the dance, but, you know. I let her go with Bryce.'

Oh.

My God.

I almost want to laugh.

He sits for a while, and then he says, like he can't quite believe it, 'So you really don't want to? Do it? Because it really felt like you . . . did.'

I shake my head and shrug. 'No. I don't.'

'So I'll go find Chelsea.'

Ugh.

'Um, Chelsea left,' I tell him. I'll leave it to her to fill in the details.

'Really?' He doesn't seem worried. 'So hey. See you around, Josie.'

'Jake, wait a second.'

He pauses at the closet door. 'What?'

'Jake, you know the butt-slapping thing you do a lot? Well, you shouldn't. It's horrible.'

He looks confused and says, 'Oh, I thought girls liked that.'

'They don't,' I say.

'No one ever complained before.' He shrugs. 'OK.' He leaves.

I don't follow Jake out of the closet. I sit in the dark, thinking.

So Jake has dumped me. Kind of. I have slut exemption now, according to Tori's rules. I can snog anyone I want. I wish.

I wish Albie would come in for his mountain rescue coat.

Though I don't need to be rescued.

I think, after everything that's happened, I'm finally in control. I'm not one of the cool gang, and I don't want to be. I'm not Jake's girlfriend but I'm not upset about that, either. I'm so much better off without him.

I'll be OK now. I've rescued myself.

I sit in the dark.

I rest my head on the closet wall.

I think about what I really want.

I've worked it out now. What I want. And I wait for a while, just in case.

I've no idea how long I've been sitting here when the door opens.

And it happens. Albie walks in.

It's Albie. 'Are you OK?' he asks.

He looks at me. I look at him. I'm not sure what to say.

I know what I want to say to him. I probably shouldn't say it.

I know what I want to say.

So first I say, 'I'm fine.' And then I say the rest, because I want to.

I decide to say it.

I say, 'I was thinking about you.'

'I've been thinking about you.'

He looks at me for a long moment.

There's a silence.

Albie says, 'I saw you come in here with Jake, and I saw him leave without you . . . And I waited, but . . . Are you really OK?'

Albie says, 'But you and Jake . . . Are you OK?'

I nod. I say, 'I had to . . . sort something out with Jake. I did. Forget it. Please. Really.'

'Jake and I broke up,' I say. I shrug. 'It's cool.'

Albie says, 'So you're not . . . with Jake?'

'You broke up?' Albie smiles. 'Uh, I'm so sorry.' He looks like he's forcing his face into a concerned frown.

I shake my head. The look on his face makes me want to laugh.

'No, really, it's completely a good thing.' I laugh.

Albie sits down.

He sits down next to me.

We talk and talk. I even mention Mum. I tell him stuff, he tells me stuff – it's effortless. It's wonderful.

And we talk for ages. We talk about life and school and even my plans for Mum's love life. Everything.

But then I don't want to talk any more. I touch his face.

Until I touch his face and he stops talking. He looks at me.

He's quiet. We sit, breathing together.

I realize I should have done this ages ago, instead of getting distracted by what other people think.

I wish I'd done this long ago. Because no matter what I thought I felt about other boys, it was nothing compared to this. This is more. I put my arms around Albie's neck. I kiss him.

I shut my eyes. I move my face closer to his. Our noses touch. I breathe in the air he breathes out. I kiss him.

He looks at me like he can't believe what I've done.

He looks at me like he can't believe his luck.

And then he kisses me.

And then he kisses me back.

We kiss. I run my fingers through his spiky hair and stroke his face. His face feels cool, but his mouth is hot against mine. He smells of fresh snowflakes. He leans into me. I lean back. We hold hands. Both hands. We stretch our arms out and interlock our fingers.

We look at each other and laugh.

We kiss again. It feels like mountain rescue. It feels like I was always here anyway, all along, in his arms.

We kiss for a very long time.

I am in a cupboard, and I'm snogging the coolest and most gorgeous boy in the whole school. And it's a big school. And we're kissing really, not snogging. In a closet, not a cupboard.

But none of that is the point at all. The point is – I am kissing Albie Windsor, the coolest boy in the school! If not the world. The coolest to me.

And the really amazing thing – I am seriously uncool.

Or I was.

And then I wasn't.

Although I also was.

And you know what? It didn't matter. I made the

right choices for the wrong reasons, and the wrong choices for the right reasons, and all the combinations of choices and reasons you can think of.

And I forgot who I was and I forgot who my friends were, and why.

And then I remembered.

I remembered, thanks to my true friends being, well, true. Friends.

And so this is it. That thing about 'being yourself', the thing everyone always says, the impossible thing, the thing I've never understood. Until now. This is it. It doesn't matter what decisions I make, as long as I make them for my true self. The self I love, the self my friends love. My friends and family – the people who love me either way, because they love ME, not my decisions. Mum, Hailey, Tori. Dad too, I suppose, and hell, maybe Kelly. Just maybe, though probably not.

Albie, though. Definitely Albie.

And so I'm kissing Albie Windsor, and I don't care if people out there think I'm cool or not. And neither does he. And he never did. It took two long parallel journeys for me to see that, but I'm here now.

I'm all me.

He's Albie.

And this is amazing.

This is my true-to-life, rags-to-riches, riches-to-rags,

duckling-to-swan, swan-to-duckling, against-all-odds, love-conquers-all story.

Split by a Kiss: The Josephine Reilly Story.

It's on Lifetime later, and repeated tomorrow.

There are two different versions.

HOME RUN

I know what you're thinking, but I don't mean THAT. Or even if I did, I probably wouldn't tell you. But I made it to the end of the year, and I'm going home to Britain. And this is the part of every good TV movie where we find out what happened to everyone. So here goes. Here's my home run-down.

And as for next year ... that's a whole new ball game.

JOSEPHINE REILLY
(AKA JO-JO, AKA JO, AKA JOSIE)

Josephine dated Albie for the whole year and she is still totally his girlfriend now. She's very sad to leave him and Massachusetts behind. Mostly him, of course, but also Massachusetts, which she can now spell. Josephine hung out with Tori in malls, and Tori hung out with Josephine in the Walnut Street thrift store. They eventually reached some kind of shopping compromise by going to an outlet mall in New

Hampshire where they were both mostly happy.

Josephine is Madison Rat's number-one fan, and she's often found hanging out at their gigs. They've played in some Irish bars in downtown Boston, Brighton and Allston, and a couple of small bars in Milltown itself. They featured twice more in the *Improper Bostonian*. They are hot. (Especially the lead singer.)

Josephine took skating lessons from Albie and can now go once round the rink, forwards, without falling over. She'll perfect the triple lutz salchow loop some other year.

Josephine discovered doughnut holes and riding the Red Line of the T over the River Charles. She is officially in love with Albie, Madison Rat, Boston and chocolate doughnut holes, in that order.

MS REILLY
(AKA SUZANNA, AKA MUM)

Ms Reilly was reunited with love, thanks to her wonderful daughter. Here's how.

Firstly, Josephine spent loads of time convincing Ms Reilly that you don't need to change yourself, not for any man who's worth it. And Rashid, as Josephine pointed out, clearly liked Ms Reilly the way she was when she first arrived in the USA and they did their first cringey Bowie dance together. Anyway, Josephine went on and on about this sort of thing, though she always seemed to end up raving about Albie and how magnificent he was.

And then there was Josephine's cunning plan, partly hatched on the night of the Winter Dance. She asked David to ask his dad to get a message to Rashid at work. The message was that Suzanna wanted to meet him at the Milltown ice-cream parlour on New Year's Eve. (Josephine had to get her father out of the way first.)

Of course, by New Year's Eve Ms Reilly was ready to try again, thanks to Josephine wearing her down. It was also thanks to Ms Reilly seeing her ex-husband again and realizing what she totally wasn't missing.

At the ice-cream parlour, a little live music was pre-arranged. Madison Rat did a killing cover version of Paul Young's *Come Back and Stay*, an eighties classic getting-back-together song that had Suzanna and Rashid crooning at each other like the embarrassing oldies they are. But Josephine couldn't complain, since it was all part of the plan.

Ms Reilly and Rashid have been together all year and Josephine thinks he's OK. More fun than Dad, less fun than a weekend marathon on Lifetime.

Ms Reilly continued to have her brain drained to the end of her contract, and she would not rule out coming back to the USA again if she can get another contract and visa. She's planning on continuing a long-distance Anglo-French relationship with Rashid, who is moving back to Paris next month.

MR & MRS REILLY
(AKA DAD AND KELLY, AKA JOHN AND KELLY, AKA BORING AND BORINGER)

Mr Reilly's visit went pretty well, especially for little Lolly, who loves her big sister, but the new Mrs Reilly really was a huge pain and Josephine decided not to ask her for fashion advice after all. Josephine did not return home to live with them, of course. She is in regular contact with Mr Reilly and has obtained new useful advice, such as how to avoid dual taxation and how, according to recent studies, circular brushing is more effective than a strict up-and-down motion.

HAILEY SMITH
(AKA MRS AMERICAN FILMSTAR-TO-BE, AKA BESTEST FRIEND THAT SIDE OF THE ATLANTIC)

Hailey also had a good time in Boston, although she had a go at Josephine a few times because she found her 'changed' and 'full of herself'. Josephine countered that she couldn't help having grown spiritually and intellectually through her Boston adventures and there was no need for Hailey to feel left behind when she could join Josephine on a higher plain. Instead, Hailey went back to England on a hairy-plane (as Lolly would say) and started going out with Jonathan's friend Grant. Josephine hopes Hailey won't get hurt but she's all ready to pick up the pieces.

VICTORIA WINDSOR
(AKA TORI, AKA BESTEST FRIEND THIS SIDE OF THE ATLANTIC)

Tori managed to stay single for nearly a week, after which she started dating a Boston University freshman named Ralph. She then dated two of his friends (but not at the same time – who would do a thing like that?) and now is with a Tufts sophomore called Topher. Josephine and Tori have been to some great parties in Somerville thanks to Tori's dating habits. There have been further parties in Tori's basement, but Chelsea and Kristy were never invited again.

Tori hasn't minded hanging out with the not-strictly-cool Josephine, and in fact often wonders out loud why she stuck with those mean girls for so long. The answer is obviously that she had yet to meet the nerdy-cool whirlwind that is Josephine Reilly.

Tori has started appreciating some straight-to-television movies, ever since Josephine broke her in gently with *Freaky Friday* – the overlooked Gaby Hoffman version. Tori still prefers the Li-Lo version, but then she would, seeing as she's the Lindsey Lohan to Josephine's Gaby Hoffman. (Josephine's mum will only watch the original Jodie Foster version.)

Tori's going to miss Josephine like mad next year, which is why she's asked her dad for a transfer to a UK school. He's thinking about it, because frankly he'd like a British royal education for his daughter.

ALBERT WINDSOR
(AKA ALBIE, AKA MY GUY)

Albie is beautiful, talented and has the greatest taste in girlfriends. He continues to date the fabulous Josephine. He writes lovely lyrics and sings them to Josephine to make her feel like the only person in the room. (This doesn't count when she actually is the only person in the room.)

Albie has now given up his job as general dogsbody for the Cooks, but not because of any dangerous liaisons with Mrs Cook. Mr Cook has fully recovered and is back in action, and Mrs Cook is getting dressed again and not needing hugs from hot teenage boys.

Albie is going to miss Josephine more than life itself, which is why he's considering a gap year working in England before he starts college. Mr Windsor is keen on this because then Albie can keep an eye on his sister's royal education. And after that, Josephine will be old enough to consider going to college in the USA with Albie. Well, those are the plans, anyway.

JAKE MATTHEWS
(AKA CONGENITALLY SEXY)

Jake Matthews hooked up with practically the entire junior cheerleading squad and a couple of sophomores in the last year, as well as seeing Chelsea on and off. He continues to be regarded as the hottest, coolest guy in the school, and those eyes have something to do with it. But the fact that he no longer slaps girls on the butt also plays a part, and that can be credited entirely to Josephine, perhaps the only girl except Chelsea who didn't swoon at his feet while hooking up with him. Well, not the whole time, anyway.

CHELSEA COOK
(AKA COOKIE, AKA CONGENITALLY GIRLY)

Chelsea hooked up with Jake all year, see above. She also had a fight with Kristy over some other boy, but no one remembers the details. She doesn't really go to the same parties as Josephine any more. And that's just fine by Josephine.

KRISTY MELBOURNE
(AKA CONGENITALLY CATTY)

Kristy broke up with Carl for some ridiculous reason, although Carl probably deserved it for being whiny and annoying. She then went out with a couple of other jocks, and got her claws out quite a lot to fight off other girls – or just because she felt like it.

DAVID MCCOURT
(AKA CONGENITALLY FLIRTY)

David dated Rachel all year. They're still together. They'll probably be together for ever even though Rachel flies into rages and storms out on him a lot, mostly when David flirts with Advanced Algebra students or any other girl who demonstrates that she has more than one brain cell. David McCourt is still hot but Josephine only has eyes for Albie and she doesn't need to ignore those other feelings any more. Much. Don't show Albie this.

RACHEL GLASSMAN
(AKA CONGENITALLY RUDE)

Rachel is with David, see above. And she still scares Josephine on occasion, but mostly she doesn't, because they're kind of friends. Rachel has stopped drawing on walls and started compiling graphic novels with David's help. And she finally painted some cartoons on Josephine's black shoes. She painted a cartoon girl with a nose. Josephine was pleased and thanked her a lot, and not only because she's been extra-nice to Rachel since she saw the Josephine voodoo doll in Rachel's locker. Apparently Rachel made the doll after Josephine's first day of school, because David made it obvious he liked Josephine, and Rachel was jealous of the 'too cute' Limey girl.

Rachel has promised she never actually used that voodoo doll, and that it had nothing to do with any of the freaky things that happened to Josephine last semester. Josephine isn't so sure, but she can't complain, because it all worked out perfectly in

THE END